ON THE HILL
OR
Not Mrs. Rossiter's Canary

Ronald Clayton

Copyright © 2017 Ronald Clayton

All rights reserved, including the right to reproduce this book, or portions thereof in any form. No part of this text may be reproduced, transmitted, downloaded, decompiled, reverse engineered, or stored, in any form or introduced into any information storage and retrieval system, in any form or by any means, whether electronic or mechanical without the express written permission of the author.

This is a work of fiction. Names and characters are the product of the author's imagination and any resemblance to actual persons, living or dead, is entirely coincidental.

ISBN: 978-1-326-95767-4

PublishNation
www.publishnation.co.uk

CHAPTER ONE

'What ho, Maxwell!' I said, on the phone from Sydney: 'I'm here, some of me. My better parts are still in the air over the Indian Ocean; I expect them to catch up in a day or two. What news out thereabouts?'

'Bad news, Wallace,' he replied: 'Extremely. Andrew Kell is dead.'

'Good Lord. He's no older than we are. How did he go? Heart? When?'

'Yesterday. He was stabbed. And hanged. And horribly mutilated. I gather they've ruled out suicide.'

'The Wagga Scientific Police are on the case, I see. This is appalling. I can barely take it in. Jayne must be beside herself. I'll be back on the 3.10.'

Going back to Wagga by train, by the XPT – formerly the Daylight Express - from Sydney Central, was a ritual with me. It took me back to the days before I could afford to fly, and the long slow haul through the south-western towns and stations was what homecoming meant. Not that it was home anymore. Venice was. Nor was it Wagga. Wagga Wagga was its permanent name now, as of course it always had been out in the wide world, but those of us who were brought up in it in the first half of the twentieth century were accustomed to calling it Wagga pure and simple, which was less insistently Aboriginal and a degree more distant from the notorious fact that Bill Kerr had built his entire career as a comedian in England on the revelation that he came from a place called Wagga Wagga. Wagga Wagga re-established itself here later, when the town began the process of learning to live up to its new status as an actual City (1946) and decided that it deserved a more dignified and resonant name, one that proclaimed its acceptance of Heritage and signified its acknowledgement of the famous fact that Bill Kerr had built his entire career as a comedian in England on the revelation that he came from a place called Wagga Wagga. And so the local inhabitants have joined the rest of the world in their Wagga-Waggery, and they take an appropriate civic pride in belonging to so internationally-renowned yet authentically Australian spot. But it was to good old Wagga that I was going back.

A Wagga without Andrew Kell, but, wasn't as good and old as it ought to have been, quite apart from the manner of his removal from it. I'd been looking forward to seeing him again, we had crucial periods of old Wagga life in common, and I'd intended to mine his memories for a project - my Memoir, an autobiographical, topographical and historical summation of Wagga's life and times and my part in them - that I'd begun to assemble. With Jayne, his wife, now widow, I had no old Wagga life in common, she being his second wife, much younger and Canberra-bred, but I'd also been looking forward to seeing her again, on account of her blonde ringlets, her long long legs and, yes, her lovely personality. Some of these latter thoughts were not to be thought on the last leg, damn, of this dismal return, between Junee and Wagga, and by the time I stepped onto the platform I was as grim and gloomy as the circumstances required.

Maxwell was waiting for me there. He'd known Andrew much better than I had, and the shock was still on his face. As we went out into Station Place and the car-park I observed, I was expecting them, the looks. We were indeed a notably mismatching pair, I the long and Maxwell the short of it. I was upwards of two yards up, he was very low-slung. He was tubby, more than very, I was slim, or perhaps spindly. I was of an aquiline, or beaked, cast of feature, he was so bushily bearded that it was impossible to make out which or how many features he possessed. Walking, talking and gesticulating together, as now, as always, we were a source of innocent merriment for all the normal, perfectly-formed people who set eyes on us. It was ever thus. Even when we were young, ages prior to Maxwell's beard, Wagga's citizens much enjoyed the picturesque weirdness of our public appearances, as we – precocious little beggars – enjoyed their enjoyment of us. So then, so now, even while our friend lay in the morgue.

We drove out to Maxwell's farmlet on the edge of town, where he told me what little he knew.

'So far,' he said, 'nothing significant's known. The few skerricks I've got have come out of the back door of the police station, from Detective Sergeant Parrot. You remember Charlie Parrot, The Man They Couldn't Drown?'

'I do,' I said: 'I was there when they tried. I wrote a humorous piece about it, which was widely circulated and much enjoyed.'

'It was on Sunday night or early Monday morning, Charlie says. They found him hanging from a tree on Willans' Hill - a pair of joggers found him, they're still in shock. A hanging corpse is a pretty jolting sight in any case, but this one was naked, its private parts had been sliced off ...'

'Dear God !... '

' ... and it had been stabbed in the guts. The probable cause of death, according to Charlie, was strangulation. And loss of blood, and shock, I should think. But this corpse wasn't a corpse when it was strung up. Its wrists were tied behind its back and it was left to choke.'

'Dear God, or have I already said that? Probably not left – watched, I'd say. The amount of hatred on show here would have needed that satisfaction. But, by all that's inexplicable, how could anybody have hated Andrew that much? Have you ever heard of anyone even disliking him? He was so easy-going, so inoffensive, such a friendly, likeable chap.'

'Someone evidently didn't think so. Maybe Jayne would know. But so far, Charlie says, there are no suspects, no apparent motives, no clues, nothing.'

'This business with the genitals – with*out* them – must mean something. There must be a motive there; unless we're dealing with a maniac who simply happens to enjoy cutting off blokes' balls. It's not unknown. Remember that butcher from Deniliquin? As for Jayne – what of Jayne? Poor Jayne.'

'I haven't tried to contact her, it's far too soon. I've sent a card, from both of us. She was away when it happened, she's away every weekend these days - there's an ailing mother in Canberra. When she got back on Monday the SS were waiting for her.'

'The SS? In Wagga? Has it come to this?'

'The Special Squad. Two policewomen and a cocker spaniel. They break bad news. The cocker spaniel, in my opinion, is a stroke of genius.'

'A blue heeler would be better. My cousin has a special race of them. Just let it off the lead, and the bad news would pale into insignificance. But Jayne, poor Jayne – is she at home?'

'I've no idea. She might well be back with her mother. Charlie will know. So will the neighbours, I suppose.'

'They might know a few other things as well, if properly pumped. Let's have at them tomorrow. Andrew wouldn't want us to leave his fate to the likes of Charlie Parrot. It's really extraordinarily fortunate that I've arrived in time to be of use; and of course now that I'm here – now that we're both here – our reputation is at stake.'

'Our reputation gives me, frankly, the pip. It's all very well for you, swanning in from foreign parts for brief nostalgic wallows. You don't have to live here with it. Ever since that blasted book came out there hasn't been a missing relative or lost ferret that somebody hasn't rung me up to demand that I track down. People stop their cars to ask me what crime I'm getting to the bottom of this morning, and whether I can tell, just by looking at them, how many unnatural acts they've performed recently. Let's leave poor Andrew to the police. I tell you, Wallace, this reputation of ours has made a victim of me. I wish I'd never been to Narrandera.'

Maxwell was referring, of course, to the Eric Connolly case, the subject of one of my more successful books here in Australia – *Eric Connolly's Comeuppance*. We had driven over to Narrandera to enable Maxwell to pursue his genealogical researches in the cemetery there – he is absolutely addicted to these grisly pursuits – while I prowled about looking for local colour: I was thinking of writing a novel that became the entirely different *Comeuppance* instead; when Lo! there suddenly came a man and a woman running and crying, followed, within the next action-packed hours, by three corpses, a naked clergyman and a police force in a state of utter bewilderment and paralysis. Suffice it to say – read the book for the rest of it – that in the course of one long hot summer afternoon Maxwell and I penetrated all the mysteries and rescued the clergyman's daughter; and the luck of Eric Connolly finally ran out.

We acquired considerable celebrity, fame even, from this exploit, which the aforementioned book – now available in paperback – has sustained and extended; but even a hefty slice of the royalties, it was apparent, had not reconciled Maxwell to the disadvantages of being a living legend in his own backyard. I endeavoured to divert his bitterness.

'Maxwell,' I said: 'I detect a bit of bile. Consider. These passing – these pausing – motorists will be redoubling their inquiries now that Andrew has been murdered, that's already inevitable. Nobody will believe you'd leave him to the police, especially after word gets around that I'm here too. Consider also how much bitterer you'll be if we abandon poor Andrew to the police and they fail to crack the case – which, if Charlie Parrot is anywhere near it, they most certainly will. Or if, by some unimaginable mistake, they should happen to succeed, think how even bitterer you'll be when it is universally assumed that we have tried and failed. But our reputation, I agree, be damned. We owe this to Andrew. He would want us to track down his murderer, to write his final page. It may well have been his last and only hope when he was hanging there on the Hill. And I promise, I really promise, not to write a book about it.'

Maxwell rolled his eyes. He wasn't convinced, or he'd had too much port. We finished the bottle and hit the sack.

Over a late breakfast next morning – black coffee and a coddled egg, to the tune or tunelessness of one of Maxwell's foibles, an irksome nagging thing by Philip Glass – I suggested that we might start the day by sifting the Kells' neighbours.

'I see this abomination has driven our traditional rituals out of your head,' said Maxwell: 'Today, your first day, we always have lunch in the bar of the Terminus with the chaps.'

Ah, the chaps. This was our term for those of our schoolfriends who still remained in Wagga. There were of course chaps and chaps; and although we were all, also of course, mates, we were mates of various kinds and degrees. Those we had the custom of meeting on my first days back had begun their careers as our mates at the South Wagga Primary School and had gone on, gone up, with us to the Wagga High School. Our first brushes with high and low culture had taken place in their company, amongst these very veterans, these doughty old South Wagga lags; and I had naturally been hoping to draw on their recollections of our primal scenes for my Memoir. Now, however, this matter of Andrew's had cast a spanner in my works.

We drove, grimly, down past the Wagga Wagga Memorial Cemetery and then West along the mighty Sturt Highway, commemorative of Captain Charles Sturt, who explored all the twists and turns of the no less mighty Murrumbidgee river in order to identify the exact spot on which Wagga could be founded.

'This will be a melancholy meeting,' I observed, 'one of our number being not in being. To speak frankly, Maxwell, I am peeved. Kell and I were together in Mr. Phillips' class at South Wagga, 2A, right next to the belltower, and I will never know now whether he could remember anything about it that I can't. And in the present circumstances the remaining chaps might well not feel disposed to rabbit rewardingly on about the days of long ago. This murder is damned untimely. My Memoir, Maxwell, has suffered a blow.'

'I'm sorry to hear that. The whole of Wagga will be sorry to hear it. But perhaps that is why Andrew was murdered, to deal a blow to your precious memoir. When you announced at the High School reunion that you were writing one a shudder ran round the room. Here we are.'

There we were at the Terminus. The Terminus hotel will deserve a place of its own in the Memoir. In the new-fangled sixties it had its name changed to the William Farrer, after a local agronomical hero; but we old stagers kept faith with its proper name, the name it bore when we used to stare across at it from the school playground and wonder what the large loud men within could possibly be doing in there. Furthermore, not only was the Terminus practically opposite the South Wagga Primary, and an aspect of its curriculum, it occupied the corner of Edward and Peter Streets, a corner of no mean significance. Edward Street, the city's segment of the Sturt Highway, and justly celebrated in song and story, was named after Edward Howe, as to whom the sole ascertainable fact is that he had an employee, John Webster, who went about the district naming things after him. (The familiarity, and incessancy, of 'Edward' – not, as one might expect from an employee, 'Mr. Howe' – suggests to me that John and Edward were the area's first gay couple.) Peter Street, named after the Scotch grazier who allegedly fixed the site of Wagga – not so: Sturt had already done it – has not so far been celebrated at all; but the Memoir will fix that. Peter Street's time is coming; for on its eastern side, some two hundred paces down from the corner – I will return to the corner anon – there stood in ancient time the ancestral mansion of Maxwell himself. And that significant corner, where we were now entering the hotel's back bar, had once been the terminus of those numerous nightly wanderings through our sleeping town during which young Maxwell and I had come to terms – though never quite to grips – with Life. There were rich dark materials for my Memoir hereabouts.

It was immediately apparent that there was little or no chance here of any serious chat about the splendours and miseries of our primary school days. Andrew Kell's exit was the only brookable topic. Gloomy greetings were exchanged. Lunch was well under way. The eight or nine chaps who'd turned up were clearly already into their third or fourth helping and we hastened to renew our local group membership by instantly ordering another round.

'When I next murder somebody,' Humphrey Hooper seemed to be saying, 'I'll murder Roy O'Hanlon, bound to. We've all got lists, you can't live in Wagga without your own personal list of removable bastards. But the point I'm making is I just can't see how Andrew could have been on anybody's list, he was just a bloody beaut bloke, he'd do anything for you.'

Hoop was the hugest fellow there, well able to murder any of us if minded to do so, and if he could actually manage to get at us across the vast barrel of his belly. His oldest and closest friend was Roy O'Hanlon, a tiny little jockey of a fellow, who always contradicted him.

'Nobody can be just a beaut bloke, you've got to be other things as well,' Roy said, 'and there's certainly somebody around who reckoned he wasn't a beaut bloke in the slightest.'

'Nobody who really knew him could've reckoned that,' Hoop replied, 'which is my point.'

'So,' said Barry Bruce, 'what you reckon is that whoever murdered him didn't really know him. That's pretty unlikely. You think some stray maniac might have just happened to bump into him up on the hill and felt like stabbing him and stringing him up?' Bazza Bruce was a purple-faced lush, but shrewd. It paid to remember that he regularly came in third or fourth in the class, apparently without ever having to swot.

'No,' I said, coming to Hoop's aid; he could be a mite slow on the uptake: 'I'm sure Hoop isn't suggesting that. This murderer couldn't have known Andrew well, really well, he means, because then his beautitude would have been so obvious that the murder could not have occurred. I'm with Roy here, though. There must have been other things in this admittedly beaut bloke's life that explain why he was killed.'

'Thanks, Wal,' said Bazza: 'Now I understand. Do you also think these mysterious other things will explain why he was not only stabbed but hung and had his balls cut off?'

'Undoubtedly,' I said: ' I... '

'It's the balls bit I can't stomach. That's bloody unnatural, that was.' This was Trevor Neely, a bit of a galoot, but his instincts were sound. 'It's hard to believe that any Wagga bloke could go as far as that.'

'What's a Wagga bloke these days?' Roy wanted to know. It was a good question, one I intended to lavish my eloquence on in the Memoir. 'These days Wagga's full of strangers and migrants. By the look of some of them they're capable of anything. Some of them probably eat balls for supper. Wagga's different now, there are people here who you wouldn't want your worst enemy to meet on a dark night.'

'Back in the old days when we were young,' I said, because there was an opening here, and it was worth a shot, 'there was... '

'Talking of strangers,' Freddy Gorman said, who was also a bit of a galoot, whose instincts were unsound, 'that wife of his could have something to do with it. She's from Canberra.'

'Jayne?' said Maxwell: 'Come off it. She was very fond of him, anybody could see that. They were very happy together. Poor Jayne.'

'That's a really indecent and disgusting thing to say, Freddy,' Roger Dunn, Dunny, declared. Dunny was our complainer-in-chief, and extremely knowledgeable on every subject he knew nothing about: 'Jayne's the last person in the world to. You've got a mind like a sewer.'

'O.K.,' said Hoop: 'That's settled. It wasn't Jayne. So who was it? Who's going to disgust us with the next theory?'

'I've got one,' said Artie Starkey, perpetual bottom of the class, unfailing failer of every exam from kindergarten on, one of my special favourites: 'Well, it's just a bit of a wonder really. What I wonder a bit is if it mightn't be one of a string of them. Say what you like, it was a pretty strange death, especially parts of it, and there've been quite a few strange deaths in Wagga in the past few years. Steve Hampson, for instance.'

'Hang on, hang on,' said Bazza: 'There are always strange deaths in Wagga, it's that kind of town, but Steve Hampson's wasn't all that strange, it was an obvious heart attack and drowning accident, and this one's an obvious murder. There's no comparison.'

'It was only an instance,' Artie replied, 'and there are others, stranger than normal. What about Donny Parker, say, or Ozzie Murray? You can't say they weren't strange. But it's only a sort of a theory.'

'We're all waiting for Wal's,' Mike McClure said: 'He probably already knows who did it.' In the period 1959-1972 Mike McClure was widely regarded as the handsomest man in the universe. His looks collapsed in early January 1973, and he had been a bitter and belligerent estate agent ever since: 'Charlie Parrot should be here soon. We've invited him specially, Wal, so you can tell him how to crack this case. Was it Eric Connolly again, do you think? It's a pretty lucky coincidence that this has happened just when our favourite famous investigator is passing through on one of his regular colonial tours.'

'Where's Eric Connolly these days, I wonder?' Bobby Fossey wondered. Bobby was a thorough duffer, but he knew it, and he could sometimes surprise you: 'There was that fellow from over near

Temora, the fellow who got into that disagreement with Donkey Taylor about the truckload of chooks, he said he heard Eric Connolly was somewhere down around Gerogery, but he could be anywhere.'

'He wouldn't try anything here,' Bazza said: 'He wouldn't come anywhere near where Wal and Maxwell might pick up his trail, he's not daft. His luck has already run out once.'

'Somehow,' I said, 'I don't sense Eric Connolly's hand in this. It's not his style; and this was a particularly stylish murder. Stabbing, hanging and castrating, I mean, amount to more than mere murder. A point is being made, a message is being sent. This murder has been designed – styled, if you will – to be noticed. How leads to why. If we can decipher the message we can get a line on the reasons for Andrew's awful taking-off, and the reasons ought to point to the perpetrator.'

'Charlie should be here to hear this,' said Mike: 'It's bloody marvellous. Wal is practically ready to name names. And Maxwell hasn't even started on it yet.'

'It wasn't a truckload, it was only a utefull,' Trev said.

'I'm not going to start on it, not if I can help it,' Maxwell said: 'And at this stage we don't know enough to know anything. If Charlie Parrot is willing to tell us a bit about what the police know, or what they think they know, there might be a clue or two worth following up; but speaking personally, I really don't want to get involved. That Narrandera business has blighted my life.'

'On the other hand,' Hoop observed, 'Andrew was our mate. We owe him. If there's anything we can do to help find the bastard who did that to him we've got to do it, which you and Wal have a special duty to, owing to you being unusually clever at this sort of stuff, if you know what I mean.'

'Hear, hear,' Mike said: 'We're counting on you.'

'Detective Sergeant Parrot, though, is a highly reliable officer,' Dunny informed us, 'which some of us don't give him enough credit for. He solved the robbery at the Commercial Club in a flash.'

'Any fool could have solved that,' Bazza said: 'It had Tommy Anderson's pawmarks all over it. He must be the most useless character in the entire country, Tommy; and the worst bloody burglar into the bargain.'

'I have a soft spot, a large soft spot, for Tommy,' I said: 'His breathtaking incompetence is part of his charm. There were moments, back in our glorious youth, in the epic wars between Wagga High and the Christian Brothers', when I owed my very survival to Tommy Anderson. What a prodigious brawler he used to be!'

'Jesus! Think of that!' Mike exclaimed: 'If it wasn't for Tommy Anderson we would never have had the benefit of Wal. The bloody mind reels.'

'To say nothing of the benefit of you,' I riposted: 'Tommy Anderson snatched you from the jaws of death at the Yanco Picnic, as many of us here present will recall. That huge Herb character went right out of control when he discovered where your hand was on his woman. If Tommy hadn't whacked him in the chops with the cricket bat you would have been a smoking pile of offal garnished with tiny little pieces of penis.'

A roar went up, Mike's penis being his proudest possession and, in his view, a national treasure. He had the grace to look discomfited. But then poor Andrew's penis sprang into our minds, and a silence fell. Into it there now entered Detective Sergeant Charlie Parrot, splendidly uniformed, whose bald and bony head presided over a gym-tooled physique and a vast, ludicrous self-satisfaction. One glance told one that he was indeed just as bone-headed as ever.

'At ease,' he said, only half-joking: 'I'll have a double whisky, I'm off-duty at this juncture. Where's Wal? Good to see you, Wal. And Maxwell too, the other half of the famous combination.'

'Off-duty?' Roy said: 'Does that mean that nobody is investigating the Kell case while you're here in the pub?'

'Not at all, Roy. The station is humming with activity. There are several promising lines of inquiry under active pursual. Some of our best officers have been assigned to this case, who they are reporting constantly to me. Real progress is being made.'

'So,' said Maxwell, 'you haven't got anywhere yet. These lines of inquiry you refer to, can you give us an idea of what they are? Some of us here knew Andrew pretty well, and we might be able to make a few suggestions.'

'How's Jayne?' Dunny asked: 'Is she bearing up? Where is she?'

'Jayne,' Charlie announced, 'is a brave and resilious woman. She is bearing up, although naturally deeply in shock. I expected that. As regarding where she is, between ourselves,' he looked about for strangers, 'I have authorised her to return to her mother in Canberra until further notice. As regarding our current lines of inquiry, on the other hand, there, I'm afraid, I'm not in a position to divulge any details whilst our inquiries are in process.'

'That's no use at all,' Bazza said: 'There are blokes in this bar who know more about Andrew Kell than all the cops in the Riverina. Also, straining in the slips, we have Wal and Maxwell, no less, the Sherlock Holmeses of the Southern Hemisphere. You've got all this expert help, Charlie, all of us just waiting to put you on the right track, and you won't even give us a hint about what you might be looking for. It makes no sense.'

'I appreciate that, Bazza,' said Charlie: 'That is the type of thing often said by members of the public. Little do they realise that any such hints rapidly become rumours, which they may easily assist the criminals to remove the clues the police are on the point of the discovery of. We have to beware of the nature of the criminal mind.'

'That is good detective strategy, Charlie,' I said: 'I congratulate you on it. The criminal mind in Wagga has met its match in you. But there are more ways than one of skinning a cat. Instead of marching up to the front door on this, and asking Charlie to tell us what his lines of inquiry are, which he won't, we might take a stroll down the back passage and ask him to tell us what they aren't, which perhaps he will. In my experience, the way forward often lies down the back passage, as it were.'

'Well,' Charlie said: 'I might be able to do something along those lines. It depends.'

'Let's try,' I said: 'For example, you wouldn't have any particular suspect in mind, as of this moment, would you?'

'No,' he said: 'Not quite yet. Early days.'

'Not even Eric Connolly?' Mike McClure suggested.

'For another example, you wouldn't be pursuing any inquiry into why the victim was assailed in three different ways, would you?'

'You're right there. That's a bit of a puzzle. We can't fathom that.'

'You wouldn't be attaching any significance to the fact that the body was found on Willans' Hill, instead of, say, in the Victory Memorial Gardens, for example? Do you reckon he was stabbed and so forth where he was found?'

'That's a strange example. That's where Donny Parker was found. But as regarding Andrew on the hill there are no indications either way. My observations lead me to believe that the path had been carefully swept with a view to concealing all clues to persons and activities. I'm pretty certain about that.'

'And for a final example for the moment, I suppose you wouldn't have found anything in Andrew's private life that could throw any light on why he's been murdered?'

'That's one of our lines of inquiry. I'm not prepared to say anything about that at this juncture.'

'Quite right. You have been very discreetly helpful, or very helpfully discreet. Well done, Charlie. Any questions, anybody?'

'Just one,' Mike said: 'Just to get one thing out of the way. We all know Wal, we all know Wal's obsession with Wagga as it used to be. We all know about this memoir he's brewing up. And as soon as he starts sticking his nose into Andrew's murder the first thing he's likely to do is go haring off into history, looking for clues back when we were all still in short trousers. That's his nature. So, Charlie, I just want him to hear you say that you haven't found anything at all that suggests that this murder has anything at all to do with our bloody past. Or has it?'

'Well,' said Charlie: 'The past is always a peculiar factor. As regarding that, I would not wish to give any indication of a definite sort at this juncture. Early days.'

At this juncture the discussion became general, and generally futile. I made several attempts, all ignored, to enter eras and areas of relevance to my Memoir. Several further helpings of lunch were consumed. Mike McClure got in several references, not all of them even-tempered, to our investigative genius and begged to be allowed to accompany us on our sleuthing, in order to marvel at it. Maxwell got into a protracted argument with Dunny over the meaning of indecency. Artie told an enjoyably filthy story about a Mrs. Rossiter and her canary. Charlie continued to absorb double whiskies, at the expense, apparently, of nobody or everybody; and to announce that he would soon go off off-duty and progress the state of this unfortunate current case. He stayed, though, until Hoop, as was our tradition, closed the meeting and proposed that we should all take lunch together on the following Wednesday, one week hence, 'by which time,' he said, 'Wal and Maxwell will have run this murdering bastard to earth.' As we wandered away, Charlie eyed us significantly and intimated that he desired a private word.

'This unfortunate current case,' he said. We were outside, on the pavement, contemplating the line of palms (*phoenix canaryensis*, Maxwell tells me) that runs the length of Peter Street – a mystery, really, as no other street in Wagga has them, and they have been so definitely, so meaningfully planted, erected, that one is baffled by one's failure to be constantly mystified by them.

'Yes,' we said: 'Yes?'

'Unfortunate, yes,' he said: 'And speaking personally, I have always had a lot of time for Andrew. He was a beaut bloke. Also speaking personally, this case, which, as I think I have previously said, I have been put in charge of, might not be completely unfortunate from every point of view, if you take my meaning.'

'Not yet,' I said: 'From what point of view, for example?'

'Well, from mine,' he said: 'If, for example, we were able to bring it to a rapid and successful solution, this would be highly desirable on all counts for all concerned. And speaking very personally, totally between ourselves, such a successful solution would be personally very beneficial.'

'Personally beneficial?' Maxwell inquired: 'How so?'

'As regarding promotion. As regarding the possibility of suitability for appointment to the Inspectorate.'

'I see,' I said: 'Andrew may not have died in vain. I gather, Charlie, that you are moving, very delicately, towards asking us to do what we can to make you a Detective Inspector – and of course we will, Charlie, as we will always be happy to help our old friends to ascend to higher things. But you must help us to help you. We need to know what the police know, and what they suspect. Your lines of inquiry must be made manifest to us. And whenever any clue, or even anything out of the ordinary, turns up, we must be instantly informed. In return, it goes without saying, we will tell you what we think, what we find; and the credit for whatever we might happen to discover, it also goes without saying, will be entirely yours.'

'Well,' said Charlie, 'I appreciate that. As regarding all that, I'll do what I can, which must never be known. We have located Andrew's vehicle and are currently analysing its contents. If anything turns up I'll give Maxwell a ring, but it must never be known.'

'It goes without saying,' I said: 'Never. Before you go, though, a word, an extra word, about the location of the body might be useful. He was found on the Hill, hanging. Where?'

'Next to the exercise trail, you'll know it. The track that goes around above the reservoir. Along there.'

'We'd like to know exactly where,' said Maxwell: 'We might pick up a hint or two. Exactly where?'

'We've put some red tape on the tree he was hung from. You can easily find it. But he wasn't completely killed there, we reckon.'

'Why do you reckon that?' I asked: 'I thought you said there were no indications either way.'

'There wasn't enough blood. There must have been most of it somewhere else. Not to put too fine a point on it, he would have bled like a pig. They must have carried him from somewhere – it wasn't from his house, there's no blood there; and hung him up on the hill. It's a bit of a puzzle.'

'Why they should have wanted to transport him up onto the Hill,' I said, 'is even more of a puzzle. Why take the risk and trouble of transporting him from this somewhere to the Hill? Unless, of course, this somewhere was somewhere else on the Hill. Adjacent. In which case he might only have been transported a relatively short and convenient distance. But why transport him at all, and why to that spot? Have you sent the dogs in? They should have been scouring the whole Hill.'

'Too right we've sent the dogs in. I couldn't find a single willing constable; that whole place must be alive with snakes. The dogs have found nothing except condoms.'

'Condoms?' said Maxwell: 'Were there condoms near where Andrew was found?'

'They're everywhere. There are scores of beggars at it all over the hill at all hours of the day and night, it's a regular brothel up there. In cars mainly, because of the snakes.They chuck the condoms out of the windows.'

'One or two of those busy beggars might not have been too engrossed to remark unusual sights and sounds,' I remarked: 'Is this one of your lines of inquiry?'

'Not as such. They're not likely to want to admit being up there. Too many of them are married. I'd better get back to the station now, they might have made a bit of progress.'

'We,' I said to Maxwell, 'had better get up to the Hill before it gets dark.'

Up we went. We drove up Edmondson Street, named after Cpl. John Edmondson, V.C. (d. Tobruk, 1941), past South Wagga Primary's grass-plot (on which – as the Memoir will reveal – I wrestled and defeated the wily Ronnie Smith); over the railway bridge, past the vast, famous, now virtually deserted Mt. Erin Convent (whose most celebrated occupant was the nun who managed to escape from it, Sister Ligouri, in 1920); on into Mitchelmore Street, named after Henry Mitchelmore, solicitor and citizen (d. Wagga, 1941) - a street that will go down to posterity, if I have anything to do with it, as the horrid, horrid obliterater of Wagga High School's western playground, historic scene of our most memorable youthful chasings and taggings – lyric grist for the Memoir's mill; left into Urana Street, so-called, presumably, because were one moved to follow it out West, one could go on and on until one fetched up at Urana; into the Baden Powell Drive, which needs no explanation from me, past the sinister School for Specific Purposes, and in, at last, to the parking-and-picnic area adjoining the Museum of the Riverina. The Hill lay all about us, bathed in the evening sun, its southern reaches embosoming the manifold delights of the Botanic Gardens, its western and north-western declivities – immediately below us, as we gazed across and down – studded with greensward, eucalypts and pines; between which, visible in streaks and patches, the exercise trail wound in and out its woeful way.

 The Hill. *The* Hill. There were several hills in Wagga's vicinity, but this one – it was really a ridge, rather, rising, at its tip, to all of 309 metres above sea-level – which dominated the city's eastern and southern sectors and was loomingly apparent all over it, was *primus inter pares*: municipally considered, it was the Hill of hills. Post-Aboriginally considered, its name was Willans' Hill, Mr. Willans having been another solicitor, whose residence had been situate on its western verge. The region into which we were gazing had, as its centre, a vile, vile, vile lake-like reservoir – trebly vile, because once upon a time, when Maxwell and I were young, a deep and ferny gully, in wet seasons a distinct creek, had been here; and for many years, when Maxwell and I were young, that gully, and all the slopes and dingles attending it, submerged now in an acre of chlorinated water, had been the very navel of our world. We had begun to explore that tract of the Hill soon after we had progressed to the Wagga High School, sited just off the western edge of it; and for many years thereafter we went there twice or thrice a week, day and night, prowling and patrolling, planning our assault on life and glory, imagining ourselves into futures far distant from the Wagga that our parents had deposited us in, and constantly, night and day, expecting the beginning of some tremendous adventure here, there, behind that tree, within that thicket, over that ridge. In this place we grew up, and all the eminences and recesses of its landscape became part of our intimate personal history. Our mutual passion for the Hill moved me early into print: while still a pupil at Wagga High I contributed a *morceau*, turgid but not unpromising, 'On the Hill', to the school magazine, *The Hill*. And many years later, years during which I fixed my residence in Europe but returned constantly to Wagga to visit parents and friends, chief among them Maxwell, when our regular ramblings about the Hill were revivings and retracings of our vanishing youth, I composed an elaborate, extensive meditation, again or still entitled 'On the Hill', and included it in a volume of essays I edited, *Secret Landscapes* – now, alas, out of print. (Not so 'alas', actually, since I intend to draw heavily on it for my Memoir.) This sacred realm – this other Eden, demi-paradise, as I could not but describe it – had now been defiled and forever changed, changed utterly, by the murdered corpse of our school-mate. We went down into it in a gloomy frame of mind.

'I'm in a pretty gloomy frame of mind,' I said, as we set off along the exercise trail: 'The whole atmosphere of the Hill has been infected by this enormity. Speaking personally, Maxwell, I take it personally. Our Hill has lost its innocence, its purity, its... '

'If what Charlie says is right it had already lost them ,' said Maxwell: 'Those widespread intercoursers have seen to that.'

'It is an astonishing thing, old thing, that in all the years we have haunted this place, day and especially night, we have never once beheld one, or rather two, of them. We may have earnestly desired to behold them, I do not altogether dismiss such a suggestion; but we have not, not a bang, not a whimper. And only two condoms, bobbing contentedly together in the creek. Standards have slipped. Good evening,' I said: for a pair of puce and panting pensioners, evidently on their last legs, came staggering past us, victims of the exercise trail: 'You're doing very well. Only six more miles to go. And be sure to attempt the Scramble Wall at the far end of the reservoir, it's compulsory.'

'Isn't one murder enough for you?' Maxwell inquired: 'That Wall will soon be festooned with red tape if we encounter any more geriatrics. And speaking of red tape, where is it?'

Indeed. We followed the trail round the reservoir's southern shore, through scrubby country where the eye of faith and knowledge could discern a few faint traces of the former gully and creek. No red tape. We turned uphill, up a steep and exercising slope. Here the path skirted an area which we had always regarded as our secret sanctuary, our last redoubt when Armageddon broke upon us, a numinous gathering of kurrajongs and antique gums and olive trees – see the final rapturous pages of 'On the Hill' in *Secret Landscapes,* if you can obtain it . We bestowed a solemn greeting on it and pressed on. Above it, the path took a sharp turn to the left and North, and began the long slow climb to the Hilltop. There, just past the turn, above the path, stood a grey-white eucalypt, stark and leafless, some forty years dead, red-taped.

'Well, well, well,' I said. There was nothing else to say. On the other hand, there was much to think. The branch from which Andrew had hung, or hanged, the only one substantial enough, was obvious; and it was also obvious – one could not avoid imagining it – that, if at all conscious, a hanger there would have had a heart-stoppingly panoramic – final – view, out over our secret sanctuary, right across to the High School and, beyond, to the Base Hospital and the far-flung purlieus of western Wagga and, farther yet, to Mount Moorong and the Pomingalarna Reserve – now, another alas, a golf-course. Despite the golf-course, if - as I explained to Maxwell, who seemed disinclined to appreciate the observation - if Andrew had still been alive, even slightly, when he was strung up here, his last sight of this world would have been of something well worth remembering.

'At night?' Maxwell said: ' Be reasonable. Only a blur of lights.'

'Still. Even so. The presence of such a view, even if invisible, would surely have been a consolation. Just knowing it was out there would be enough for me.'

'For you, yes. For me too, marginally. But not, I think, for Andrew, or for anybody else. We mustn't mislead ourselves. You were asking Charlie whether there might be some significance in the fact that Andrew's body was found up here on the Hill. What we have to remember is that the Hill is a place of great significance for us, but for everybody else it's merely the nearest bit of convenient Bush.'

'I was forgetting that. True. We are not as others are. Charlie, you must have noticed, didn't think that question worth answering. And it still seems to me to be a somewhat peculiar place to hang a body. '

'Surely not. It's practically next door to where Andrew lives, lived. Sunshine Avenue is just over there, just a street away. However he came here, it's the closest piece of secluded ground to his own house. If he was going to be killed or carried anywhere out of the way, this is much the most likely spot.'

'Spot is what I meant. Not the Hill in general - this particular spot right here, where the body was found. Doesn't it strike you as somehow peculiar?'

'Every spot is a particular spot. You're letting that memoir do your thinking for you. I must say I think Mike McClure hit the nail on the head when he pointed out your tendency, to put it mildly, to look for the roots and springs of almost everything that happens hereabouts back in the land of lost content when we were young. If, despite my pleas, we are going to have a look at Andrew's murder, could you possibly make a supreme effort to concentrate on the here-and-now and put our blessed past aside?'

'Agreed. I shall restrain my tendencies. Nonetheless, Charlie didn't actually agree with Mike that the past could be discounted. "The past is a peculiar factor", quoth he, displaying much uncharacteristic wisdom. When is the past past? Whether Artie was also displaying uncharacteristic wisdom is another question entirely. I'd like to know more about those previous deaths he was wondering about. There has always been a certain shrewdness beneath his inanity. And of course I must be sure to register their various passings in the Memoir.'

'Oh God, you're already doing it again. Mike's words of warning have been thrown away.'

'I'll keep them in mind, I promise. I promise I won't let that interfere with the here-and-now, which, as far as poor Andrew is concerned, is already the there-and-then. But sufficient unto the day is the discourse thereof. Let's go.'

We sat there, though, for half an hour or more, more or less in silence, taking in the view – Andrew's view, I named it – and reflecting on the day's passages. At the going down of the sun, Wagga is surely – who could doubt it? - one of the most beautiful places on earth: as the lights came out and the river mist arose it was still, in spite of this atrocious murder, one of the Great Good Places. Maxwell and I were honour-bound to do what in us lay to keep it so.

Before we wended our way to the car-park we went on up to the municipal look-out on the top of the Hill, from which we surveyed all the kingdoms of the world and the glory of them; after which, on our way back, I inspired another couple of senior citizens. We drove on over the Hill, into Lake Albert Road – named after Lake Albert; which was named after Prince Albert, and why not? – and on to Maxwell's welcoming farmlet.

Food. Port. Sleep.

CHAPTER TWO

We were up with the currawongs– Maxwell's garden, or arboretum, being their regional H.Q.; and we were but half-way through our scrambled eggs, to the delicious warbling of Emma Kirkby and her consorts when, Duty having called up Detective Sergeant Charlie Parrot equally early, the phone rang, and it was he.

'Andrew's car,' he announced, 'contains certain items which I would welcome your opinions regarding. Don't come to the station, it's full of police officers. Meet me down at the Beach, about eleven.'

'Trusty Charlie,' I observed: 'Delivering on his promises with all the passionate promptitude of one who sees before him, just within reach, the Crown of Life, the Inspectorship.'

Maxwell thought this unduly cynical. Before and after eleven, we thought, we should try to have a few probing words with some of Andrew's other friends and workmates. Maxwell thought that Jayne would know more friendly names than he did, she and Andrew being, having been, on the dinner-dancing fringe of Wagga's *beau monde*, a world he wotted not of; but that we could drop in on his place of work on our way down to the Beach.

'Dinner-dancing? Andrew was middle-aged,' I said, 'like us.' Maxwell shot me a look. 'Later-middle-aged, which makes it worse. I'm sorry to hear that he hadn't put away childish things. Think of all the invaluable reading-time he wasted, dinner-dancing.'

'He had a non-late-middle-aged wife, an obvious non-reader. Women must be amused. Jayne loved dancing; Andrew told me they'd even gone so far as to take tango lessons.'

That silenced me. We drove into town and down Baylis Street, Henry Baylis having been the magistrate who, in 1863, was bailed up, wounded and robbed by the celebrated bushranger, Dan 'Mad Dog' Morgan, who was later shot, beheaded and had his scalp made into a purse. Such is life. We parked, naturally, in Morgan Street – named, disappointingly, after Wagga's first doctor. A short stroll took us into the Plaza Arcade, so-called because it was within sight and sound of the celebrated Plaza Theatre, the cinema in which, at Saturday matinees, many of our youthful dreams – the Memoir will throb with them - were engendered. In the depths of said arcade, past the inimitable Ron Gillman's tailoring surgery, a brace of Gift Shoppes and a louche beautician, were the premises of Klever Kitchens, now and forever without their popular Head of Sales.

Maxwell's saucepans were Klever Kitchen's, and he was greeted there as a valued client and a known friend of Andrew's. Mutual condolences were exchanged. I was introduced; the Manager reckoned he'd read something of mine somewhere, perhaps in a book of some sort; and I allowed that that was within the bounds of possibility. Maxwell then explained that we were helping the police with the whys and wherefores of Andrew's death. Was there anything at all unusual in his mood or behaviour in his last few days? The Manager urged me to call him Doug. Doug said that the police had already asked them this question and the answer had to be No, he was just his usual self, he was a beaut bloke right to the end. A pert girl in Reception, quite pretty, green eyes, said she thought he'd been a bit gloomy really, normally he was quite a joker, but not so much lately; but a chap from Repairs said he'd told him a very funny story last thing last Friday, he was definitely in good spirits then. What story? I asked. The chap said he'd been hoping we wouldn't ask that because he couldn't remember the crucial details and it was far too filthy for mixed company but it had something to do with a canary. I remarked that that story was doing the rounds and we already knew the punch-line. The pert girl said she hoped I would tell it to her sometime, she was really noticeably pretty. Maxwell intervened and wondered whether the police had examined the contents of Andrew's desk? Doug said they had, there was nothing personal there. Only that little chain, a girl in Sales said - plain, but with nice ears. Not even, I asked, a picture of his wife? Not even, Doug said. Unusual, I said. Don't you for example, I said to the pert girl, have a picture of your boyfriend on your desk? Sometimes, she said, it depends on my moods. Doug said that nobody could be more devoted to his wife than he was but he didn't have a picture of her, it was a matter of personal style. Like dancing, I said, where personal style makes all the difference, particularly in the tango. There are those, I said, who say that those who haven't seen Andrew do the tango haven't lived. The pretty pert girl said she wouldn't say that, not in the slightest; at the firm's Christmas dinner-dance at Romano's Andrew and the tango were poles apart. But as for Jayne, I said - wouldn't you agree that Jayne's tangoing was a thing of beauty and a joy for ever? Doug said that Jayne hadn't been there on that occasion and maybe they should all be getting back to work now. What little chain? Maxwell asked. The salesgirl with the ears said That one there, pointing towards a desk that had evidently been Andrew's; on which, on closer inspection, a small gold chain was hanging from a letter-rack. She went on to say that the big bald detective, immediately identifiable as our Charlie, had said he thought he might as well leave it here for Jayne to pick up, it was an intimate kind of thing; and Doug said that as a personal friend Maxwell might like to pass it on to her, he'd be likely to be seeing her before she'd be likely to want to come down here. Maxwell accepted the mission and the chain. We asked the Klever Kitcheners to give him a ring if they remembered anything possibly useful, and departed. The pretty pert girl followed us up the Arcade and said she remembered who I was, she'd greatly enjoyed *Harry Donnelly's Coming*, which her boyfriend couldn't make head or tail of, but there were a couple of parts of it that perhaps I could explain to her one evening when I was free. Maxwell intervened and said I was never free but I said I might be, just give me your phone number, which she did; and then we were out and away.

 We drove on down Baylis Street, took a hard right – Maxwell's motoring angles tended to the acute – skirted the huge and horrid Civic Administration Centre – situate in, and virtually abolishing, the Civic Centre Gardens which, time was, were the site and stage of the fabulous Miss Wagga contest, wherein I used to bear the part of major-domo and municipal Town Crier (Oyez! Oyez!) until tumultuously objurgated off the stage by dolts and ruffians in the mid-1950s: a moment that I have ever regarded as one of the turning-points of modern Australian history. There were rich pickings for my Memoir in this vicinity and I began to sketch them for Maxwell as we swung left around the Civic Theatre, words fail me, and then right into Cross and Church Streets, where there were several churches and the Riverina Playhouse, a doleful, ill-assorted building which now squatted where the vasty, smelly municipal gasworks had once upreared its fumy head; but 'pickings' seemed to provoke him and he demanded to know instead why, in my late middle-age, I needed to make a fool of myself by trying to pick up girls who were young enough to be my children, or indeed grandchildren?

'Firstly,' said I, 'if picking up was in motion I was not the prime mover. Secondly, because picking up was definitely in motion, so the interesting question is Why? We can discount looks, charm, sexual panache. If she'd been going for those she'd have gone for you. Was it perhaps a wish to sit at the feet, say, of a distinguished literary figure? Perhaps. She might be that sort of a sort. Fame, famously, is a potent aphrodisiac. Thirdly, whatever her wishes might turn out to be, I am prepared to throw myself into a nocturnal interview with her and run the risk of her boyfriend's choler because, Fourthly and finally, she was a critical or at any rate a criticising witness of Andrew's attempt to execute the tango at a dinner-dance from which Jayne was absent, and as to which Manager Doug was suddenly suspiciously keen to bring the discussion to an end. So there.'

While I was enunciating these truths we were shooting past: St. John's, C of E, where – time was, again – Maxwell and I had appeared before the public as altar-boys, suave and stately attenders on the legendary Archdeacon, later Bishop, Davies; St. Andrew's, Presbyterian of course, no comment; the previous location of the Christian Brothers' High School, inveterate foe of heroic Wagga High, now (heh! heh!) a brasserie and retirement apartments; and St. Michael's cathedral, seat of *episcopus corvopolitanus*, whose current occupant, a man of parts, was an admirer of G.K.Chesterton. Another hard right took us down into Cabarita - aboriginal for 'beautiful place by a river' - Park, a camping-and-caravan reserve in which nameless things have ever been done, and on - past the Wagga & District Pipe Band Pavilion, thoughtfully sited well away from human habitation - to the Beach, Wagga's historic lido on the mighty Murrumbidgee. There, stern and erect between the Lifesavers' clubhouse, in which even more nameless things have ever been done, and the site of the former refreshment kiosk, Charlie Parrot awaited us.

'This must never be known,' he said, ' unless I say. I can't have it known that I've brought these clues out to show you. Take a quick look at these.' He produced a buff envelope and laid out its contents on a picnic table: a postcard, a cuff-link, a copper bracelet, four cigarillo butts, three spent matches, two Wrigley's spearmint chewing-gum wrappers, empty, and one crumpled can of Foster's, also empty. 'What do you make of them?'

'Is this a selection,' I asked, 'or the lot?'

'Most of it,' said Charlie: 'I couldn't bring the blood, which is certainly a major clue. There are evident signs of serious conflict in the vehicle.'

'Serious conflict?' said Maxwell: 'What do you mean exactly?'

'I mean blood,' said Charlie: 'Blood in several areas of the interior. As if a considerable amount of violent struggle had taken place in it. The Scientific Police are already pretty confident that that blood will be proved to have belonged to the deceased we are concerned with.'

'It might also belong to somebody else as well,' I said: 'Violent struggles tend to involve more than one participant.'

'Which I have often observed,' said Charlie: 'That blood will be closely examined for all manner of clues. The likeliness of a lot of it belonging to poor Andrew has been made very likely by this further additional item.'

He now produced a plastic bag containing a brown leather wallet.

'This wallet belonged to poor Andrew,' he said, 'as is proved by its various cards and documents. It was found under the driver's seat. He must have lost it during the struggle in the vehicle.'

'These other items that aren't supposed to be a selection look like a selection to me,' I said: 'In any normal car there would have to be much more more miscellaneous stuff. Where's the rest of it?'

'Very shrewd,' Charlie said: 'The Scientific Police have gone through the vehicle with a fine-tooth comb, and there was nothing else there. It is their considered view that it has been carefully stripped of virtually all of its contents. Furthermore, and speaking personally as an experienced investigator, that is also my view.'

'How such careful strippers managed to overlook these various items is something of a mystery,' Maxwell said: 'I wonder why?'

'Because, possibly,' I responded, 'they are utterly insignificant. All the real clues have been carefully removed. These items are so insignificant that it would have looked extremely suspicious if they had not been overlooked. The beer can, for example. There can't be a single car in Australia that doesn't have an empty beer can knocking about in it. If there hadn't been a beer can here we would have been in no doubt that these items had been planted in order to mislead.'

' Really?' said Charlie.

'It's therefore just as possible,' said Maxwell, 'that the beer can has been planted here to remove the suspicion that the other items might have been.'

'Amazing!' said Charlie: 'So you reckon there's a certain sinister intention here to misdeceive the police?'

'We don't reckon anything yet; except that there seems to be something fishy about these clues,' said Maxwell: 'But I can definitely say that the Wrigley wrappers and the cigarillo stubs didn't belong to Andrew, he didn't chew gum and he didn't smoke. We're also missing a match: we have four butts but only three matches.'

'Very acute,' Charlie said: 'I shall instruct the Scientific Police to conduct a further search. But the smoker in question might have chucked that match out of the window. It's a fairly common practice unfortunately, especially in summer.'

'Who belongs to the copper bracelet,' I inquired: 'I recognise the type. Whoever's missing it either has or fears the rheumatics. Had or feared. Does that sound like Andrew?'

'Not as far as I know,' Maxwell replied: 'I certainly never noticed him wearing one. Jayne will know. Poor Jayne. She'll surely also know whether this cuff-link' – it was round, blue, and had a silver spiral on it – 'is Andrew's. When's she coming back?'

'The day after tomorrow,' Charlie said: 'Poor Jayne. I've spoken to her on the phone, her and her mother. She says she'll do all she can to help but she's completely baffled by it, she can't imagine why or who. The mother sounds like a real battleaxe.'

'The ultimate exhibit is this postcard, which may perhaps be a little less insignificant than the rest,' I said. This postcard depicted a section of Fitzmaurice Street – 1st Lieutenant John G. Fitzmaurice of the 95th regiment of foot was a fellow-officer of Sir Thomas Mitchell, Colonial Surveyor-General, who judged that Wagga was the proper place for a memorial of his colleague's life and works – back in the days when David Jones (decamped 1971) was the big department store there. All vehicles within sight were utilities. Four pedestrians were discernible, two of whom were in the act of turning around to look at the other two. A pitiless blue sky overarched acres of rusty tin roofs. The Hill, in the near distance, was drought-riddenly yellow. *Welcome to Wagga Wagga, Garden City of the South* it said. It bore, on its reverse, no address, no message.

'In what way less insignificant?' Maxwell wanted to know. So, by the blank and bewildered expression on his face, did Charlie.

'I haven't the faintest idea,' I said; 'but it's an odd thing to have left behind in the car. It's an even odder thing to be there in the first place. Is it Andrew's? If it's not Andrew's why would somebody bring it into his car? It's an old postcard, 1950s or 1960s. Should we be looking for a collector or hoarder of old Wagga postcards? Does the date matter? Or the street? This item raises so many questions that it simply must mean something.'

'Where was the car?' Maxwell asked.

'On The Boulevarde. You know, off the Lake Albert Road,' Charlie said: 'Mr. Jackson reported it. It was on his nature strip.'

Mr. Jackson was a notable citizen, a former municipal Librarian and an illustrious Rotarian – another man of parts. He is due to make a memorable appearance in my Memoir.

'The Boulevarde,' Maxwell reminded me, 'is within a block or two of the eastern end of the Baden Powell Drive. The Hill and its exercise paths are only five minutes away.'

'So they are,' I said, 'and Lake Albert itself is just down the road. I seem to remember that our old schoolmate Steve Hampson met his end in Lake Albert. Such a pity. I don't suppose that there were any postcards or cigarillos or beer cans in the vicinity of that tragic scene?'

'Beer cans, probably. He was quite a drinker, Steve was,' said Charlie: 'But none of the others as far as I can recall to mind. It was a straightforward heart-attack with drowning in consequence. Poor

Steve. By the time they got to him he was too far gone to be regenerated, even if Tommy had known how.'

'Tommy?' I said: 'Tommy who?'

'Tommy Anderson. You must remember Tommy, the school villain. He's the town villain now, we have to keep arresting him, he's a real nuisance. But underneath, in my opinion, he's not all bad, he's got a lot of loyalty towards everybody he was at school with, for example.'

'Here and now,' Maxwell said, 'Andrew's … '

'Why was Tommy there?' I inquired: 'Lake Albert isn't the most obvious place for him to be. Did he just happen to be swimming past?'

'No, he wasn't, he was on the shore. Or so I've heard. He apparently became aware of Steve in difficulties. He seems to have dived in to help him. My view is that he was out there, in the proximity of the Lake clubhouse, with the intention of discovering where their safe was.'

'I think,' said Maxwell, 'that we have got as much as we can, for the time being, from these items you have shown us. If anything further occurs to us we'll let you know.'

'Well,' said Charlie, 'I understand. You'll want to have a bit of time to have a think about these clues now before you come up with any conclusions. I'm relieved to notice that we seem to be on the same wavelength in regard to this obvious attempt to pull wool over police eyes. Whoever they are, they have failed to succeed. I can smell a set-up as soon as I see it. And you two probably can even before that. I'd better get back to the station, they'll be wondering where I've got to.'

We promised to have a think, and he took off.

We took a stroll on the beach and watched the turbid stream. It was surely exactly here that Captain Sturt had planted his founding feet; it was the only strand of sand, the only inviting landing-place, in the neighbourhood. Its latter history has been full of incident. It was here that I was taught, with much misery and many startling sinkings, to swim. It was here, one hot and thundery evening, on a Wagga High outing, that I first *saw* S.E.X. – Gary Doggett, dead and gone, and Sonia somebody, a scrubber, but exceedingly toothsome. It was here – he had obviously forgotten all about it, he would certainly not have had this meeting here if he had remembered it - that several feckless fools failed to drown young Charlie Parrot. And it was here, virtually here, only a couple of hundred yards downstream, in Dixieland – a dance-floor and approved trysting-space, daringly suspended over the river – that my mother had her first dance with my father, wearing – she, not he – a gorgeous green dress held together with pins. I could almost hear the music.

'Lunch,' I declared: 'At the Tourist Hotel. We might run into Tommy Anderson there, it's one of his haunts.'

'I don't know why you bother with that malignant layabout,' said Maxwell: 'He's an extremely unappetising character, nobody can stand a bar of him. What do you see in him? The only thing he's ever managed to do is be the most incompetent crook in the district.'

'Incompetent he certainly is,' I replied; 'but he is, as you also say, a crook. It makes no sense to be investigating a crime of this magnitude without making contact with the local criminals. Tommy is our way in; and he might have heard something, or be able to pick something up. Layabout he may be, but he's never been malignant to me. I helped him in a few exams in ancient times, and I once wrote a letter for him to a girlfriend, which worked. All things considered, Tommy and I are cobbers. You will notice that I say nothing about Steve Hampson.'

We drove down Sturt Street, past the police station and the court-house (1900-02), round Romano's' corner – Romano's, in our day, was Wagga's grandest hotel, and shards of that glory still clung to it – and into Fitzmaurice Street. I planned to include a noble threnody on this legendary street in my Memoir. Who else in this day and age would be capable of commemorating – a remote family memory, this – the site and delectability of Mrs. Perkins' Pies? For most of the city's history Fitzmaurice Street was Wagga's main street, where the principal stores, solicitors, accountants, stock-and-station agents and hotels, especially hotels, had their premises; but Wagga grew away from it, southwards, so that Baylis Street became the main street and Fitzmaurice fell into decline and dilapidation, its proud establishments abandoned or re-located, particularly its noble array of fine hotels, a dozen or more in its palmy days, of which a mere four, mere basic boozers, now remained (What a falling off was there, O my countrymen!), one of them the Tourist. In we went, and the resident basic boozers regarded us with profound incuriosity. We ordered the basic Australian lunch, steak and beer; and I looked around for Tommy, who was not, I soon saw, there.

'Where's Tommy?' I asked; and then, because one needs to strike the right comradely note at the outset: 'Where's that old bastard today? Fuck me, I reckoned the lazy bugger was bloody certain to be in here about now.'

The barman rebuked me for swearing. Apparently there was a woman on the floor, but still conscious, at the far end of the bar.

After a minute or two's general muttering in distant corners, a very old battered fellow with an extraordinarily lumpy nose rose up and tottered over towards us. When he arrived, 'He's not here,' he said.

'So I see,' I said: 'Where is he? I'm an old friend, he wouldn't want to miss me.'

'I know who you are, I was at school with you,' he astonishingly said: 'Rory McFadden, South Wagga 5A.'

'Rory!' I tried to exclaim: 'Of course. And you're looking so well!' I had no memory of him at all: he must have sat right up the back. Or perhaps it was the nose. 'We must have a chinwag real soon. At the moment, though, it's Tommy I need to talk to.'

'We haven't seen him for a few days, not since Saturday' old Rory said: 'He'll turn up soon, he was saying he expected you back here about now and he wanted to be sure to have a chat with you. He actually wanted to tell you how much he liked one of your stories he'd just read, something about an Eric.'

'*Eric Connolly's Comeuppance* , that would be,' I said: 'I'm surprised – gratified, of course, but surprised – that he should have tackled it, it's full of long words. What did he say about it?'

'He said it was a real bugger to get into, but if you managed to there were a few pages towards the end that made everything worthwhile.' Rory said.

'That's pretty classy literary criticism,' I said: 'I long to discuss this further with him. Where is he?'

'He said he had a thing to do out in the country, somewhere out Boree Creek way he said,' Rory said, 'but I dunno what.'

'We'll hear about it soon enough, never fear,' I said: 'It'll be in the paper, in the police reports.' There were widespread chuckles and noddings of heads. 'How was he, when last seen, the old beggar?'

'Good,' said Rory: 'In a good mood. Very joky really. He was telling us this story that Artie Starkey had just told him, you remember Artie, he was at school with us, well Tommy could hardly stop laughing about this story, it was about some woman and a canary...'

'Ah yes,' I said: 'Wagga's current side-splitter. This joke is following us about. Did he say when he'd be back?'

'No, he didn't. He just said he was on to something that was going to make him a mint. But he often said that.'

'When he comes in, tell him I'm here. Tell him to give me a ring.' I gave him Maxwell's number and he tottered back to his corner.

Over the steak and beer we considered how things stood. The car, we reckoned, had been left to be found, and quickly. ('Why quickly?' Maxwell said.) Abandoned cars were two a penny in most areas of Wagga but not, most emphatically not, on Mr. Jackson's nature strip. If you wanted to make absolutely sure that something would be promptly and responsibly reported, Mr. Jackson, throwing open his curtains in the morning and discovering an intolerable trespass on his front lawn, was your man. Not only had the car been left to be found, it had been left stripped and ready for investigation. The assorted owner's junk that all cars contain had evidently been removed; the items remaining in Andrew's were, apart from his wallet and, possibly, a cuff-link and a bracelet, notably un-Andrewish; and it was therefore fairly likely that they too had been left to be found. ('Also quickly,' Maxwell said.) But why? It appeared probable that, as Charlie had been – surprisingly: he was less bone-headed than he looked – quick to pick up, they had been left as apparent clues to baffle or mislead the police. Baffling them would be better done by leaving no clues at all; but if they were meant to mislead them they seemed, uselessly, to lead in no discernible direction. What wild-goose chase, equipped with these clues, could the constabulary go blunderingly off on? I had a feeling that cuff-links had a well-established role as vital clues in detective fiction, although I couldn't immediately think of any examples. In a traditional detective story the postcard might appear to be leading us into Fitzmaurice Street because here we were in it; but we were in it only because I happened to want to meet Tommy Anderson and it happened to be lunch-time – and besides, the postcard's view of Fitzmaurice Street did not include the Tourist Hotel. Maxwell continued to fret over the missing match. Things stood at odd angles.

Steak and beer bring on naps, and we returned to Maxwell's farmlet to have them. By tea-time it was time, we thought, to gather some of Andrew's neighbours' impressions. Up and over the Hill we chugged, down Baden Powell Drive, past the sinister School for Specific Purposes, and then hard right into Macleay Street; which, by the bye, was named after Sir William Macleay, magistrate, publisher, legislator and – mark this: there was a time when we out here knew what was owed to Intellect and Learning – one of the founders of Sydney University. A harder left brought us into Sunshine Avenue, named after the sunshine, of which Wagga has much too much. The Kells' house was in the first block, within sight and stroll of the Hill, and we averted our eyes from its drawn blinds and closed curtains. Next door to it, Maxwell said, there were the Rodds, Bill and his missus, on one side, and on the other, renting from yet another dentist who had retired down the coast to Bermagui, there were a couple of unattached females who, according to Andrew, were mutually attached. Further down the street there was Vic Hopkirk, whom he knew the Kells knew, who would be quite a surprise, and also Miss M.E. Paddock, Head of Girls at Wagga High for most of the twentieth century, though now – under protest - retired, a terror to us all, who now must be at least one hundred and fifty. These, I could tell, were not promising interviewees.

We tackled the Rodds first. Theirs, like everybody's up here, was a commodious brick bungalow with a wide verandah and boundless lawns, swept and garnished. As we trekked across the latter I was momentarily transported back to our high school days, to the time when Sunshine Avenue, and Grandview Avenue, its northern partner – named after the grand panoramic view to be had from it over All Wagga and Environs – produced a remarkably rich and continuous crop of tantalising teenage schoolgirls, girls with *golden* legs, who wore their tunics higher, just a touch – or Miss M.E. Paddock would have notified police and parents – above the knee, who sported brighter eyes and bolder bosoms than their scraggy sisters from the other side of the Wagga tracks. We used to marvel at their splendid equipment, at their sheer sexy self-possession; and for many yearning years we inclined to a climatic explanation of their numbers and wonders. The air up here was evidently balmier, more favourable to lushness and rampancy, than down town on the river flats. The Sunshine and Grandview girls were a race apart. The real explanation, when it eventually came to us, confirmed this judgment. These streets, aloft on our southern slopes, had views, had a breath or two of cooler air in our long hot summers, and were therefore much in demand and commanded higher property-prices than lowlier regions. Those who could afford them bought, settled and bred here. Moneyed men and pretty women tend to go together; and pretty women tend to make pretty daughters. In more recent times, as the town expanded and developed into the present megalopolis, other even cooler and more spectacular eminences for the wealthy, now even wealthier, to throw up their palazzi upon, to the South and West and out around Lake Albert, were incorporated into the city, and the glory days of Sunshine and Grandview Avenues departed. Ichabod. They were still among Wagga's better class of streets, their bungalows were ample, their inhabitants were comfortably-off and generally respectable, but they did not nurture and harbour the beautiful people, as of yore; and it was of that yore – their and our prime (O world! O life! O time!) – that I wished my Memoir to sing. Alas! The golden girls had vanished from these streets, and as soon as I attempted to summon them back Andrew's bloody corpse now threatened to drive them away. As we trekked across the verandah Bill Rodd appeared at the screen-door.

'G'day,' he said.

We said G'day and Maxwell introduced me as another old friend of Andrew's. Bill came out onto the verandah and we surveyed his lawn for a while, shaking our heads.

'A foul business,' he said at last: 'It's been a terrible shock.' His hair, which stood on end, seemed to confirm this remark. His crest of hair and improbably huge conk – the second, so far, today – made him a far more convincing parrot than Charlie Parrot. But such is life.

'A shock, yes, terrible,' I said: 'But was it a terrible surprise, if you know what I mean?'

'No', he said, giving me a very parroty look.

'I think what he's wondering, Bill,' Maxwell said, 'is whether it came as such a terrible surprise that somebody would have wanted to murder Andrew?'

'Not these days,' Bill said: 'There are so many madmen about. You never know when someone will have a go at you.'

'That's true enough,' said Maxwell: 'Have you noticed any of these apparent madmen hanging about up here, any strange-looking strangers?'

'Not during the day, not more than usual. But if they came at night we'd be watching the TV, there could be scores of them out there, we wouldn't be going out to find out, if you know what I mean.'

'I do,' I said: 'But leaving these madmen aside for a moment, were there any unusual sights or sounds next door, last Sunday?'

'The police asked that, and I told them No, nothing at all. Andrew went off on his jogs in the afternoon, every Sunday he went, and we would have been having our tea when he came back.'

'If he came back,' Maxwell said: 'Were his lights on that night?'

'We were watching the TV. We didn't look out.'

'A jogger, was he?' I said: 'What time did he jog off? Which way did he go? Up towards the Hill?'

'Up that way, yes. And it would have been aroundabout two or so, as usual. His last jog, poor chap.'

'And did he normally come back from his Sunday jogs after you normally wouldn't be looking out ?' I said.

'Normally. It depends on what's on the TV.'

'I don't suppose you happened to notice whether he used his car that night?' Maxwell asked.

'We were watching the TV. We have to have it on loud, the wife's on the deaf side. And afterwards there's the sleeping pills; so no, we didn't.'

'Other neighbours may have been tuned to other and quieter programmes,' I said to Maxwell: 'Unless you have further questions I suggest we thank Bill for his valuable time and help, and ask him to convey our best wishes to the lady of the house.'

Maxwell agreed; we all said G'day; and we trekked back into the street. Next, we went to the unattached/attached females, who declared that they had already co-operated repeatedly with the police, that they had had quite enough of being badgered (and here they looked closely and rudely at Maxwell, as if weighing the possibility that he might indeed *be* a badger – he was particularly bushy this evening), and that they had no knowledge of the habits of the Kells. They had seen no lights, they had no interest in noticing any lights. As for the car, they said, closing the door, they had told the police that it had driven away soon after midnight that night, and they could put a time to it because the dreadful clashing of the gears had woken them up. Which, they said, opening and shutting the door, might have been due to Mr. Kell being drunk and incapable, and if so it wouldn't have been the first recent occasion either.

'So you do know something about the habits of the Kells,' I said to the door; which did not reply.

We went across to the houses opposite, facing, the Kells'. Nobody there had noticed anything unusual recently, although one old fellow volunteered the opinion that there were more idlers and layabouts hanging around up here these days than there ever were back when Detective Inspector Cloke – that was back when I was young and easy – ruled the streets. Nobody there had seen the late jogger return; which wasn't unusual, we were told, because he often returned late, after dark. Nobody there had noticed any lights; which would have been unusual, we were told, if Jayne had been at home, but wasn't because she wasn't, because Andrew apparently tends, tended, to do whatever he does, did, around the back. We then went around the back, into Grandview Avenue, and consulted the people there – one of whom was certainly one of those golden girls of yore, but I couldn't recall her name – whose back fences abutted on the Kells' backyard; and here, at last, we had sight of lights. A grim, thin fellow who was something in haberdashery somewhere – a poignant memory assailed me here, of Paulls', *The Premier Drapers,* in Baylis

Street, one of my mother's favourite haunts, dreadfully stacked with complicated corsets - had gone out for a bit of fresh air and a smoke; and late, it was after midnight, the Kells' lights had come on, and ten minutes later off, and soon afterwards, just as this thin smoker was going in, their car went off too, in which whoever was driving it seemed to be having a spot of trouble with the gears.

Vic Hopkirk was our next stop. Maxwell had said he would be quite a surprise; and he was. I remembered him as the suave and *distingue* sales manager of the Don Jones Tyre Service, defunct decades ago. What came out of his front door at us was a wild and dishevelled creature with a grotesque grey mop of matted hair and eyes that seemed to be not only red but revolving. He hailed us as old friends and faithful allies. He informed us that Satanists had assassinated Andrew, who - the Satanists - had been hiding in his – Vic's – shrubbery and infesting the neighbourhood during the last couple of weeks, awaiting their opportunity to strike their deadly blow. Or it was the Papists. He adjured us to pray continually, to avert the wrath to come. We asked him why these Satanists or Papists should have wanted to assassinate Andrew. 'Because,' he whispered, 'of Jayne, who even the surrounding Methodists would like to make a meal of, whose two breasts are like two young roes that are twins, also clusters of grapes. So pray, pray.' He bolted inside, presumably to do so. We beat a stately Anglican retreat.

What came out of Miss M.E. Paddock's front door at us was a blast from the past. There she exactly was, in no particle changed – the iron-grey plaits coiled tightly round the tiny head, the icy glitter in the invigilatory eyes, the merciless mouth, and below, all below, sheathed in bombazine, the magnificent bullet-proof corsetry. It all came back in a flash. So did we, apparently.

'Mother!' she shrilled into the dark backward and abysm of the hall: 'Here are those two young rascals we were speaking of last night.' She looked down on us from her full height of five foot two. 'To what do we owe this interruption? It's tea-time in this household.'

We reeled. The Mother had to be at least two hundred years old; and she was evidently still taking nourishment. Maxwell de-reeled quicker. I was disordered by suddenly remembering that in my final year at Wagga High I had borrowed a book from Miss Paddock – I couldn't remember its title, but I could remember that I had never returned it.

'We must apologise for disturbing you, ma'am,' he warbled: 'We won't detain you for more than a moment. We're helping the police with their inquiries into Andrew Kell's death, and we were naturally wondering whether you, or indeed your mother, had any suggestions to make, or had been aware recently of any unusual sights or sounds.'

There came a cry from the dark abysm. 'Throw them out !' it cried: 'We want no more of that sort around here.'

'Quite so,' I said, recovering: 'Your mother has put it in a nutshell. But who are these others of that sort who you want no more of – '

'*Whom* you want no more of,' she said.

'Whom you and your mother want no more of? Are they perhaps persons who, whom, who are not the sort who belong in this part of town, strangers, lurkers, objects of suspicion?'

'Indeed they are, and some of them have gone to considerable trouble to disguise their appearances. I have had far too much experience in detecting wigs and false moustaches to be imposed upon,' she said, 'for an instant. But I have reported this, *viva voce* and in writing, to the police, and I see no need to repeat it to you.'

'Quite so,' said Maxwell: 'But just before we leave you to your tea, is it your view that these disguised persons seemed to have a particular interest in the Kells, and if so, why?'

'Young man,' she said: 'I am much too busy to have views. But it is certainly Mother's view that the Kells have been the centre of attraction; and my knowledge of local human nature leads me to suppose that since these persons we are referring to are male, and since Mrs. Kell is a young woman in the prime of life, no special effort of mind is required to read the riddle.'

'Throw them out at once!' came another abysmal cry: 'Or I'll come and do it myself. These crumpets are getting cold.'

'We're off,' I said: 'It has been a real privilege, ma'am, to see you again, so unexpectedly, after all these years. You bring back so much. I long for a longer chat, but cold crumpets are an abomination, and we must hope that they are not lost beyond recall.'

'You haven't changed, have you?' she responded: 'Facetious, that's what you always were. You still are. It ruins all your books.' I caught Maxwell nodding, as if in agreement. 'Speaking of books: you borrowed one from me and have not yet returned it. Bring it back.'

'Ah,' I said: 'It had slipped my mind. What was its title?'

There was a frightful clanking and grinding noise from the abysm. Mother was coming.

'That's for me to know and you to remember. Be off,' she said.

We fled.

Driving homewards, we reviewed the neighbours' offerings. It seemed tolerably clear that the Kells had been under observation lately. The presence of strange loafers had been picked up by the old fellow opposite; they had woven their way into manic Vic Hopkirk's shrubbery; and they had been detected, irrespective of their disguises, by the infallible Miss M.E. Paddock and her unimaginable mother. They were likely to be local loafers because those disguises were pretty obviously intended to prevent any pre-or-post-murder recognitions in and around Wagga. They were most unlikely to be Sunshine/Grandview Avenue locals because it is a well-known fact that if people know you and you put on a disguise you at once become extremely conspicuous and the object of much unwelcome hilarity and speculation. 'Is that well-known?' Maxwell asked. 'It is,' I replied: 'Trust me. I am a veteran of the Venice Carnival. I know.'

Back at Maxwell's, over a glass of wine and an omelette, we considered the lights and the car. Two scenarios presented themselves. One, Andrew had come back late, very late, from his jog, had entered the rear parts of his house and briefly done there whatever he did, and had then got into his car and after experiencing some, perhaps alcoholic, difficulty with the gears, driven away. Two, Andrew had never come back from his last jog, having been nabbed in the course of it; and somebody else had later entered the rear parts of his house and briefly done there something or other, and had then got into his car and after experiencing some difficulty with unfamiliar gears, driven away. We could not choose between these possibilities, so left them to bask in our minds until we had more to go on.

'That more,' I said, 'should be coming the day after tomorrow, when Jayne comes home. She must be able to tell us more about Andrew's life and habits.'

'Speaking of Jayne,' Maxwell said: 'We surely can't credit the Hopkirk and Paddock notion that all this lurking and disguising has to do with Jayne? I mean, a certain amount of prowling and peeping might be occurring, she's a woman worth spying on, but not on this scale, and not on the way to such an atrocious murder.'

'You say true, or trueish. Poor Vic is evidently in the grip of religio-sexual fantasies about her, and Miss Paddock as evidently believes that all men are always in the grip of sexual fantasies. So, doubtless, does her mother. Glimpses of Jayne would surely be a bonus, not the main aim. On the other hand, it is a well-known fact that when there's a woman in the case, the case will have something to do with a woman.'

Two of the three messages on Maxwell's answering-machine were from two of the chaps – Mike McClure, of course, and Dunny Dunn. Dunny said he wanted to help us, and he had something to tell us in private. Mike wanted to know whether we'd solved the crime yet, and if so he hoped we'd bring the prisoner along to our next lunch so that he could try out his new uppercut on him. The third was from Detective Sergeant Charlie Parrot, who seemed to be whispering. 'We've found Kell's clothes,' he whispered, 'which they contain items of interest. I'd appreciate your opinions. I'll give you a ring tomorrow morning.'

It was while we were listening to Charlie's whispering that we realised we were also hearing something else. There was somebody outside, near the window. Maxwell snatched up a convenient swordstick and threw himself through the back door. I, assisted by several excited cats, fell out of the front door. We met at the window, where somebody had not waited for us. It was too dark to go a-hunting. A passing, reconnoitring thief; or an eavesdropper on purpose? Closed windows henceforth, in case.

Port. Sleep.

CHAPTER THREE

Charlie rang during Beethoven and bacon the following morning, his voice sonorous and Sergeantly, emphatically unwhispery, which told us that there were no policemen within earshot at that moment. Andrew's clothes – or clothes that Charlie said he was morally certain were Andrew's – had been found in close proximity to Tichborne Crescent, strikingly close to where his car had been discarded. The Wagga Scientific Police were currently on the scene, on the job; and no unauthorised person – in which number, Charlie said, he regretted to say that we too, or two, were unfortunately included - would be permitted to enter the area until their investigations had terminated. As soon as the experts had withdrawn, he said, he would let us know, and would appreciate a meeting with us there.

We eased our impatience with Schnabel's Beethoven for an hour or so. The phone rang, but it was Dunny Dunn, hoping to have a private word with us in the course of the day. We promised to ring back when we knew how the day would develop. The phone rang again, but it was Roy O'Hanlon this time, wondering how we were getting on, and whether we might have a drink and a bit of a natter, say tomorrow. We said tomorrow. The phone rang again, and now it was yesterday's pretty pert girl from Klever Kitchens, Veronica she said, she said she thought I might have misheard her phone number when she gave it to me so she'd rung Maxwell's just in case, she was wondering whether I'd be willing to explain a few hard things in that book we were talking about over a drink one evening, perhaps tomorrow, perhaps even better tonight. I said tonight, I was ready to be explanatory tonight, and in Romano's, I suggested, where Andrew's tango had caught her eye. I hardly had time to remark to Maxwell that the case was hotting up when the phone rang again. It was Charlie, who said Come; and we went.

It was a short drive from Maxwell's, through streets devoid of any significant historical, literary or autobiographical associations; except, of course, for Tichborne Crescent itself, which commemorated the celebrated Tichborne Case, commemorated in Wagga because the Tichborne Claimant dwelt here, Arthur Orton/Tom Castro, the outstanding liar, confidence trickster and tall story virtuoso in a town and district famously rich in them. Charlie awaited us at the Berala Street end of the Crescent – Berala: aboriginal for 'musk duck', by the way. An adjacent house and garden, festooned with anti-entry tapes, was evidently the site of the bloody discovery – made, Charlie informed us, in a backyard shed by a passing local checking constable. Charlie conducted us in to inspect the shed and its surrounds, where nothing that might have counted as a clue to anything had survived the attentions, and the boots, of the Wagga Scientific Police. He then produced his exhibits, enclosed and untouchable in polythene wallets.

    The clothes – a blue jersey with a white V and collar, and grey flannel track-suit pants – were dirty and bloody, the former particularly dirty and the latter particularly bloody. Charlie was confident that the Scientific Police would be able to tell us that these further bloodstains also belonged to Andrew because, he said, the jersey couldn't be a coincidence, it was a Wagga High rugby jersey and, as we must remember, Andrew was in the Firsts back in the old days, on the wing and bloody fast, so this could only be what he must have been wearing. His train of thought, though logically rocky, seemed to be going in the right direction. Charlie pointed out that the right-arm sleeve was missing, had apparently been ripped off; and he then brought out an envelope, and extracted from it a page of paperback-sized print which he said had been found in the pants' back pocket. I do not intend to pollute these pages with the contents of that page. Suffice it to say, it concerned and concluded the adventures of somebody called Fiona, whose body – it was evidently quite some body – was the site of operations – the open-cast mine – of a kiltless Scotchman, Hamish, whose massive block-and-tackle and sovereign indefatigability were at last – it was page 169 – bringing the ululating Fiona to the point at which she – in our revolting author's words – Got Her Fill. The blank back of the page was not, when Charlie turned it over, blank. Roughly printed in red biro were the words: *museum carpark on Hill at midnite.*

'What do you make of that? That's a clue,' said Charlie, 'if I ever saw one. Speaking for myself, it seems to tell us that Andrew drove his vehicle away from his house in the region of midnight on the night in question and also and further that he drove it to the Museum car-park up on Willans' hill, which is not very far from where he was unfortunately found on the following morning.'

"It alas tells us nothing about how and where he was occupying himself before this midnight meeting.' Maxwell said: 'He can't have been jogging all that time. And there might be traces of what happened to him in the car-park.'

'Exactly,' said Charlie: 'I have already given orders for it to be closely searched.'

'Just think of it,' I said: 'It took 169 pages for Fiona to get her fill. One wonders what she could have been getting in the preceding 168. It's a pity, on purely technical and literary grounds, that one will never know.'

'We'll take a look at the car-park ourselves,' said Maxwell: 'We're on our way up that way this morning.'

'I'd better be getting back to the station,' said Charlie: 'The Scientific Police will be wondering where I've got to with their exhibits. They'll be raring to get at them.'

When he'd gone we strolled around the corner into The Boulevarde, and on along it to Mr. Jackson's nature strip, last resting-place of Andrew's car, a bare three hundred and thirty yards – we paced it out – from his bloody clothes. This area, we agreed, we could not but agree, was significant. There was a story here. Lightning had struck twice in it. Andrew's killer or killers had been here, and had left some of him here. Was this where his or their lair was, or was it as far as possible from said lair – in, if so, Wagga's far north-west, out towards the Racecourse (scene of the world-famous Wagga Gold Cup); or was it conveniently on the way to his or their lair, out Lake Albert way? Had Andrew, alive or dying, been here? Why were the clothes hidden, and evidently not very expertly, in that particular shed, just there – because it was on the way away from the car, and the first convenient hasty hiding-place, or because, having carefully stripped or salted the car, the killer or killers saw no point in hanging on to these soiled and sordid items and had simply, carelessly, chucked them aside? Unanswerable questions. We looked about, hoping for a sign. Henwood Park, a bowl of dust at this time of year, lay before us, and showed no such sign. ('Henwood' preserves the name and fame of S.N. Henwood, a major subdivider hereabouts). The adjacent streets – most of them evidently named in aboriginal fashion: Barinya, Moani, Immarna, Coolibah &c. – showed no sign of anything. We were at a stand. But perhaps, somewhere down even these meaningless streets, some new and enlightening find was awaiting its finder, perhaps that very same passing local checking constable who had happened on the stash of clothes. We needed him to do more of his local checkings. We would talk to him as soon as Charlie could arrange it.

Meanwhile, this morning, we had other fish to fry. Maxwell's mobile put us in touch with Dunny Dunn, and the private word he wanted to have was scheduled for three in the afternoon in, at his insistence, the Calvary Hospital garden. This word had to be very private, he said. We then drove up to the Museum car-park on the Hill and gave it a once-over. It was passably clear, we agreed, that the note in Andrew's back pocket was the very note that had drawn him to this spot on his fatal night. Whatever suspicions we might harbour about the items left and found in his car, this fragment from Fiona's herstory looked to be the genuine article, there being no point in tricking the police into believing that he had come here on Sunday night when that could give them no misleading clue as to where and by whom he had been killed.

'That Fiona fragment,' Maxwell said, 'doesn't tell us what Charlie thinks it does. It doesn't tell us that he drove his car here, only that he was invited or summoned here. He might have walked, or jogged. It's within easy jogging distance.'

'Quite so,' I said, not having noticed that: 'It doesn't settle the question we were revolving last night. Mesmerised by the midnite, Charlie jumped to that conclusion. Which is almost enough to convince me that we should jump the other way, and suspect that Andrew's car was driven off by somebody else.'

Our once-over of the car-park revealed nothing relatable to Andrew. We joined the exercise trail and made our way around to Andrew's hanging-tree. It was more than passably clear from

Charlie's account of what the police had (not) done where Andrew had been found that they had scarcely searched the surroundings at all. They came, they saw, they were conquered. All about, in that high, dry, unfathomable grass, they suspected, there lurked multitudes of snakes, gnashing their fangs. They would not venture in. They might have been right. But this had nothing to do with us. No snake had ever offered violence to us on the Hill. On the Hill we and the snakes were brethren. Elsewhere, in all probability, we would have fled shrieking. Here, however, on our own holy ground, we were bold and qualmless. We plunged in, in quest of whatever stones the police had left unturned.

Uphill, eastwards, where the grass was thinner and patchier, a swift, thorough casting-about turned up a condom, a few choice pages from a nudists' magazine and (aha!) an empty packet of cigarillos. Downhill, westwards, we entered the tract of kurrajongs and olives that I have already described briefly here – and more fully, much more eloquently, in that essay in *Secret Landscapes* – as our secret sanctuary, our last redoubt, the hidden holy heart of our Hill's mysteries. This, of all spots on earth, was the spot where, if something was there to be found, we would be able to find it. We were not able to find it. We went uphill again and cast about afresh, and it was while we were so engaged that we noticed – Maxwell noticed, I was under a Lachlan pine at the time – that we were being watched.

The gentle reader may think it unsurprising that two mature gentlemen crawling in, out and around a clump of trees should have attracted attention. *Au contraire*. In all our many years of activity on the Hill we had never been watched, or, which comes to the same thing, we had never been aware that we were being watched. In present circumstances, this was a sinister development. With infinite cunning we both hid our awareness and watched our watcher. There was a spinney of gorse south-east of our position, and a face with binoculars was discernible at the edge of it. No casual observer, this. The possibility, though, that he was a crouching birdwatcher could not be dismissed; but it could be tested. I rose up and strode towards him, pointing southwards and calling out 'What bird is that?' Instantly he vanished, failing the test. Last night we'd had a listener, this morning a watcher. Either one by itself could have been accidental, happenstance; both not. We were under observation. Our investigation of Andrew's death was of interest, perhaps of concern, to a person or persons unknown.

'If only we had our throwing-sticks with us,' I said: 'We could have immobilised that fellow and found out what he's up to.'

'Not without some strenuous practice,' said Maxwell: 'I haven't had a throwing-stick in my hand since you were here last. Andrew's death has driven our weapons out of my mind.'

'We'd better start our practising with them again at once. We only ever need a couple of concentrated sessions to bring our old skills back up to scratch. They would have come in useful here today.'

The skills and weapons we referred to dated back to all those years ago when the Hill had been both our home-from-home and the battlefield on which we were constantly readying ourselves for total war – for Armageddon, indeed – against nameless and numberless foes of the darkest dye. We had accordingly developed and mastered a range of simple, brutal weapons – coshes, prongs, throwing-sticks, garrotters &c. – in order to deal with our huger, hugely-armed opponents whenever they should dare to appear. Regularly, whenever I returned to Wagga and the Hill, Maxwell and I returned to our marvellous youth by practising with these instruments of destruction, believing, or keeping alive the belief, that we could still wield them potently and give a good account of ourselves on that day of reckoning. Andrew's murder, as Maxwell had remarked, had so occupied our attention that so far our traditional practising rites had not resumed. From now on, we resolved, we would get back into the swing of them.

Meanwhile we got back into searching our sanctuary, where Maxwell re-examined a remote thicket and discovered a cache of unused, ready and waiting condoms. The news that there was a considerable amount of intensive intercourse going on on the Hill had not come as much of a surprise, but we had never imagined – and we had never encountered any indication – that the intercoursers were in action here, even here, in our very sanctuary. Barricadoed behind a network of prickliest gorse, and protected, as we imagined, by the Hill's magical prophylactics, it had always seemed proof against such unseemly invasions. Alas, though, no. This was a grievous blow. I raised my eyes and fists towards the unfeeling heavens, preparatory to uttering a series of dismal exclamations; and I saw, stuck on a branch of one of our sacred kurrajongs, a strip of blue jersey-like material. We fetched it down. We fetched *them* down – because beneath it, looped on that branch, was a strip of dark-blue flannelette, a numinous object as I immediately realised, on which, in gold, was inscribed the immortal legend P.S.A.A.A. First.

'This,' said Maxwell, regarding the bit of jersey, which was streaked and spattered with dried blood, 'if I am not mistaken, is the poor dead winger's missing sleeve. But what's this?' regarding the piece of flannelette: 'And what's it doing here?'

'This,' I said, as impressively as possible, ' is a pennant, an immensely potent pennant. I have one of them myself. It's on my wall at home. P.S.A and so forth stands for Public Schools Amateur Athletics Association. First is self-explanatory. Pennants such as these are bestowed on the winners of the annual regional schools' championships. I won mine in 1957 in Yanco. You will be gratified to hear that my record stood for many years thereafter. The hop, step and jump has never been the same since.'

'You astound me, as usual,' said Maxwell: 'I suppose, though, that this is not your pennant. Whose is it? And what's it doing here?'

'Andrew's, it has to be. It goes with the football jersey. They corroborate each other. Andrew won one too, that same year. The reason why he was on the rugby wing was because he was a super sprinter, incredibly quick out of the blocks. He won the one hundred yards.'

'And what's it doing here? What are both of these things doing here? Observation and experience tell us,' Maxwell told me, 'that sportsmen stay attached to their old togs long after their triumphs have been forgotten by everybody else, except, of course, people like you; and this sleeve is obviously a part of Andrew's jogging clobber. We can wonder how it came to be ripped off, there might have been a fight, but it's part of the clobber, it goes with the jogger. The pennant isn't. He surely wouldn't have been flying his old pennant while he jogged. It's out of place here, it makes no sense.'

'The sleeve, too, is out of place,' I pointed out, 'here, up in this tree. It's been left or put here on purpose. The sleeve, I agree with you, probably arrived on the jogger, but the pennant must have travelled separately; and neither of them found their own way up the tree. Perhaps that, though, is their point. That is where and why they make sense. If we bring our superior powers of psychological penetration to bear we can crack this conundrum wide open.'

'Holmes, you amaze me,' said Maxwell: 'I can't wait to know all.'

'These,' I said, 'are Andrew's trophies, the signs and relics of his golden age, when he was young, famous, victorious, adored – when he had a future. Like so many of us, old fellow, he must have felt that his real life was back there, in the 1950s, when the crowds were roaring him on and the girls were falling at his feet – '

'You're doing it again,' Maxwell said: 'You're galloping off into ancient history.'

' – It must have been obvious to him that it has all been downhill since then. Since then, this shining star has been occupying a salesman's desk at Klever Kitchens and endeavouring to learn the tango. No wonder he preserved these proofs of his former greatness. Now. Allow me to speculate. Whoever killed him not only knew him but knew exactly what these bits of cloth signified. Positioning them here proves that. Further. The odds are that anybody who knew this would be not only local but *au fait* with the sporting achievements and ethos of Wagga High.'

'There's a bit of a jump there,' Maxwell said.

'That's my hop and my step. Now for my jump. We might well be looking for this villainous whoever among former students at Wagga High; even among students who were at Wagga High when Andrew was there -'

'That's a jump too far. You're obsessed with Wagga High. All that's needed is someone who knew what these items meant to Andrew. But here we are again, as prophesied, right back in our schooldays, looking for clues in ancient history. I notice that your bold conjectures do not include the possibility that this was a Christian Brothers' murder, in revenge for repeated sporting defeats.

I notice, too, that you haven't explained why you think these scraps of material have been hung up here.'

'Think of them as aerial grave goods. They were hung up near where Andrew was hung up, *in memoriam,* as a tribute to what he once had been and done.'

'As a mark of derision, more likely. You don't make a point of cutting off a man's balls, and then take the trouble to leave him a tribute. *You* might have hung him up a tribute, but no other murderer would have done something so bizarre. I would also beg to draw your attention to the fact that these grisly relics have been hung up, not where Andrew was, where there is already a large and convenient tree, but down here, out of sight of the body, tucked away where no tribute-seeker would think to find them.'

'They weren't out of *his* sight, they were right there where he could look down and see them while he died. Given time, and the public's tendency to haunt the vicinity of ghastly murders, they would have been found. And another confirming thing that he had to see is right out there in front of him on the western edge of the Hill, Wagga High itself, the scene of the triumphs that these remainders are reminders of. Derision is a possible motive, I accept that. Some wretches are capable of anything, even of sneering at a P.S.A.A.A. pennant. But be they trophies or sneers they are indeed profoundly out of place. They are in *our* place, in the heart of it, polluting it. These murdering fiends have picked exactly the wrong spot to hang out their spoils. If they wished to provoke me, us, into pursuing this investigation to the bitter end they could not have picked better. They have undone themselves. They have set us on their trail, and their discovery and comeuppance is their own doing.'

Further searches, terrestrial and arboreal, produced nothing detectable. Maxwell's mobile informed Charlie of our finds; and he undertook to inspect and collect them. We agreed to meet for lunch at the Union Club hotel. We caught no glimpse of our watcher on our way back to the car-park, which convinced us that we were still being watched.

The Union Club hotel – it displayed practically the last remaining array of Wagga Lace, the elegant decorative ironwork that had graced most of the verandahs along the main street in a bygone era, ours – served a good steak. We were deep into it when Charlie arrived. A double whisky (on us, apparently) later, he viewed our recent trove; and seemed disappointed, even a touch critical of our failure to unearth anything more interesting. Cigarillo packets and nuddy magazines, he said, were as common as condoms on that hill. The jersey sleeve he sadly nodded his head at, and declared that the First XIII jersey was now a complete exhibit, which would be filed accordingly. For what it was worth, he continued, his view was that it had been torn in the course of a struggle prior to death. Did we agree? We agreed. 'Highly probably, in my view, in the course of that struggle in his vehicle. But what's this?' he said, turning the pennant back and forth: 'What's this P.S.A. stuff about?'

I told him; and I spoke of trophies, golden days and so forth. He scratched his head.

'Maybe,' he said, 'if you say so. There might be something in it. Wagga High has constantly been a frequent source of local crimes. But why was it up that tree? How did it get there? You don't expect to find a thing like this stuck up a tree like that, do you?'

'These are excellent questions, Charlie. They do you credit,' I said: 'Maxwell and I are pondering them like nobody's business. On the other hand, those dogs of yours, the ones you sent in where policemen feared to tread, aren't up to snuff. How could they have missed these things; or do you train them to sniff no higher than the average Australian crotch?'

'I don't train them,' Charlie said: 'I shall convey your comments to Constable McIvor.'

'Or perhaps they didn't miss it,' Maxwell said; 'but even very clever dogs find it hard to show people what they've found if the people won't come in and take a look at it. What you need, Charlie, isn't better dogs, it's braver policemen.'

'Or, indeed, more commanding commanding officers,' I said, 'of Inspectorial calibre.' But I could see him reddening: he wasn't equal to this raillery: and it was important to keep him co-operative. 'However, we have certainly seen deft and decisive leadership yesterday and today. All is most definitely in order in that respect. And speaking of leadership, Charlie, we'd very much like to have a few words with that clever local constable who found the clothes this morning. Will you arrange that?'

'I'll see what I can do. It's pretty irregular, of course, and he might prefer to not.'

'Command him, Charlie,' said Maxwell: 'Haul him in, and give him his orders.'

'The problem is you're not official, you're only in this because I've let you. But I'll see what I can do. And by the way, we found that other match that you couldn't detect. In his car, you'll remember. The match that must have been dropped by the cigarillo fellow while they must have been talking in his car after Andrew drove it up there that night.'

'I remember,' said Maxwell: 'Let me congratulate you and your staff.'

Off he went with our finds. As we left, ten minutes later, we literally bumped into Clive Brady – or he as literally bumped into us.

'Well, well. It's the ineffable Wal, of all people,' he said: 'Welcome home, Wal. I somehow gathered you weren't due back this year. How are you getting on? And Maxwell, old chap, how are you?'

'Well. We're both well,' I said: 'And how are you?'

This enthralling and wide-ranging conversation expressed, by not expressing, a mutual reserve between Clive and me, a wary circling, which had emerged during our Wagga High days, when we competed against each other in various debates and public-speaking contests. He was, there was no doubt about it, a very good speaker, very good indeed, really stylish and persuasive; and I don't mind admitting that he won a couple of competitions that I thought I should have won. Strange, how some of these juvenile rivalries are never outlived, are always *there*, waiting to be awakened, throughout our lives! My Memoir will contain sage reflections on this.

'Well. Very well,' he said: 'Never better. Dreadful news, this, about poor Andrew Kell. Poor Jane.'

'True,' said Maxwell: 'Too true. I hear you're running for Mayor.'

'Standing rather than running is how I'd put it. The only other candidate is a woman whom nobody can abide.'

'Mayor of Wagga Wagga,' I said: 'Now that is an office worth aspiring to. Scores of civic projects – roads, culverts, children's playgrounds, water-treatment works – will sweep into history with your name attached.' I simply could not help myself. 'I envy you, Clive. I hope you romp home. I'll be sure to tell all my international friends that I am acquainted with the Mayor of Wagga Wagga. They'll be thrilled.' Maxwell was flinching all the way through this address.

'Ever witty Wally,' Clive responded: 'We all feel the lack of you. Scarcely a day passes when people, ordinary colonial people, do not come up to me and cry 'Where is Wal? Where are his exhilarating words?' If and when I become Mayor I'll be sure to send you down into history in suitable company. We're building a new abattoir out at Bomen. I'll name it after you. Meanwhile, I wish you both success in your investigations.'

Off he strolled, superbly-suited and perfectly-groomed (whereas Maxwell and I were acmes of scruff), fair-haired (while I was greying and Maxwell was blizzard-white), slim (which Maxwell was not), self-possessed (which I, at that moment, was not); and destined, it was obvious, to be the most successful and powerful townsman, locally speaking, of his, our, time. I fumed.

'You are well-matched, you two,' said Maxwell: 'If I didn't love you dearly I wouldn't know which of you I could dislike more.'

It was time for Dunny Dunn. We drove westwards along Morgan Street so that I could enjoy the sign at the front of the Wagga Wagga Endoscopy Clinic, *Please Use Back Entrance*, and then southwards up Docker – after, supposedly, a certain Judge Docker – Street and on past the Base Hospital. Off Docker, perched on a little hill of its own, was Calvary Hospital – in our era it was known as Lewisham, after the Sydney suburb where its ministering nuns had set up their first abode. Here, the Sisters of the Little Company of Mary tended to all ills and orientations; and the garden before it, set with seats, walks and a concrete grotto for spiritual uplift provided exercise and refreshment for patients, locals and lovers alike. I knew it well. This was my end of town. However, the garden I had known in my tenderer years, and could still see and feel – in whose murky, ferny recesses I was often wont to moon poetically, wondering and wandering about - was altogether wilder, darker, junglier than now. Dunny awaited us in one of the few remaining recesses, behind the grotto, He seemed nervous, and twitched at every sound.

'I haven't got much time, I'm due back,' he began: 'I've got something for you, a possible sort of possibility.'

'Why are we here?' I asked him: 'It's a lovely spot for a chat, but unusual. It's so out of the way that it's actually quite conspicuous.'

'Conspicuous? Do you think so? Is anybody watching us?' He shrank into a fern.

'No. Nobody,' said Maxwell: 'But perhaps you'd better tell us what you've got before somebody notices us hiding here in the undergrowth. The Little Sisters may fall upon us at any moment.'

'I didn't want any of the other chaps to know I've been talking to you. I mean, talking to you about this. But some of us were having a drink at the Commercial Club a night or so ago, me and Mike and Trev and Artie Starkey, and Artie, who I know of course doesn't have what you or I would describe as ideas as a rule, ideas worth having, although I always say he's a chap who has his feet firmly planted on the ground, anyhow, Artie went back to that idea of his he had at the Terminus, you know, the one about Andrew's death being possibly the latest in a line of strange possible ones among people we went to Wagga High with What's that?'

'It's the sound of a bird leaving a tree,' I said: 'Go on. I remember what he said. '

'Well, you'll remember we thought there weren't any that could be murders, not of anybody we went to school with. Well, this is the point, Artie said he could remember something strange about the way poor Donny Parker went because there was a Wagga High tie involved.'

'How did Donny go?' I asked: 'When? Remind me. Poor Donny.'

'Five or so years ago it must be,' said Maxwell: 'I'm sure I mentioned it to you at the time. He had a heart attack, in regrettable circumstances. *In medias res.* In the act of sexual congress with a person who was not his wife. A person who was not a woman.'

'I've heard of stranger things,' I said: 'It's not what you would call a usual death, not in Wagga; but although it has unnatural features it's natural enough at bottom. What's especially strange about it?'

'He was that year's Master of the Masonic Lodge,' Dunny said, 'and he would have been the next Chairman of the Chamber of Commerce. And on top of it all it happened in the Victory Memorial Gardens, in the old boathouse on the Lagoon. On Anzac Day.'

'Had I been there,' I said, 'I should have saluted. That was surely poor Donny's most memorable achievement. Strange, then, yes, I grant you that. But what about the tie?'

'Ah,' said Dunny: 'What Artie said is that someone who was in a position to know told him that it didn't really look like a heart attack actually, it was more a kind of strangulation, there was a lot of bondage about it, but it was hushed up.'

'I'm not surprised that it was hushed up,' Maxwell said: 'It was deeply embarrassing on every front. There's absolutely no reason to imagine murder here.'

'The tie?' I said: 'The Wagga High tie?'

'He was strangled with a Wagga High tie,' said Dunny: 'Or anyhow that was wound tight around his neck, this someone told Artie. But Mike and Trev still said they couldn't imagine it could be murder, the particular tie couldn't matter, but I thought that maybe, even so, you two might be able to imagine it, and we should run it past you to see if you thought there was anything in it. But the others said not to, it didn't hold water, and if you heard about it, especially Wal, he'd do exactly what we were warning he'd do at the Terminus, he'd bolt off into the past, and then there'd be no chance of ever finding Andrew's murderer. So we agreed not to.'

'I see,' I said; 'but why are we hiding and whispering here; and why are you so on edge?'

'I wouldn't say I was on edge. I'm cautious, is all. I thought it wasn't up to us to just decide that there was nothing in it, you should. And if, if there is a connection, then, you know, the walls of the Commercial Club have ears, they're very leaky, and there might be somebody around who might have been hearing about what we were talking about, and there's something else, which I don't like to mention because I know you get on with him and I need a promise that he'll never hear I mentioned him.'

'Who?' I said: 'You have our promise.'

'Tommy Anderson,' he said: 'Donny and Tommy didn't get on, which isn't surprising, Donny was one of our most highly looked-up-to figures, until the unfortunate end of course, and Tommy's the complete opposite. I'm not accusing him of anything, I don't have anything to go on, but I know Donny was very jittery just before he passed away and once near then when I happened to mention Tommy to him he went very pale and started to tremble. But probably that's got nothing to do with anything What's that?'

'Dogs,' said Maxwell: 'Or wolves. Perhaps we'd better creep our separate ways. Somebody might be on our track. You did the right thing, Dunny. These possibilities will be carefully pondered.'

'This has been very helpful, Dunny,' I said: 'Are there any more strange Wagga High deaths that you and the others have been able to bring to mind?'

'Not at the moment. We've racked our brains,' he said: 'But not a word to the others, please. I don't want any of this to be even guessed at.'

He put on a pair of dark glasses and padded off.

'Tommy again,' I said, 'although in this case we must take account of Dunny's obvious prejudice against him and the fact that, as he admits, he has nothing to go on. Half Wagga goes pale at the mention of Tommy's name.'

'Your prejudice in his favour must also be taken into account,' said Maxwell: 'But there's no sign of Tommy in this business of Andrew's. Until there is, let's concentrate on that. Donny's admittedly strange death can't become a murder because of a tight tie. A degree of strangulation is often employed, I gather, to heighten sexual pleasure. Bondage can have unpredictable consequences.'

'Really? You astound me, Maxwell. What on earth is the world coming to? But why a Wagga High tie? He wouldn't have been wearing that, forty years on.'

'He was regressing. It's a well-known syndrome. And speaking of regressing, I can't help thinking that there has to be some other explanation for that pennant. Charlie didn't even recognise it. I suspect it's because you're so proud of your own little strip of flannelette that you imagine it must have been important to Andrew and his murderers.'

'Perhaps. Still, it's a mystery, it's got something to do with something. I was actually rather surprised that Charlie didn't know what it was. Of course he never won one. Only footy, and being one of those bone-headed forwards, red in tooth and claw, evidently mattered with him. Blinkered, then and now. I noticed that he's still insisting on Andrew's having driven his car to the midnight meeting. Dunny was in a strange state, didn't you think? I've never seen him so jumpy. Or so fluent, in a weird kind of gabbling way. '

'You're out of touch. He obviously felt he was going back on an agreement with his mates, saying what he'd promised not to say. He was under stress. Mateship is not yet dead in this part of the country. What was really strange was hearing that Artie was inside the Commercial Club. I shouldn't have thought they'd let him through the door, not after the mounting of the waitress incident only four years ago. Memories are long in the Commercial Club.'

We paced back to the car, in reflective mode and mood, passing the Mary Potter Nursing Home, where both our mothers spent some of their last days. We drove home southwards, up past the Showground, scene of the annual Wagga Show, which seemed to my young self to be the most immense and spectacular event in the universe, and my Memoir will record many momentous moments thereat – including the famous occasion on which I won seven successive bibles in a quiz in an evangelical tent; up athwart Fernleigh Road - named after 'Fernleigh', a former homestead - adown which there used to live one of my early girlfriends, a plaited blonde, who introduced me to hand-holding and Puccini, whom I amazed with my poems until she discovered that I was transcribing them out of a volume of Swinburne – my first (and last!) literary theft; out through the suburb of Tolland (God knows why so-called), which did not exist when I left Wagga – these were paddocks – and therefore still does not really exist; and off, eastwards, along the Red Hill Road, so-called because the earth hereabouts is notably red – God and Maxwell know why. As we entered Maxwell's gates I uttered a small exclamation.

'Aha!' I exclaimed: 'I can tell you something that Donny and Andrew and Steve have in common. They were all in the school production of *The Mikado*, you remember, the one I starred in as Ko-Ko.'

'Practically all of us were in *The Mikado*, even the school dog,' said Maxwell: 'It was virtually impossible to get out of it. Half of Wagga have that in common, and are alive to tell the tale. I was in it, Charlie Parrot was in it, even Clive Brady was in it, for God's sake.'

'And what a nauseous exhibition he made of himself. He sang like a sick cat. Whenever he opened his mouth the music-lovers absolutely hurled themselves at the exits. But I do not wish to dwell on that aspect. I dwell, instead, on Ko-Ko. Allow me to sing for you,' and I sang: *'I've got a little list, I've got a little list, And they'll none of 'em be missed – They'll none of 'em be missed.* Sinister, wouldn't you say?'

'Not unless you're confessing to several murders. Ko-Ko's little bloody list has nothing to do with the case. If this was a crime novel, and the clue to serial mayhem turned out to be a patter-song from *The Mikado*, you would be the first to fling the book into the garbage. It's far too far-fetched.'

'Nevertheless,' I replied: 'It remains a striking coincidence, which I intend to keep in mind. Sometimes it's the bad books that get closest to life. And death. Tommy Anderson wasn't in *The Mikado*, he'd left school by then. Let's discuss a bottle of shiraz.'

While discussing it, windows tight shut, we decided that Maxwell would try to set up a brief meeting with Jayne tomorrow. Tomorrow, too, we were due to meet Roy O'Hanlon. Tonight, however, I – and I, I insisted, alone – would go to Romano's and, greatly daring, expose myself to the wiles of pretty pert Veronica from Klever Kitchens. Maxwell said that if I had pleaded with him to accompany me he would have refused, he had no desire to witness Spring and Autumn frolicking together, and how could I imagine that she might be of any use to us? In dealing with women, I replied, it is always wise not to imagine anything in advance; but, I reminded him, the initiative here is hers, it is she who wishes to have contact with me, and there had definitely been something odd about our conversation about Andrew's tango, possibly his last tango, at Romano's.

Maxwell thought that the only odd thing about that conversation was the weird and disconcerting way I'd launched into it; but disconcerting, I said, was my trade and bent, and I would try a little more of it this very night. Meanwhile, I said, how about a little light practising with our weapons? We retired to the seclusion of Maxwell's back paddock and after an hour or so of painful rustiness we began to recover a few, and a few degrees, of our ancient dexterities.

Later that night, in Romano's, I was practising with another weapon. Veronica had her boyfriend with her, a large sulky person, Rex apparently, who displayed a boundless contempt for all human achievements except sporting, specifically Australian Rules, prowess, and the craft of woodwork. I was able to tell him that I obtained the highest mark ever recorded for woodwork theory in my first year at Wagga High, and the lowest ditto for woodwork practice, but this seemed not to interest him in the slightest, although Veronica found it hilarious and frequently touched my knee in delighted appreciation while I was recounting it. Rex apparently soon decided that he would spend the rest of the evening at the bar, occasionally lurching across to urge Veronica to have another cocktail; which she was always very willing to have. She, close up – and she got closer and closer up as time went on – was really more than particularly pretty. Her eyes were large, lustrous and an unusual shade of greeny-blue; her ears were unimprovable; her nose was pertness itself; her hair was up, tending to blonde, and looped with a silver ribbon. She wore a blue shift, off the shoulder – shining shoulders – which floated and shimmered down to, I would say, six inches above the knee – entirely embraceable knees; and when she was sitting down, and she generally was, the blue shift rose most delectably up to, I would say, twelve inches above the knee. Her thighs, since we have now arrived at them, were perhaps a smidgeon plumper than the ideal, unless one happened to prefer thighs plump - as, so it happened, one did. I haven't mentioned her breasts because, so far, they hid in the shift. Meanwhile, I was trying to concentrate on her (large, ripe) mouth, because out of it there flowed a great tide of nonsense.

'This *Eric* book,' she said, producing an obviously unread paperback copy, 'is one of my favourites. It's amazing. How you can be so clever is amazing. It must be amazing to be so famous and yet to come from Wagga.'

'It's amazing,' I said, 'to be here with someone so fresh and responsive as you. You are exactly the sort of young, luscious and vibrantly intelligent person I write for. Let me autograph *Eric* for you. And it strikes me that I should write a part for you in my next novel. Would you like that?'

'Oh yes please,' she said, bringing her knees into close conjunction with mine: 'That would be amazing. I'd do anything for that. What sort of part would you say?'

'Well,' I said; and here Veronica had to lean across me to place her cocktail on a table, and her (slim, capable) hands, returning from that long and risky journey, required a period of recuperation on the inside of my left thigh. The inside of her right thigh immediately called for a sympathetic rub in return. 'Well,' I said; and there was so much closer-upness at this point that it was much more difficult to remove my sympathetic hand than to leave it, gently rubbing, where it was. I persevered. 'Well,' I said : 'What sort of part would you like? You can have anything, anything at all. But how about one in which I can bring your lovely legs into the action? I feel I need to show you dancing.'

'My legs?' she said, looking down at them, and at my sympathetic hand between them: 'I've never thought they were all that much, but I'm really happy you like them.' She put her hand on mine, and we gently rubbed together for a time. 'And dancing? Dancing is one of my favourite feelings. It can be amazing.'

'I could describe you dancing, for instance, the tango. Is the tango one of your favourites? Perhaps you've danced it with poor departed Andrew Kell?'

'Perhaps. But Rex is coming back, so we'd better talk about *Eric*.'

We disentangled ourselves, and our knees were together and apart when the lurcher fetched up. I was describing the sudden appearance of the naked clergyman. Rex, definitely Rex, recommended another cocktail, which Veronica said she was looking forward to, and to prove it she drank off the current specimen at a gulp. Off he took himself; and she swivelled back: 'Naked? Completely naked?' she said: 'That must have been amazing. I wish I'd been there.'

'It wasn't a pretty sight, I assure you. If only it had been somebody like you instead. But that happens only in dreams. Tell me, why can we talk about naked clergymen when Rex's around, but not about Andrew Kell?'

'It's not just Rex. Somebody might overhear.' There was nobody anywhere near. 'We need to be somewhere private.'

Rex was around again, delivering the next cocktail. As soon as his back was turned she leant down to place her cocktail on the floor beside her, and paused there, evidently rapt in thought. The blue shift's top fell open, and her breasts, not large but perfectly-formed, perfectly-nippled, presented themselves. We paused. She raised her eyes and watched me looking.

'Private?' I said, a little hoarsely: 'Perhaps we could go out for a stroll?'

'Perhaps,' she said: 'Or perhaps you could take a room here for tonight, and I could come back after Rex has taken me home.'

'Say no more,' I said. I went to the desk and took a room, room 33. 'Room 33,' I said when I came back.

'Lovely. I think I can remember that,' she said, leaning down to pick up her glass. The shift did its thing; the breasts were still there, still perfect, and surely somewhat larger than before. She tossed off her cocktail. 'I'll be back in about an hour. Rex,' she called: 'We need to go now.'

Rex came, and after she'd thanked me for our simply amazing chat about *Eric*, they went. Rex, in that oafish modern fashion, put his hand on her bottom as she passed through the door.

In the intervenient hour I rang Maxwell and explained – into a disbelieving silence at the other end of the line – that something crucial had come up and I'd be back for breakfast. And then I went for that stroll: down Fitzmaurice Street to the Tourist Hotel where, as I expected, that woman was still or again on the floor at the far end of the bar, Rory McFadden and his confederates were ensconced in their corner, and Tommy Anderson wasn't. Tommy, Rory told me, didn't seem to be about, he must still be out around Boree Creek somewhere, but it was a bit strange that he hadn't been in touch yet, normally he would've been by this time, but anyhow Bill, Bill Dwyer, you might remember Bill, he was a couple of years behind us at South Wagga, and even then he was very spotty, he was going down there loading this morning and he'd be asking around. I said yes, it seemed a bit strange, and although I didn't know anybody who could look after himself more totally than Tommy I was a bit worried. Rory undertook to ring me as soon as Bill returned. I returned to Romano's and took up station in room 33.

After an hour and a half she tapped on the door. Her hair was now down, the silver ribbon around her throat. She sat on the bed. I was sitting in an armchair, with insistent springs.

'Well,' she said: 'This is amazing. I never thought I'd ever be alone in a hotel room with a famous writer. I'm sorry about the time. Rex wanted to stay, and I had to put him off. Isn't that light bright!' She waved at the mini-chandelier. 'This one,' she switched on the bedside lamp, 'will do.'

I arose from my springs and switched off the chandelier. 'Far too bright,' I said: 'Here with you, who glow with youth and beauty, a single candle would be illumination enough.'

'Oh, you're just saying that. Don't go back over there, I can hardly see you now. Come and sit here.' She patted the bed beside her. 'My mother always used to tell me not to be bold. But I feel bold tonight.'

'Boldness be my friend,' I said, sitting where she was patting: 'Before we get too comfortable, although I simply can't imagine how I could get too comfortable with you, I want you to tell me a bit about Andrew Kell, especially any bits that you didn't want anyone to overhear.' I was back on track, having had an hour and a half to recover from the sights and stirrings in the lounge downstairs.

'Oh Andrew, yes, he was bold all right, I mean most men are, that's what I've found, which I don't mind really, it's quite exciting really, but he was always trying it on, hands up skirts and so on, he even used to try it with Brenda, you might remember her, the plain girl in Sales, so it wasn't even much of a compliment, was it?

While Andrew was thus appearing to me in a new and sordid light, Veronica's shift, as if by magic, was clambering up her thighs.

The twelve-inch mark was history. I needed to be strong, to look away, but the only adjacent objects to be looked at were her knees, and these, poor creatures, were now so exposed, so abandoned, that it seemed only decent to give them a consoling massage. While I massaged she continued.

'So, you know, it wasn't a surprise when he turned up at the Christmas party here with a strange girl, when I say strange I mean she wasn't his wife, and she was far too young for a man of his age, she couldn't have been much older than me really, and nobody knew her, though I thought Doug did, Doug the manager. I don't think she comes from Wagga.'

'Doug knew her? That's interesting?' Massage, massage. 'I wonder who she was? Were she and Andrew tangoing together?'

'That's what they called it, but it was ridiculous, she had no idea, she just clung onto him, he didn't seem to have much idea either, it was just an excuse to get hold of her in lots of places, and although he seemed really keen on them it was the sort of dancing where you could see that her legs weren't all that special, they weren't much better than Brenda's even. But you mustn't ever say that I said Doug knew her, though he knew her, you could tell, and I really trust you to not say anything about anything here tonight. Oh, it's getting amazingly hot in here, don't you think? I'm really stifled.'

She stood up, and in one of those amazingly deft and graceful movements that women have in their genes, she drew her shift over her head and cast it on the floor.

'Oh,' she said: 'I'd forgotten I wasn't wearing a bra. Oh well, you've seen them already, haven't you? But I'm a bit embarrassed.'

'There's no need to be embarrassed. They are splendid, splendid. Both of them are simply splendid. You ought to be very proud of them.'

'But I'm still embarrassed, because look at me, I've hardly anything on' – only brief briefs, also blue – 'and look at you, you're still fully dressed. It's not fair. Unless you take some of yours off I'll have to put mine back on. I mustn't be too bold.'

'Perish the thought. But it won't be a pretty sight.' I discarded shirt and singlet, and she at once began to explore, with fingers and (pink, pink) tongue, some of my outstanding moles and dimples.

'That's amazing,' she said: 'It really makes me wonder what the rest of you is like.'

'It wouldn't be fair to show you. And you might never recover. I couldn't possibly consider it. Those are tantalising briefs.'

'These?' she said: 'I shouldn't be taking these off, not just out here in the room. If you want, I'll take them off in the bed. But you'll have to ask me very nicely.'

'Please,' I said.

'Oh, all right. But you'll have to come in too. And you can't come in in those scratchy trousers.' She slid under the sheets, and a moment later, in a blue flash, her briefs were winging their way over my head.

'I hear and obey, though it won't be a pretty sight. Or have I already said that?' I tore off the rest of my togs.

'That's really amazing. You can come in now.' She threw off the sheets and afforded me a full-length view of all of her.

'Before we get even more comfortable,' I croaked, coming in, 'I wonder whether you ever saw Andrew and this strange girl together again?'

'I didn't, but Brenda did,' she said, climbing on top of me: 'She saw them not so long ago, out at the Winery. She said they were in and out of each other's mouths like nobody's business. So it wasn't a one-night stand. Have you got any objections to one-night stands?'

She had, or I had, her left breast in my mouth at that juncture, and it was some little time before I could reply.

'None whatsoever,' I said, 'although I have a strong preference for five-night stands.'

'Greedy,' she said, positioning herself on the *point d'appui*: 'And I thought you were a real gentleman.'

This was almost the end of our useful conversation at this point; and it would be otiose, perhaps even offensive, to go on and on and on about our goings-on. You must imagine them. There was, however, a further exchange of some significance. Towards dawn, as we were going on again, she looked up at me and said, roguishly: 'There's another reason why we're doing this.'

'Reasons?' I said, also roguishly: 'So there are reasons? What's the reason other than this other one?'

'Oh, that's having it with somebody famous, every girl wants to do that, though I've never had it so continuous with anybody before. You're really amazing. How do you keep it up?'

'It's a trade secret. And what's the other reason?'

'My mother. She used to say how much she'd liked it with you, and as soon as I saw I had the chance to sort of follow her and have what she had I jumped at it.'

'So you did. I'm very glad you did. Your jumping' – and we did a little of something like it just then – 'is beyond compare. But is it possible that your mother has mistaken me for someone else? For me, if so, there has never been a more fortunate mistake. I can't believe I can ever have met your mother' – the wild idea that Veronica might just happen to be my daughter came and went. 'If she's anything like her daughter I would certainly remember her.'

'I'm sure you can remember her, she could remember everything about what you used to do and she was exactly right, it's exactly the same. I know you'll remember Robyn Lee, she was your girlfriend for a while at Wagga High, and the two of you used to go up on Willans' hill and do a lot of this.'

This put me right off my stroke. I had a vision of Robyn, excited and experimental, and I could now see her in her daughter. And another vision, of the Base Hospital tower, eight storeys high, and of Robyn jumping off it.

'Robyn. Yes, of course, of course. I was really passionate about her. You have inherited all her amazing qualities. I was so very sorry to hear of her passing. I simply could not understand how such a beautiful and talented creature could do such a dreadful thing. Were there any signs beforehand? If you can bear to talk about it.'

'It's three years ago, I'm used to it now. It was a complete mystery. After her divorce from Daddy she went from man to man for a while, she couldn't seem to settle, but she was very happy towards the end so nobody could have predicted it. Don't stop. On the day she did it she told me I'd understand one day but I didn't know what she was talking about until afterwards and I still don't understand it. In a way we're bringing her back, you and me, in this bed.'

'We are, we are. But how awful for you, you poor lovely thing. And – forgive me, but I owe it to dear Robyn to ask this question, and it was such a strange death – was there never any suspicion that she might not have done it all by herself?'

'Not when there was a large crowd of people there who were watching her do it, and some of them were climbing out and trying to stop her. She was determined to do it. But you're spoiling the mood. Let's go back to where we were.'

We went back, and went on. Dawn arrived. Sleep came at last. I awoke as she slipped out of bed and into her shift.

'Got to go,' she said: 'They'll be wondering. It was amazing. I'll give you a ring when I feel bold again.'

She looked wonderfully pert as she closed the door; but less pretty. Skinny, really. Like her mother. Doubtless, she would look pretty again by the evening.

I dressed, and drove to Maxwell's for breakfast.

CHAPTER FOUR

Breakfast was grim. Maxwell did not know what I had been up to, but he deeply disapproved of it. Over a small half-boiled egg and a great deal of Philip Glassy yammering I revealed that Veronica was the daughter of Robyn Lee who, in case it had slipped out of his memory although it had been an impenetrable secret at the time so maybe it was never in it, had been a brief but brightly-burning flame of mine in the old Wagga High school days, and who had thrown herself off the Base Hospital tower three years ago.

'I remember that,' he said, 'but I don't remember her.'

'It's a very rememberable death,' I said: 'It surely deserves to be included in our list of strange recent Wagga High deaths. It's strange, don't you think, that the chaps haven't mentioned it?'

'Not at all. Firstly, the chaps are chaps, and the strange death of a mere sheila is easily overlooked. Secondly, it was such an obvious public suicide that it doesn't count as the sort of strange death they've been mentioning – the sort that Artie apparently thinks might not be what they seem. And thirdly, you seem to have needed the special assistance of her daughter to remember it yourself. If the chaps had had Veronica to inspire them their memories too might have suddenly improved.'

'*Touche*. I may well be affected by late-onset feelings of guilt. I should have kept in touch with Robyn. I might have been able to dissuade her from her fell fall. I shall dedicate my next story to her; or the next but one. Veronica comes next, and she does so, old bean, on account of the light she sheds on Andrew's courting practices. Brace yourself.'

I proceeded to describe, to Maxwell's amazement, Andrew's wild and womanising ways, his up-skirty hands, his unbridled tangoing and his passionate osculating of a mysterious female friend, to whose identity Manager Doug was apparently privy. Maxwell plainly put some of this down to Veronica's inflamed state of mind, being unwilling to accept that there was a whole rampant side to Andrew that he had never even suspected; but he agreed that we should, with the utmost delicacy, try to see if Jayne had suspected it, and that Manager Doug should be probed for the name and location of the mystery girl. At this point Charlie Parrot rang in. He confirmed – the Scientific Police had confirmed – that the scrap of jersey we'd plucked from one of our kurrajongs was Andrew's. No further news, he said. He supposed we would be seeing Jayne soon, poor Jayne, she was back now, when would we? This very day, we hoped, we said.

'I recommend that,' he said: 'She might have some valuable clues. I have decided to leave that side of things to you. She was in a highly unreliable state when I tried to conduct an interview with her soon after the unfortunate event. I have purposefully held back my team from investigating Andrew's personal items and surroundings, to give you an undisturbed chance of seeing if there's something you can see there, I know how famously keen both your eyes are. There has been no police presence in the home in question as yet, and I have instructed Jayne to not touch anything among Andrew's effects. I hope you'll be able to give me some progress before long. After all these days I'm a bit disappointed that we still don't have anything tending to a suspect yet.'

'He fears he sees the Inspectorship slipping away,' I said: 'But I think we're on the verge of cracking it. All we have to do is find the verge. And now for Jayne. *Andiamo.*'

Jayne had invited us to morning tea. At eleven sharp we were there; and so, opening the door, was she. Her blonde ringlets always lifted my heart, and she had a most enjoyable face, only a little lined; her breasts, as Vic had correctly observed, were like two young roes; her legs, in blue slacks, tight slacks, were long and lissom, lovely things; and of course she also had a lovely personality, which was somewhat muted now, naturally, by present circumstances. We got through the social preliminaries pretty quickly, and then there came a silence, into which I cleared my throat.

'It goes without saying,' I said.

'Then don't say it,' she said: 'Maxwell said it all in his card from both of you. There's nothing more to be said. He didn't deserve anything like this.'

'That also goes without saying,' Maxwell said; 'but you said it as if you think he deserved not this, of course, but something. But perhaps I misunderstood you.'

He hadn't, there was no mistaking her inflection. She tipped up her chin and laid her eyes on us, blue-grey, lavishly-lashed; and smiled.

'You didn't. He certainly deserved some sort of comeuppance, if I'm allowed,' she looked at me, 'to use that word. He wasn't the most faithful of husbands. Over the last two or three years he did a lot of chasing, and catching. You wouldn't have had any idea of this, Maxwell. He respected you too much to let on. He was in awe of you, he really admired your wonderful mind and all the clever things you know. We all do. But inside the man you knew there was another man. There always is.'

'Do you think it was that other man who's been murdered?' Maxwell asked her.

'That I can't say,' she said, 'because I can't imagine how anybody could come to be murdered like this.'

'If we knew more about him, about the man inside,' I said, 'we might be able to imagine it. Detective Sergeant Parrot has asked us to help.'

'Detective Parrot,' she said, 'has been very sympathetic. But he said he would look around the house for clues, and he spent just five minutes here on the Monday before I went back to Canberra, and as far as I'm aware he hasn't been back since.'

'He has extraordinarily sharp eyes, has Charlie,' I said: 'Even as a lad he was famous for them. Perhaps he detected all the clues he required in those first five minutes. He must have left no stone or room unturned.'

'He sat where you're sitting all the time. To be quite frank, he only had eyes for my legs.' Involuntarily, we followed his example. 'I was in a state of shock, but I noticed that.'

'We've begun to get inklings of Andrew's other man,' I said: 'What would you like to tell us about him?'

'Well, there's not much to tell really, and it's really the same old story. He had affairs, which might be my fault partly, I don't know, and at first he was very, you know, discreet.'

'Affairs with whom?' I asked.

'I'm not going to tell you. They were very discreet, hardly affairs at all really, just, well, a few nights here and there when husbands were away. You know the type of thing.'

'Husbands?' said Maxwell: 'Would I be right in conjecturing that these various wives belonged to the same social circle that you and Andrew tended to move and dine in?'

'The dinner-dancing circle,' I said: 'The tangoists.'

'You might say that, although he never mastered the tango; he didn't have an ounce of rhythm in him.'

'You can thank your lucky stars that you have never had me as a partner,' I said: 'How did you find out about these very discreet affairs?'

'The girls told me, of course, the wives. It wouldn't have been fair otherwise. Andrew didn't know I knew, he thought it was a complete secret, and I couldn't bring myself to tell him.'

'I can understand that,' Maxwell said: 'Do you think the husbands of those wives knew? If they did they would surely have been extremely irritated. They might even have been vengeful.'

'I don't think so. It's not the sort of thing you tell your husband. And there was never any sign of anything like irritation. But these people are our friends. I simply can't imagine any of them murdering Andrew, to say nothing of cutting off his Oh I can't say it.' She hid her face in her hands.

'Quite, quite. There's no need to say it,' I said; 'but you must see that that unsayable act strongly suggests a motive of a sexually fraught and punitive nature. That seeming so, we need to be looking at those who might have reason to have such a motive.'

'I see that, I do. All I can say is that none of our friends could have had enough of that motive to want to do a thing like that, that's all.'

'O.K.,' said Maxwell: 'Point taken. Now, Jayne, apart from these husbands and wives, these unmotivated friends, might there have been anybody else, anyone you've heard any rumours about, who Andrew might have included –'

'*Whom* Andrew might have included,' I interjected, I and Miss M.E. Paddock.

' – whom Andrew might have included in his affairs?'

'I did hear,' Jayne said, 'that there was somebody new, somebody much younger. Friends mentioned seeing them. But I don't know who, I never inquired. To be frank, he could do what he liked, I'd had enough of it. And of him. He'd become so much coarser too, especially lately, perhaps due to this new girl he'd found. Always telling such filthy jokes. On that last Friday, the last time I saw him, he practically drove me out of the house by insisting on telling me a revolting story about some woman and a canary.'

'Ah yes,' I said: 'That story is certainly going the rounds. Afterwards, as I suppose, you went off to Canberra as usual?'

'Yes. I've really been too occupied in Canberra to care very much about things here. I'd already told him I wanted a separation. Such a comedown really, after six years of marriage. If it wasn't so common it'd be tragic. Or do I mean comic?'

She meant both, of course; but the little whimsical touch at the end was meant to let us know that she was also putting the whole thing behind her, and that she'd given us the only version of her side of this story that she intended us to take as true. As she'd sketched it for us, though, it was a touch too neat, too one-sided. Attractive women, I have found, are frequently much more cunning than one realises. But they can be undone, as it were, by innocence and courtesy.

'Speaking of Canberra,' said Maxwell, 'I hope your mother's health is improving.'

She blushed. Her very cunning compelled her to suspect that Maxwell's remark was loaded: that he had some notion, or more than a notion, that her mother was not her sole occupation in Canberra. 'She's not well. I mean, she's difficult, she's very demanding, she takes up more and more of my time these days, I need to be over there every weekend really.'

'Really?' I said, artfully raising my eyebrows and glancing across at Maxwell: 'You're telling us you're fully occupied over there looking after your mother. Yes?'

'And yes,' the blush was back, and those grey-green eyes flashed defiance and dislike, 'I'm seeing somebody else there, which you can hardly blame me for after what I've had to put up with here. He's been a huge support.'

'We're delighted to hear it,' I said: 'You'll pardon me for asking, but is this friend from Canberra one who is also wholly incapable of taking a gun or a knife to what you had to put up with here?'

'Andrew often said you were a nasty piece of work. I see what he meant. He never liked you, did you know?' She was pale with anger, blonde all the way down: it really suited her: I had never seen her look so devilishly desirable. Why Andrew had gone elsewhere was one of life's unfathomabilities. 'But if you're asking for information, he's not, I mean he's the last person who'd be capable of anything like this; and I was with him all the time all through the weekend. Besides, he knows we're separating, so what motive could he have?'

'We're delighted to hear that he has no motive and such an excellent alibi,' I said.

'Andrew was a dedicated jogger, apparently, particularly on Sundays,' Maxwell said: 'Did he have a favourite route, do you know?'

'I never paid much attention, I'm afraid, but I gathered he mainly went up on Willans' hill, which doesn't surprise me, I hear it's overflowing with young girls these days. I always thought he was too old to be out jogging.'

'Too old?' I said: 'Come, come. He was no older than we are. But joggers are a race apart. Age cannot weary them, nor the years dismay. In Andrew's case, I should have thought that the lust for fitness goes back, went back, to his youthful prime. He was quite an athlete as a schoolboy, a highly promising sprinter. He won the hundred-yard dash at the P.S.A. championship in 1957, did you know?'

'Oh, I know. He often brought that up, he was very proud of it. He even has the blue ribbon to prove it, he's got it pinned up on the wall of his den in there.'

'I think,' Maxwell said, 'if you're agreeable, Jayne, we'll take a look at Andrew's den, if that's what it's called.'

'Of course. I haven't been into it since. I couldn't bear to. And Detective Parrot particularly asked me not to. It's through there.'

She indicated a doorway, and through it we passed into an enclosed, louvred rear verandah. Its end wall bore shelves bearing books and boxes; a settee faced a back door, a sash-window and the back yard; the floor was a pock-marked parquet; and a desk and chair stood centre-stage. I went at once, as is my wont, to the bookcase, to survey the books, only one of which, disgracefully, was mine. That one, though, was a surprise: *Secret Landscapes* : which I would never have supposed Andrew to have had any interest in or capacity for. We live and learn. Not all the books were books: closer inspection revealed that filed among them was a run of Wagga High school magazines – *The Hill*, you'll recall – from the 1950s, when he and we were fellow-pupils there. Even closer inspection revealed that the run was not complete: one was absent, a pleasant surprise really, as it contained an excruciating poem of my own penning, which I had long wished to suppress. (I do not here reveal the year, for that reason.) It was a small but distinct relief to know that there was at least one household in which it wasn't discoverable, festering. (Had it not been absent, I would have been tempted to secrete it about my person and find a bonfire for it.) The absent *Hill* – a thought struck me, to which I'll return – had left a gap, and in that gap, I now noticed, there couched a map – of Wagga (Wagga), its streets and regions, internal and outlying. One two three black biro crosses marked spots of some apparent significance. There was also a biro arrow drawn across the bottom right-hand quarter of the map, pointing to what, at first glance, appeared to be Tichborne Crescent, near where the car and clothes had been found.

'At second glance,' said Maxwell, studying it, 'this arrow seems to point to Coolibah Street or Moani Place, desolate regions in which nothing of note has ever happened. I regret to say, however, that this map puts a cross on the Victory Memorial Gardens, and another one out on Lake Albert. I had hoped that this fantastic story of strange linked Wagga High deaths would die of its own incredibility, but here it comes again.'

'Thinking aloud,' I said, 'I think that those two crosses signify Donny Parker and Steve Hampson. This third cross' – I pointed at one on the town's south-western fringe, on the railway line to Uranquinty and Melbourne – doesn't ring any of my bells, but no doubt a name will occur to us in due course. Another cross should now be planted here' – I pointed at the Hill, and again that thought returned – 'in memory of Andrew. Still thinking aloud, I conjecture that Andrew and Artie have been thinking along similar lines. And thinking aloud for the third and final time on this occasion, since it is conceivable that thinking along these lines got Andrew murdered, we need to warn Artie. He could be next in line.'

'I just can't believe this. It's too far-fetched,' Maxwell said: 'This is Wagga, after all. I was fond of Andrew, he could be good company, but he was also, frankly, a bit of a nong. He could get hold of some pretty ropey ideas and get carried right away by them – Atlantis, secret Egyptian codes, a nest of Nazi war criminals hiding out in Walla Walla: for any sort of conspiracy-theory he was as the moth to the flame. If he actually thought there was a connection between these various deaths there almost certainly wasn't.'

'Artie is also, and much more so, a nong. It's not impossible that here in Wagga two nongs might make a right.' I replied: 'Let's see what else we can unearth.'

The boxes were full of nondescript odds and ends, and hundreds of bar coasters, and offered no clue to anything. The settee was extremely uncomfortable, although a search of the cushions brought nothing pointful to light. On the desk there was a fine large reproduction of one of Ingres' Turkish bath/harem paintings - very arresting, but why down here, why not up on a wall? Under it, almost out of sight, peeped forth a photograph from the 1950s of South Wagga Primary's Class 5, Mr. Gersback's, out of which virtually everybody we'd grown up with stared mutinously into the future. All the chaps were in it, named and numbered, including Andrew; and somebody who might have been young Rory McFadden; and of course ourselves, our little faces already glowing with intellect and sensitivity. Little Tommy Anderson's face, I noticed, had a biroed ring around it.

'Little did we know then what life held in store for us,' I said, perhaps unnecessarily: 'This is the sort of photograph that I tend to moon over, the past being my particular patch. Movingly, it catches us all at the last moment when we were all together. Class 6 split us up and down and apart forever into A, B, C and D streams. Andrew,

I should have thought, would tend not to moon over those historic moments. Why is it here?'

' He was evidently an extremely secret mooner; he certainly never gave me any hint of it. More likely, he knew you were due, so he was refreshing his South Wagga memories in readiness for you and your memoir.'

'How thoughtful. This is a most poignant item. It vastly increases my determination to find the swine who prevented us from comparing notes.'

Desks have drawers, which we could not leave unexplored. Another poignant item came to light. Near the bottom of the bottom drawer lay a copy of my third novel, *In the Course of Events*, a rollicking farce with, suddenly, a spectacularly tragic conclusion – one of my best plots; but its sales have been disappointing. Why here? Why not in the bookcase? I was asking myself as I drew it out – but before I reached speech I realised that this was no merely poignant item, there was something telling in it, it contained a bookmark, a postcard, that same Fitzmaurice Street – utilities – four pedestrians – *Welcome to Wagga Wagga, Garden City of the South* – postcard that had been found in Andrew's car. On the back, as before, nothing.

Immediately, naturally, I looked at what – pp.144-5 – the bookmark was marking, in case it could tell us more than that that was where Andrew had ceased reading. It seemed not to: these were pages of Wildean persiflage and repartee, of no relevance to anything outside the novel. The postcard itself was, if anything, the thing. It linked whatever had gone on in Andrew's car on the fatal night with whatever had been going on in here, in Andrew's mind and den.

'These identical postcards are telling us something,' I said: 'Or was Andrew just a collector of old Wagga postcards? Let's see if Jayne knows anything about any of these things.'

Jayne, appealed to, conquered her reluctance to enter the domain of the deceased and joined us at the desk. We wondered whether he'd been mentioning any of our old cobbers – former schoolmates, for example: Donny Parker, say, or Steve Hampson, or Tommy Anderson or anyone at all? No, she said, she couldn't recall him mentioning anyone. Had he seemed to be on edge lately – excited, meditative, expectant, moody, unusually anything at all? No, she said, he'd been a bit irritated during the last few weeks by Clive Brady coming here badgering him about canvassing for him for mayor but apart from the increasing coarseness he'd been just the same as ever, if anything even more relaxed and carefree than usual. Tears came into her eyes, and Maxwell and I contemplated the backyard until she recovered herself. There might be files or personal papers or diaries, Maxwell suggested, in which he might have jotted down observations, appointments, stray ideas and so forth which could give us an inkling of his recent train of thought. No, she said, as far as she knew there was nothing of that sort, and as far as she could tell he didn't have trains of thought, it was only ever just straightforward instincts with him. Was there a computer in his life? I asked: boldly, because I didn't know the first thing about such things, it was still fountain pens and manilla folders with me. No, she said, he was always just thinking of getting one, but he had no more chance of mastering a computer than he had of learning to tango. Speaking of dancing, Maxwell said, he'd heard that a regular bout of it was just the thing for those twinges of rheumatism that tell us we're getting on, although many people swear by copper bracelets; did Andrew? He'd never mentioned any twinges, she said, and he'd never worn any copper bracelets. Bracelets remind me of cuff-links, Maxwell said, smiting his brow, because there was one of Andrew's in his car, blue with a silver spiral, which we'd meant to bring back. Which there was no need to, she said, because it couldn't be his, he didn't wear them. I pointed out the gap in the series of *Hills* – was the missing issue in another part of the house? Not that she'd noticed, she said, but she'd never even noticed those old magazines before. She might have noticed some of these old postcards before, I suggested, indicating it, which Andrew might have been collecting. No, she'd never seen one like it before, and the only things he collected were bar coasters. Maxwell indicated the Ingres print and commented that Andrew's interest in art had never come up in any of their conversations, to which she replied that it was news to her too but since the picture had lots of naked women in it probably an interest in art didn't come into it. I see, I said, that he'd been reading *In the Course of Events*, which relatively few people had taken to, what did he think of it? She said he'd never liked any of my books, too pretentious he'd said, so she supposed that that's what he would have thought.

'Going back to those old *Hill* magazines,' I said, 'they were probably as valuable to Andrew as his blue P.S.A. ribbon hanging up on the wall here – where?'

'There,' she said, pointing to a blank space over the back door: 'Oh, it's gone. And that window has been left open.'

The sash-window was, if not quite open then not quite closed. We unlatched the back door and immediately made out that the fly-screen on the window had been forcibly deprived of its snib and now hung loose. Jayne would have noticed that, she said, before she'd left for her weekend in Canberra, but as far as she could see at first glance nothing was missing except that stupid ribbon and why would anybody want to take that? She further said that she was tired of answering our questions.

'You've been very patient and helpful, Jayne,' said Maxwell: 'We're most grateful. We'll show the map and the photo,' he scooped them up, 'to Detective Sergeant Parrot. He'll be very interested in them. Wal, I think we should now take our leave.'

'Just before we take it, where did Andrew keep his car keys?' I asked.

'There,' she replied, pointing at a small cupboard to the left of the door: 'But they're not there. I'm told they're in the car.'

As we were stepping out of the door Maxwell suddenly produced the little gold chain that Klever Kitchens had entrusted to us. 'Andrew had this on his desk at work,' he said: 'Is it yours?'

'It is not,' she said; and slammed the door on us.

We took a stroll, down towards Wagga High, and considered where we stood. Maxwell seemed less rubicund than usual. I recognised on him the pale cast of thought. Even while we were strolling he had opened and was studying the map. There is nothing like a map to stir the imagination. Think of *Treasure Island.* Think, if it has come your way, of my early novel *Helena*, in which the right interpretation of the map at the front reveals the whole plot. In this map of Andrew's, as it seemed to me, there was a gap. Whatever convinced the chaps that Robyn's strange death was a mere suicide and not strange enough to deserve notice had apparently convinced Andrew as well – the Base Hospital, scene of poor Robyn's Leap, was crossless. I, though, wanted it noticed: in part, no doubt, because I felt a pang of guilt about it, and in part because I now owed it to her daughter. That was Maxwell's view. He was also, as he looked for ways of testing or discounting the sudden central importance of this map, inclining to the idea that the crosses marked merely the deaths, not the strange and suspicious deaths, of three of Andrew's friends; although he admitted that he'd never heard Andrew refer to Donny or Steve as friends. The third cross continued to elude us. The arrow ditto. And despite Maxwell's emollient words about the Class 5 photo I was surer than ever that Andrew had been meditating on its line-up of victims (and murderers?) shortly before he went out to be murdered himself. But whatever his meditations may have been, I could not help feeling that we were being drawn back, by that photo and those postcards, into the 1950s and 60s, *our* era, *my* era. It was almost as if my yet-unwritten Memoir might hold the key to this ghastliness on the Hill.

Our findings in Andrew's den pretty well persuaded us that on the night of the murder somebody had entered the house through the window. That somebody – not Andrew: Charlie was of course probably quite wrong – had switched on the lights, taken the car keys and the pennant, and driven away. The somebody knew where the keys and pennant were, which suggested that he had been in the house before, even that he was acquainted with the Kells; but Maxwell counter-suggested that Andrew's mutilated state implied torture, and torture could easily have extracted the location of the car keys – but not, apparently, of the house keys, so maybe the first suggestion was the likelier. Once inside, what might the somebody have been doing during the few minutes the lights were on? What, apart from the pennant, was being searched for? Was it found? Taken? I could not but suspect that there must have been other evidences of Andrew's thoughts and suspicions about these strange deaths, less carefully-hidden than our map, and that they had been spirited away. It even occurred to me that Andrew, knowing I was coming, had hidden that map where only I would be likely to find it, in case something should happen to him. Maxwell thought he would have left more than a map with three crosses on it in that case, there would have been a few hints and guesses tucked in there with it, and he doubted that he could have foreseen Charlie Parker's keenness to involve us in an investigation. I had my doubts about this; but I had no doubt that taking and placing that pennant was such a bizarre and somehow *intimate* thing to do that close acquaintance with Andrew and/or the 1950s/60s world of Wagga High had to be absolutely central to the why and how of his strange death.

'Further to which,' I said, 'a thought struck me back there while I was considering the *Hill* magazines and contemplating the Hill on the map. In the note that summoned Andrew to the museum car-park Hill was spelt Hill, capital aitch. A Wagga High person, I reckon, is much more likely than other local mortals to think of the Hill as the Hill and not merely as Willans' hill, small aitch. This is another clue to the world this death has emerged from.'

'It's a possibility,' said Maxwell, 'but people print in upper and lower case at random, and persons of our vintage might have hyphenated the car-park. Do you think that's significant? You're trying too hard to make this connection. The only connection between these very different deaths is that they occurred to people who were at school here when we were. Wagga's cemeteries are already full of people who were at school here when we were. You and I are getting on.'

'Once upon a time,' I replied, 'these dead ones and we were all in the same class, South Wagga 5, and the odds are that the bearer of the third cross will have been in it too. Four of our former classmates, therefore, are strangely dead; five, if we grant Robyn honorary membership. There are only ten of us, ten little niggers, left. The chaps, if now put to it, may be able to subtract yet more. I repeat, if Andrew's death has anything to do with what seems to have been his suspicion that these deaths are linked, little Artie may be in danger. We have to tell him. We couldn't save Andrew, but I could never forgive myself if we failed to save little Artie. Even Dunny might be at risk; but I can live with that.'

Our stroll had brought us to the borders of Wagga High, and my mind was naturally flooded with memories of our years of adventure there. Our teachers, especially the lunatics among them, rose up before me. Our fellow-students, ditto, especially the dead ones. We strolled through the grounds of that incomparable institution, hearkening to the furious shouts of the teachers and the answering gales of irreverent laughter – loved, familiar sounds; and sadly noting the disappearance of many of the tracts and sheds among which we had pursued our education and other activities there in the good old days. *Eheu! Ichabod!* The mood was shattered by the arrival of a trio of security guards, who told us to be off because we were trespassing, and plainly regarded us as a pair of hardened paedophiles. We had no sooner begun to tell them who, whom they had the temerity to be giving their oafish orders to than Roy O'Hanlon came through on Maxwell's mobile wanting to know where and when we would be meeting him today. He suggested, and we agreed, that we should come to his house for a few cold early-afternoon beers. This exchange having interrupted our flow of castigation, we let the ignoramuses off lightly, and made a dignified departure.

We drove down to the Tourist Hotel in quest of tidings of Tommy Anderson, whose persistent absence had begun to ruffle my mind. Rory McFadden came at us in a rapid totter the moment we entered the bar.

'Where have you been?' he wanted to know: 'I've been trying to ring you all morning.' I'd given him Maxwell's home number, and nobody was at home. 'Something's up with Tommy.'

'Something's always up with Tommy,' I said: 'What is it this time?'

'He's disappeared. Bill here,' he said, indicating Bill there, still very spotty, who was on his way over – over the woman on the floor at the far end of the bar – to join us, ' is just back from loading down in Boree Creek and there was Tommy's ute all right but no Tommy anywhere about. Nobody knows where Tommy is. You tell them, Bill.'

'His ute was just sitting there by the silos with the keys in it,' Bill told us: 'A couple of passing blokes noticed it. The Boree Creek people hadn't, but nothing registers out there under a couple of weeks usually.'

'What do you reckon?' Rory asked: 'It's a bit of a mystery. He even left his wallet on the seat apparently. There wasn't any money in it but, not by the time the passing blokes passed through. Or so they said.'

'I find that reassuring,' I replied: 'Tommy always left his things everywhere. Most of his spells in gaol have been due to his habit of littering the scenes of his crimes with personal effects. He's behaving quite normally here. What I reckon, since you ask, is that he's on the prowl, there's some farmer's wife who needs a good seeing-to, and he's simply lost track of the time.'

They didn't think much of that. Heads were shaken, lips pursed. Utes just left anywhere out there, Bill said, were liable to lose all their parts, which Tommy would know, and Rory said that even Tommy couldn't possibly keep it up for three days, he was our age, so a woman couldn't be the explanation. I allowed that these objections had weight; and agreed to reconsider Tommy's disappearance if he hadn't surfaced by the end of the weekend. Maxwell gave Rory his mobile phone number, and he promised to ring us with any news. We then repaired to the Union Club hotel in case Charlie was, or wasn't, there. To Maxwell, as we went, I remarked that I was actually not reassured by Tommy's abandoned truck and wallet. Tommy lived a dangerous life, and he lived it very ineptly. It was all too likely that something was, indeed, up with him. If it was, was it a sinister coincidence, or only the merest accident, that we had been discovering a copy of my *In the Course of Events* in Andrew's den drawer, for I had set that rollicking farce with its tragic conclusion in Boree Creek? Might Tommy's be the next strange Wagga High death on the list? But I was in danger of developing an obsession here. We agreed that we shouldn't bring Tommy's possible plight to Charlie's attention because it would only distract and confuse him, one problem at a time was all he could cope with, and Tommy would be ropeable if he knew that we'd involved the police in his affairs. Charlie wasn't there.

We consumed chops, in quantity. By the time we'd disposed of them it was early afternoon, time for Roy. We drove West, along Forsyth Street – named after our first Mayor, George – and turned left, southwards, into Murray Street. At once, two revelations broke upon us. One, strictly speaking, broke on me, although I communicated it promptly to Maxwell. In my South Wagga schooldays when, a tender youngster in uncertain control of my bike, I ventured into Murray Street – named, by the bye, after one F.J. Murray, whose land lay hereabouts – I was regularly assailed and pursued by a mob of ruffianly boys and hysterical dogs – whether the boys sent the dogs out or the dogs the boys I was pedalling too frantically to judge – and the memory, ripe and ready for my Memoir, of my many hair's-breadth escapes rose up and smote me the moment we turned the corner. At the same moment, give or take a heartbeat, we both knew who belonged to the third cross on the map: Ozzie Murray, struck down and swept away by the midnight mail on the line behind his Ashmont farmlet six or seven years ago. Artie had mentioned him in the Terminus as a possible strange death, but his name and fate had dropped out of sight since.

 Roy O'Hanlon was a tiny fellow, but he was a very big drinker of beer, and there was a lot of it waiting for us on his back verandah. Of course he wanted to know how much progress we'd been making. One possibility we were exploring, I said, was that Andrew had come to believe that a series of local, apparently accidental deaths over the last few years were actually murders, and that it was while he was pursuing his investigations that he met the murderer and his fate. Which deaths? Roy wanted to know. Maxwell listed them, and included Ozzie's. Ozzie, Roy said, is one of the bees in Artie's bonnet because it was widely-known that he was in an alcoholic daze when he met that train but Artie reckons he wasn't a drinker so somebody must have got him drunk on purpose, which seems pretty bloody unlikely, even teetotallers have occasional binges, but he was surprised to hear that Andrew had got hold of the same crazy idea, because who in the world would want to murder Ozzie, he was as harmless as they come? He never went anywhere or did anything or even knew anybody as far as anybody knew, he and those sisters of his were just holed up in the old Murray place in Ashmont doing nothing at all, the sisters were still there doing it. Even if Andrew was wrong about, say, Ozzie, I said, somebody might have thought he was close enough to the truth about one of the others to get rid of him. Not in that way, Maxwell objected, not including castration, because castration surely implies some sort of sexual dimension, and that has nothing to do with murdering somebody to stop him revealing that somebody was a murderer. That, I agree, I agreed, opens an intriguing gap between what looks like Andrew's murder-theory and Andrew's murder, as if, I said, there might be not one but two distinct lines of mayhem, Andrew being their point of intersection. 'More beer,' Roy said: 'I'm losing the thread.'

We had some more beer, during which Roy remarked that he'd told the chaps that it was only a matter of time, and hardly that, before I started dragging what happened to Andrew back into the bloody past and probably into our bloody schooldays too, because that bloody memoir we all knew I was writing would take charge of me and sweep me away. Like poor Ozzie, Maxwell remarked, in spite of his ceaseless efforts to drag me into the present. I then remarked that our common past was a vast repository of stories, far too many for a single Memoir to encompass, but stories that featured old hatreds and deep-seated antagonisms might be relevant to the case before us. Perhaps Roy could remember some particular hatred and antagonism involving Andrew that might give us a clue, although I for one had never noticed anything of the sort. Roy remarked that that didn't surprise him because I was always so self-centred that I couldn't be expected to notice much else, but apart from the hatred and antagonism between me and Clive Brady, which wasn't relevant, the only example he could remember connected with Andrew was the angry period when Tommy Anderson was getting over Andrew getting off with his girlfriend at the time, that very busty little Yvonne thingamy, after the Intermediate Social, but we were all only fourteen then and that couldn't be relevant either.

'Good old Clive,' I said: 'I had a pleasant chat with him only yesterday. He seemed to be in fine form. I trust he's now outgrown that old adolescent rivalry, as I did long ago.'

'Of course he has, it's been fifty years since,' Roy said: 'When I was talking to him a couple of weeks back he said he knew you were due and he was looking forward to seeing you again.'

'Ah,' I said: 'I fear I still unsettle him. He had to pretend yesterday that he didn't know I'd be here. He couldn't bring himself to admit that he was expecting me.'

'These adolescent traumas are full of interest,' said Maxwell, 'but to return to Andrew, there might be something relevant in what you say about his conquest of Tommy's Yvonne.'

'I remember Yvonne. Even now, fifty years on,' I said, 'I can picture the exact shape and volume of that marvellous bosom of hers. It all comes back to me now. So does the Intermediate Social. So does Andrew in his snaffling heyday. This will get a mention in the Memoir.'

'It's not that ancient feat I had in mind,' Maxwell said: 'It's his more recent feats of a similar sort that might be relevant. He seems to have been having quite a few girlfriends in recent times, and very recently one in particular. Do you know who?'

Roy said he didn't know, the only thing he knew was that women were more trouble than they were worth and only a fool would believe anything they said. While we were on the subject of women, I said, there was one, one I'd always had a soft spot for, Robyn Lee, who'd had a pretty strange death, all things considered, which couldn't of course be suspected to be a murder but was strange enough, despairing enough, to make me wonder whether there was more to it than met the eye. Roy said he didn't know, the only thing he knew was what we all knew about Robyn and that was that she had very poor judgment, she couldn't be stopped from doing anything and she often did it with anybody, anybody at all, even real ratbags and no-hopers.

Roy's phone rang at this point. Detective Sergeant Parrot had received information, he said, that we were currently in the Roy residence and he wished to indicate that at five this afternoon he would be in the Union Club in the hope of receiving a progressive progress report on our day's inquiries, which, he wished to speak frankly, had not been progressive in the slightest so far apparently. We said we'd be there at five. Roy said that Charlie was getting up himself these days, and the way he'd started talking made it practically impossible for the locals to understand what he meant until he clumped them on the head, but he was a good deal smarter than he sounded and you couldn't afford to underestimate him. As for our inquiries, he said, we seemed to him to be making a lot of progress in a lot of useless directions, but on the other hand he was used to being wrong and of course he wasn't anywhere near as clever as we were. We tried to explain to him that cleverness wasn't anywhere near as important in a case like this as local experience and an instinct for what was likely and unlikely in the circumstances, but he just shook his head, he said all of it was just far too unlikely for any of his instincts, and hadn't we better be thinking of getting off to meet Charlie?

We got off accordingly. We didn't need much in the way of instinct to know that Roy wanted to get rid of us. It was barely 4 p.m. He'd seemed suddenly to become ill at ease, dismissive and defensive, as if our talk had entered territory into which he wouldn't venture. I opined that the weather changed when Robyn Lee's death came up. Maxwell thought it changed earlier, when Andrew's young girlfriend came up. For a man who normally knew a whole lot about almost everything locally suddenly to know nothing about these two subjects was pretty surprising, which left us, Maxwell pointed out, with the usual three alternatives: he didn't know, he didn't want us to know, or he didn't want to know he knew. Evidently, I said, I need to go more deeply into Robyn's strange death with Veronica; and we still have time enough, pre-Charlie, to hie to Klever Kitchens to arrange to interview her again, and also to extract the name of Andrew's co-tangoer from Manager Doug. Just for the record, I added, Andrew didn't snaffle Yvonne thingamy from Tommy after the Intermediate Social. That was the one and only occasion on which anybody snaffled anybody from Mike McClure. Andrew would certainly wish me to make honourable mention of it in the Memoir.

Veronica and I engaged in some energetic eye-contact when we arrived, to the effect, on my part, that I wanted to see her outside afterwards and, on hers, that she was as willing as possible. Brenda, the plain girl in Sales, happened to intercept one of my more telling glances and reeled away among the frying pans. Manager Doug gave us a cheery wave and retreated into his office; we followed him thither. He claimed to be very busy, and fiddled futilely with papers on his desk. We needed only a few moments of his valuable time, we informed him, and the quicker he gave us answers to a couple of simple questions the fewer those moments would be.

'What questions?' he said.

'The first question, Doug,' I said, 'seems a bit strange to me, but Detective Sergeant Parrot is particularly keen that we should ask you it. That dance that Andrew and his young friend were dancing at your Christmas dinner-dance, was it really what you'd reckon was a tango?'

'I don't know much about dancing,' said Doug, 'but – '

'Neither do I, Doug,' I said: 'I'm with you there.'

'That young friend you're mentioning,' said Maxwell: 'How young is young? I've heard she's about twenty-five.'

'Twenty-five!' I exclaimed: 'Come off it, Maxwell. She's much younger than that, isn't she, Doug? When I saw her the year before last, she looked about eighteen.'

'Eighteen!' Maxwell exclaimed: 'These young females always baffle you, you've never been able to gauge their age. If you reckoned she looked about eighteen she was probably either fifteen or well over twenty.'

'Doug'll settle this,' I said: 'She's certainly older than fifteen or sixteen, isn't she, Doug?'

'Oh yes,' said Doug: 'About twenty, I'd say.'

'There you are,' I said: 'Doug's got it. About twenty is about right. As a matter of fact, Maxwell, when you mentioned twenty-five just now I thought you might have been thinking of her mother. Of course she's older than that, she has to be, but when I saw her not so long ago she hardly looked it. She's very well-preserved, wouldn't you say so, Doug?'

'Her mother?' said Maxwell: 'Are you sure you've got the right woman. Clarry Harmer told me she was looking very old for her age.'

'Clarry's crazy. Or I have indeed got the wrong woman. She's quite tall and blonde. She – '

'She's short and squat. She's built like me, apparently - that's what Clarry says. Doug'll know. Short or tall, Doug?'

'On the shortish side, I'd say. But it's some time since I saw her.'

'She'll be shorter now,' said Maxwell: 'I wouldn't be surprised if she was developing a bit of a hump by now. Widows often do.'

'Widow? What are you wittering about? You and Clarry have certainly got the wrong woman. I saw her husband strolling down Baylis Street as large as life only two days ago. I say her husband because I hadn't heard they're divorced. Are they, Doug?'

'Not that I've heard, but I've heard he's a difficult bugger, just like his father, you know.'

'Was his father difficult? I hadn't heard that, Doug. Difficult in what ways?'

'He used to attack people without warning, apparently for no reason at all. You must have heard of the time he nearly throttled old Archdeacon West.'

'Ah yes. Old Dudley Davies. It all comes back. It's been really good to talk to you, Doug. I wish we could natter on but Maxwell has to see a man about a dog and we'd better be off.'

'About that dance you were asking about. I think it was a tango.'

'Good, good. That's what we were hoping for. Detective Parrot will be delighted to hear it.'

We hung about out in Baylis Street, waiting for Veronica, and I congratulated us on the skill and cunning of our interrogation. 'Masterly,' I said, 'is the only word for it. A consummate double-act, quite in our old style. He hadn't the faintest idea where we were leading him. Billy Davies was two years behind us at Wagga High. His daughter shouldn't be hard to track down.'

'I don't understand why we didn't just ask him who she was,' said Maxwell: 'I'm sure he would have told us.'

'You scientific bods,' I said, 'are so unimaginative. Speaking of which, not a word about this girl to Detective Parrot. He'd be into her, boots and all, before you could say Ned Kelly, and all too probably ruin several lives. The police, I have always maintained, should be kept well away from nubile young women.'

Bang on cue, Veronica, faintly perspiring, appeared. That night, boyfriend Rex was taking her to a disco. Tomorrow night at eight in Romano's she would be free, and she said she had something very important to tell me.

Over we went to the Union Club hotel, where Charlie was inhaling a double of what turned out to be our whisky.

'Well?' he said: 'What clues have you managed to get from Jayne? I'll be interviewing her myself tomorrow. We need some progress here. The Superintendent has been asking me how close I am to making an arrest.'

'Tell him you're very close,' I said: ' Say that you need only a few more days to tie the whole thing up. And speaking of tying things up I'm suddenly reminded, by an odd but obvious association of ideas, of another old schoolmate of ours, Donny Parker. You remember Donny, of course, and the strange strangled death he died in the Victory Memorial Gardens. Poor Donny. Pure accident, I'm told, the consequence of accidentally excessive exercise. Is that the considered opinion of an experienced investigator like yourself?'

'It was before my time. I wasn't involved in the investigational bureau at that date,' Charlie said: 'Another double, Rowena. Less ice. But now you ask, I can remember having the thought that there was something peculiar about some of the ways he was hung up. Poor Donny, it must have been a really uncomfortable way to go. My professional opinion, at this distance of time, is that it was the kind of accident that required a bit of assistance, particularly the strangling angle. Donny would've had to be an acrobat to get his neck into that position, and also he would've needed a stronger noose than a Wagga High tie. But there you go, I wasn't involved in the investigation, and you two fellows weren't around to solve it. Why are we wasting all this valuable time talking about Donny? What about the clues you must have gathered from Jayne? What have you got for me?'

'Ah yes, the clues,' I said: 'These clues, Charlie, are numerous and striking, very striking indeed, as I'm sure Maxwell will confirm.'

'Very striking,' he confirmed, 'indeed.'

'So very striking,' I said, 'on the whole, that a day or two's further analysis and investigation will have them pointing straight at the culprit. Almost all of the pieces of the jigsaw are already in our hands, and we are engaged in deciphering the pattern, the sinister pattern. In a day or two, Charlie, you can strike. Wagga will be amazed. Just at this moment, however, when the whole appalling story is beginning to crystallise in our minds, our thought-processes, particularly Maxwell's, must not be interrupted. We cannot stay and delay to explain; we must press on. But before we go, Charlie, there is one clue that you might be able to shed light on. We have found evidence suggesting that Andrew's murder might not be entirely unconnected with the strange death of yet another of our old schoolmates, Ozzie Murray. What do you make of that?'

'Ozzie Murray? ' said Charlie: 'There can't be any connection there. Poor Ozzie's was as accidental as possible, I've rarely experienced a clearer case. About the only person who ever seemed to imagine that it wasn't was Tommy Anderson. Apparently they were friends. Apparently they saw a lot of each other in the period before the tragic accident. Tommy kept coming to see me to see if we'd picked up anything strange about it. Of course there was nothing. Drink and railways never mix, I've always said that.'

'Another straightforward tragic accident, I see,' said Maxwell: 'There's a lot of them about. We are evidently an accident-prone generation. If only Andrew had survived another year or so he might have had a fatal accident instead.'

'True, too true,' I said: 'But before we go, and we must go immediately because Maxwell has an urgent appointment, we cannot leave the subject of fatal accidents among our Wagga High mates without mentioning Robyn Lee, poor Robyn, and her dreadful leap into the unknown from the Base Hospital tower.'

'That was suicide, pure and simple,' Charlie said: 'I've never experienced a clearer case.'

'But why?' Maxwell said: 'Why would she have done something like that?'

'Who knows?' Charlie said: 'Women are prone to unreasonable acts of such a nature. Robyn, poor Robyn, had very poor judgment. Even back in our schooldays she couldn't be stopped from doing anything and she frequently did it with anybody at all, even no-hopers and ratbags. But I can't say that I know anything about her unfortunate deceasement.'

'I'm sure you're right about poor Robyn,' I said: 'Everybody says the same. I was fond of her, even so. And I'm fond of dear old Tommy, whose name has just come up. I'd like to have a chat with him about poor Ozzie's passing. All the years I've known him I've never actually known where he lives. Do you happen to have his address?'

'More or less. We keep having to visit him to bring him in for questioning. It's in Moani Place, I can't happen to recall the exact number but it's down at the Tichborne Street end. Give him my regards.'

'We will, we will. He'll appreciate that. We'll be in touch, Charlie, just as soon as we've crystallised those clues. Have another whisky on us.'

'Suddenly Tommy's everywhere,' I said, as we went back to the car: ' I caught myself wondering why his name wasn't coming up in connection with Robyn's suicide. As to which, which you must have noticed, there seems to be a lot of local unanimity about poor Robyn's poor judgment. Charlie and Roy described her in virtually the same words.'

'I noticed,' said Maxwell: 'And virtually exactly is closer than just virtually. They must have been talking about her.'

Tommy's persistent unavailability, which had begun to be worrying before lunch, was seriously hampering our investigations by sunset. His neighbours, I suggested, might have inklings of his whereabouts. Where was Moani Place? ('Moani', of course, means 'kangaroo') Maxwell said he knew where, we could drive there on the way home. We did so. He drove out along the Lake Albert Road. He turned left into The Boulevarde, past Mr. Jackson's nature strip. He turned right into Berala Street, past that backyard shed. He turned left into Tichborne Crescent and right into Moani Place. I was flabbergasted.

'I'm sorry to be saying this,' Maxwell said, 'but your old mate Tommy is not merely everywhere; he is also somewhere. And that somewhere is here, right around the corner - we can pace out the exact number of yards at our leisure – from the last resting-places of Andrew's personal effects and his car. You keep telling Charlie that we're on the point of cracking this case, in defiance of the fact that no case in the history of detection has ever been further from being cracked; and now, suddenly, out of the blue, a shower of clues has descended upon us. All of which point in the direction of your old mate Tommy.'

'Wait a moment,' I said, deflabbergasting speedily: 'You go too far too fast. We have found no skerrick of evidence connecting Tommy with Andrew's death. And how many kinds of idiot would he have to be to be littering his own surroundings with the signs and remains of his crime?'(I must admit that my voice trailed off towards the end of this query.)

'Quite,' said Maxwell: 'As you yourself have often remarked, Tommy is famous for being precisely that kind of idiot. What do you mean, no evidence? Our current hypothesis – *your* hypothesis, and the only one we have – is that Andrew's murder is one of a series of strange deaths, Wagga High deaths. We have noticed Tommy lurking suspiciously in the neighbourhood of one of them, giving the victim of a second the jitters and hovering, also suspiciously, around a third. And now here he is again, a short stroll from Andrew's relics. If your hypothesis has anything going for it it is going straight for Tommy.'

'All right, conceded,' I replied, '*pro tem.* If we can find him we can cross-examine him about them. Until we can find him we have to find out a bit more about them than mere hearsay is telling us. Meanwhile, since we're here, let's take a look at Tommy's emoh ruo.'

Moani Place housed thirteen bungalows, twelve of which were spick and span. The thirteenth, a tumbledown in a jungle, was obviously Tommy's. We banged on doors and shouted through keyholes. We peered through windows too murky to be peered through. Tommy remained unavailable. We visited his neighbours, none of whom had seen him for days or knew or cared where he might have gone off to. His nearer neighbours, we noticed, were disinclined to tell us anything about him, as if fearing we might carry their comments back to him. Their caution was natural and understandable: Tommy was a pretty frightening character. A distant householder, however, on the far and safer side of the cul-de-sac, gave us something to chew on. Tommy was a real pest, a bloody noisy bugger, he told us, especially at night, especially late at night, and especially last Monday night, when he and his mates were having a really riotous party, crashing and banging about until nearly one in the morning, which he was just about to go across and complain about but it stopped just before he'd got his pants on and since then thank the Lord there hadn't been a peep out of him. We set off back towards Maxwell's homestead, chewing on this. As we drove past that backyard shed at the top of Berala Street we remembered that we had still not managed to achieve a few words with the passing local constable who had happened on the stash of Andrew's clothes. Tomorrow we would press Charlie to exert his authority and produce him.

Tomorrow we would also do something else, I announced, while recuperating from one of Maxwell's chilli extravaganzas. I closed the windows in case of eavesdroppers. 'That noisy party in Tommy's house would seem to have been taking place after he went to Boree Creek and disappeared. He might have come back for it, but then he wouldn't have left his vehicle down there, would he? Perhaps that party wasn't a party and those mates weren't mates. Something has happened to Tommy, I feel sure of it. And if, as we have been coming to suspect, there is indeed a connection between Tommy and these strange Wagga High deaths, it's not impossible that this unlikely late-night party might be connected with it.'

'It's not impossible that this unlikely party might be connected with the connection between Tommy and all these deaths? Charlie is going to love this. I think we should ring him up immediately and tell him we've had a breakthrough.'

'By which I mean something like this,' I said: 'It seems to me that Tommy has been having suspicions about Ozzie's death, and perhaps he noticed something peculiar about Steve's. Giving someone the jitters when you're someone like Tommy is pretty normal behaviour, so Donny's strange death shouldn't count against him personally. Now. Andrew seems to have been having suspicions about these deaths, and he's been murdered. Tommy – '

' – Let me guess. Tommy's been murdered. You've discovered yet another Wagga High murder! I don't believe this,' said Maxwell, apparently preparing to tear his hair: 'You're so determined not to believe that your old mate Tommy could possibly be a murderer that you want to make him a murder-victim instead.'

'It's not impossible.' I said: 'And you're right, I can't believe that Tommy could be a murderer. It is at least possible that Tommy's suspicions have come to the attention of whoever is really responsible for these murders and both Tommy and Andrew have been disposed of for the same reason. I admit that Andrew's castration and so forth doesn't seem to quite fit in with that, but there are always loose ends in life and death. You know how happy I am to be proved wrong. What I want to do tomorrow is to find out a bit more about these other strange deaths.'

'It's Tommy, Tommy, Tommy isn't it? We're supposed to be investigating poor Andrew's strange death, and no wonder we're making no progress – you want to investigate every other strange death instead.'

'One day should do it,' I said: 'We have to see where Tommy fits in. One way or the other, Tommy's disappearance, I now sense, is close to the heart of the matter.'

Maxwell tore his hair and went to bed. I finished the port and went to bed.

CHAPTER FIVE

It was a bacon-and-eggs morning, to give us strength of purpose and clarity of mind.

In Wagga (Wagga), a strict etiquette governs Sunday morning visiting. Sunday mornings are out of bounds, except for family members within the first two degrees of propinquity. Our townspeople might have gone to church, or they might not; and we think it indecent to have it known whether they have or haven't. And then there is the Sunday dinner, generally a leg of lamb with all the trimmings, to be got through; and then there is the nap. Three p.m. is absolutely the first available slot. Our morning, therefore, was free. We practised with our weapons for another achy hour or so; after which we were charged with chores by Maxwell's taskmistress wife. Down-town we went, obediently touring supermarkets and fruit and veggie merchants, with a side-trip to Bargain Booze. Homeward bound, we took the scenic route up and over the Hill, thinking that we might pay a restorative visit to our secret sanctuary there, and look again, in sombre Sunday mood, at Andrew's last vista.

As we turned into Baden Powell Drive we descried a considerable crowd of cars and people in the Museum car-park. We parked and mingled. There was a general movement into the Museum's foyer, which we joined, and anon found ourselves wedged and trapped between a cabinet of aboriginal curiosities and three of the largest women on earth. A vista that I at least would have gone to great lengths to avoid lay before us – there was a ribbon waiting to be cut and, scissors poised and waiting to give tongue, was Clive Brady.

I will spare you his speech. Of its kind, I admit, it was good. Quite good. Pretty good. But it was a loathsome kind. It reeked of false humility. It continually focused attention on the speaker by insistently and conspicuously directing attention away from him, towards something else. And that something was, I was mortified to have to behold, what, on the far side of the waiting ribbon, a glittering golden plaque described as The Clive Brady Reading Room. I gnashed my teeth. At long last Clive concluded, the scissors did their stuff and the mob surged into the CBRR, mad to start reading. We tried to get out before CB noticed us. In vain. His sharp little eyes had taken us in, and he sashayed over.

'Wal. Maxwell', he said: 'Welcome. Good of you to come. This is such a teeny little local event, very small beer beside the various international gatherings you generally attend, Wal, and I know how busy you both must be, tracking down poor Andrew's murderer. I was chatting to Superintendent Wilkinson a couple of nights ago at the club and he seemed to have formed the impression that you fellows are getting nowhere, but I told him that it probably only looked like that, and that behind the scenes you were no doubt absolutely racing towards your goal. I hope I'm right.'

'Right enough,' said Maxwell. I was momentarily hyperventilating. 'Why does this reading-room bear your name, Clive? Are you a generous benefactor of the Museum?'

'Pretty generous. I do what I can. Those of us who have stayed on in Wagga Wagga have a responsibility to keep our cultural flags flying. It's also the kind of thing that looks well on the record of a prospective mayor of the city. Don't you agree, Wal?'

'On both counts, yes, especially the latter,' I said: 'And who knows? One of these days some of my books on teeny little local subjects may merit a place in the CBRR, perhaps in a special little corner cabinet of their very own. If that day should ever come, Clive, those international gatherings will call to me in vain. I'll be back in Wagga Wagga in a jiffy, I'll open that cabinet, and I'll bring the ribbon myself.'

'I'll start a subscription immediately,' he said: 'I may even contribute to it myself.'

'Wal,' said Maxwell, 'we are tracking down poor Andrew's murderer, remember. Let's hit the trail.'

The exercise trail took us away from this agitating scene – away and up, I still gnashing, to our secret sanctuary and, looming above it, Andrew's fatal tree. Gnashing as I was I could not help regretting that I had not done as Clive had done, and long before he did it. His motives, it went without saying, were disgustingly, transparently self-promoting. Mine would have been, if not pure, purer. A reading-room bearing my name would have been a peculiarly appropriate endowment and monument, for many – even most – of my works owed many of their incidents, circumstances, characters and reflective passages to my life and times in my native place. Even now, when I knew the world, Wagga was as alive and kicking in me as when it was the only world I knew. It deserved well of me, but I had made no adequate return. Maxwell did not wholly sympathise with my feelings in this matter, suggesting, as we ascended the final slope, that a possibly perfectly adequate return might be never to mention the town in my writings again.

We spent a few refreshing minutes among the olives and kurrajongs of our secret sanctuary, which Maxwell admitted had been properly and movingly mentioned in my writings. We then went on up to that spectral gum, poor Andrew's last look-out, and looked out from it at his terminal view. It seemed so obvious now and here, knowing what we now knew and could conjecture, that Wagga High was the key to Andrew's murder – and, in all probability, to those other strange deaths that we, and he, had begun to detect; for there, full in his view, his last sight on earth, as he had been O so carefully and cruelly positioned to see, out across our sanctuary and the reservoir in the vale, exactly at dying-eye-level, stood the central *massif* of Wagga High.

We passed rapidly, eyes averted, through the Museum car-park, and brought our goods back to base. Maxwell's missus told us that Detective Charlie had been ringing and wanted to be rung back. This we did. Charlie informed us that he was on the point of sitting down to his Sunday dinner, but he had taken the trouble of looking up Tommy's number in Moani Place, it was 13. We reminded him of the passing constable we wanted to interview. He smote his brow (we heard the smite over the phone). That constable was away in Victoria on a special mission; but he would arrange for his recall at the earliest possible juncture. Charlie went on to say that he felt he ought to let us know that the Superintendent was showing unmistakable signs of being completely fed up with the lack of progress in this case. I replied that we were confident we would have a major breakthrough to report within twenty-four or forty-eight hours at the outside. Maxwell tore his hair.

It was leg-of-lamb-time and we consumed one. A short nap took us to 2.45. Ozzie Murray's sisters were our first port of call, on the old Murray property in Ashmont. (Ashmont – in case readers are still interested – is one of our suburbs; it bears the name of the Salmon family's homestead on an adjacent mont.) We drove out up the old dog-legged Sturt Highway, along Dobney Avenue (T. Dobney, Mayor, 1910-11). Off it, in the good old days, our days, farmlets ran down to the southward-bound railway-line; these days, those farmlets were mostly awaiting the archaeologist under suburban development; but one or two fragments of the past yet remained, and one of them was the Murrays'.

We waded through a wilderness of thistles towards an extensive, extensively decrepit, mansion. Two sizable females occupied the verandah and watched our approach.

'Narelle! Joelene!' I cried, activating my famous memory: 'Lovely to see you again! And you're both looking amazingly well!'

'I know you,' said Narelle, or perhaps Joelene: 'You're the boy who thought he was the cat's pyjamas.'

'Exactly so,' I said, 'though I have learnt humility since.' Maxwell shot me a swift look. 'And this is Maxwell, an old friend of Ozzie's at school and elsewhere.'

We spent some time refusing cups of tea and lamingtons, and raised the subject of Ozzie's tragic death. Narelle or Joelene said of course it was tragic but it was also a kind of blessed relief really and they'd been expecting it for some time. We understood, we said, that although of course he hadn't been much of a drinker there was a strange air of alcohol in the circumstances. They seemed surprised. They asked us how we knew. We said we'd just heard a passing rumour, was it true? They said they were disappointed to hear that such a rumour had got about, Detective Sergeant Parrot had promised to keep it a secret for the family's sake, but yes Ozzie had taken to drink in a continuous way, night and day but especially night, due to a stream of disappointments in love because he was too shy to really try and of course he was embarrassed by his looks and he got that way that he needed to have a bottle of brandy constantly ready within reach and during the nights especially he would be wandering about inside and outside the house and up and down the paddocks with his bottles and often in the morning they'd find him fast asleep out by the railway-line, he always had a friendly feeling for trains, so it was no surprise when he was run over by one, poor Oz, he had a lot to offer but somehow he was never able to offer it. True, we said, very true. His friends, we suggested, no doubt tried to help him, particularly close friends such as Tommy Anderson.

'Never heard of him,' said the other one: 'Who's he?'

I gave them a vivid and detailed description of Tommy, but there was absolutely no persuading them that they'd ever clapped eyes on him: they were adamant that they knew all of Ozzie's friends, all four of them, and this Tommy wasn't one of them. Ozzie had never mentioned him. They had never heard of him.

We withdrew, and reflected, in Maxwell's car, on our current position. This death didn't seem to be a strange one – not even, out here, a particularly unusual one. Maxwell and I could think of several similar cases, even in our own families. Nonetheless, it might have been a murder. One could easily imagine somebody – Tommy, to humour Maxwell – creeping up on the sleeping sozzled Ozzie and heaving him into the path of the night mail. But if – to humour me – Tommy had not done that, then why did both Tommy and Andrew apparently suspect that an apparently straightforward accident wasn't? If Tommy wasn't one of Ozzie's four friends his marked interest in his death was either extremely suspicious or a sign that he was suspicious about it.

Although we hadn't been able to find Tommy in or around Ozzie's not-so-strange death, according to Charlie he was right in the middle of Steve Hampson's out at Lake Albert. I thought we should find out more about that at once. Maxwell thought I was so intent on clearing my old mate Tommy that I was losing sight of the main line of our investigation. It would be truer to say, I said, that I was now bent on trying to prove that he was our serial murderer, even though I didn't believe that for a moment. The whole hypothesis of the Wagga High murders depended on Steve's and Donny's deaths – since we seemed to have drawn a blank on Ozzie's – and if it fell, there fell with it what had come to seem the likeliest version of Andrew's murder. We set forth to forthwith pay a call on Steve's widow, the former Judy Fawcett, whose legs I had hymned – attaching them to another, fictional owner - in *Eric Connolly's Comeuppance*. They were still worth hymning when we viewed them in her garden in Dalton Street – named, I always prefer to believe, after the hero of my first novel. She was gardening in her garden, assisted therein by a middle-aged gent. whom we took for her second husband, Steve's replacement. Judy's face had never been arresting, or even noticeable, and it was now less so. Those legs, however, were still in fine fettle, ugly green wellies notwithstanding.

'Judy!' I cried: 'Lovely to see you again! And you're looking amazingly well! This is Maxwell, an old friend of Steve's at school and elsewhere.'

She knew me. We chit-chatted for a time, and she introduced us to Herbert, her younger son, who apparently resided over in Cootamundra with wife and family of four and was paying her a weekend visit, to help in the garden. After admiring some of her plants I brought the conversation around to the old days, the carefree years of youth and promise (and legs), and I mentioned that I was working up my Memoir of exactly those days and their glorious doings. She said she'd heard about that forthcoming memoir, everybody she knew knew about it; and I also then mentioned that I wanted to touch on dear old Steve's departure from the land of the living with all the delicacy and accuracy at my disposal. 'I understand,' I said, 'that the poor fellow's heart gave up the ghost while he was paddling his canoe.'

'Yes,' she said: 'He had a history of heart. The doctors told him it was in a very fragile state but he just went on over-exerting himself right to the end. He was that sort of man.'

'I hear,' I said, 'that another old friend, Tommy Anderson, tried to resuscitate him.'

'Tommy Anderson?' Herbert exclaimed: '*The* Tommy Anderson? He wasn't there. I was, and by the time a couple of chaps and I got Dad to the bank it was far too late to do any resuscitating. Tommy Anderson wasn't anywhere in evidence.'

'Evidently you know Tommy,' I said: 'Do you know him well?'

'Not personally, not at all,' said Herbert: 'But I'm a solicitor, I used to practise here. Tommy's a well-known figure in the local courts. I can't imagine how you can have got the idea that he was present at Dad's death.'

'I can't remember. I must have misheard somebody saying something,' I replied: 'I'm glad we've cleared that up. I hope readers of my Memoir will be properly grateful.'

We had a bit more chit-chat; we admired more plants; we declined afternoon tea; we withdrew.

So. Donny was now the only shot in the locker. The Wagga High murders were evaporating before our eyes. Tommy, as Herbert Hampson had just put it, wasn't anywhere in evidence.

'It's a real stroke of luck,' I said as we walked back to the car, 'that we happened on Herbert, a vital witness, just when he happened to be over from Cootamundra on gardening duty. Tommy's right out of Steve's death and he's really only on the far fringe of Ozzie's, apparently asking questions about it. So far, the hearsay from Charlie is null and void wherever we've tested it. Much more disturbingly, wherever we've tested our ruling assumption that Andrew was questing after strange Wagga High deaths we're finding ordinary, everyday run-of-the-mill Wagga deaths, illustrative of several of the common ills that flesh is heir to. Either our ruling assumption is wrong or Andrew has been ridiculously, hopelessly and systematically wrong all along. Either way, we have no line on his murder. Utter failure and widespread jeering, fleering and sneering in the Terminus are staring us in the face.'

'I warned you,' said Maxwell: 'I told you how loopy Andrew could be. Once a bee got into his bonnet he could lose all contact with reality. But maybe we've simply been attaching far too much significance to those little crosses on that map. Maybe they mean something else. What seems to be becoming clear at last, surely, is that Andrew's murder isn't one of a series, which the uniquely awful manner of it should have convinced us of from the outset. Now that we also know that your Tommy hasn't been a serial murderer, at any rate of Wagga High veterans, perhaps we can let him alone at last and go back to hunting for the murderer of Andrew Kell.'

'Perhaps,' I said: 'But I continue to feel the need to get Tommy off Andrew's map. That arrow worries me. Whatever the crosses mean, the chap who put them on the map has been murdered. He also put that arrow on the map, and the chap it appears to be pointing to has mysteriously disappeared. However you look at it, something's up.'

'There's a lot there that we don't actually know,' Maxwell said: 'We don't know that Andrew put the crosses and the arrow on the map, and we don't even know that the arrow apparently pointing to Moani Place is pointing at Tommy Anderson. There are twelve other houses within range.'

'True, technically true, *mon vieux*,' I replied: 'But Tommy's name has been constantly coming up around whatever those crosses mean or don't mean – he's really always been on the map in one way or another; and every probability under the sun points to its being a fair bet that the arrow points to him.'

'O.K. Tommy's file stays open,' said Maxwell: 'Meanwhile, let me remind you, we have another open file in front of us, of immediate and obvious relevance to Andrew's murder. The traditional motives are still the best. *Cherchez la femme*, or have I already said that? After all, the excision of the balls has always made that the likeliest explanation.'

'By Jove, you're right. We've been neglecting our female lead, Andrew's fair young friend the tangoer, and a real goer according to Veronica, who is undoubtedly an expert in these matters. Speaking of whom, I'm due to give her an additional interrogation this evening after eight. Meanwhile, the curious case of the one strange Wagga High death that nobody seems to regard as strange continues to tantalise.'

'Before the tantalising resumes, we might have time to probe the whereabouts of the Davies daughter. Indirectly, naturally. I can ask Heather Whittle where they live.'

Heather Whittle, one of Wagga's innumerable old maids, was permanent President of the Wagga High Old Boys' and Girls' Association, and was rumoured to keep extensive files on us all. I had occasionally endeavoured to persuade her to divulge the contents of my own file, but she always denied that it, or any such, existed, maintaining that there was no need for them because Miss M.E. Paddock knew everything about everybody who had ever passed through the school's portals and she would obviously outlive us all.

Heather, however, kept up-to-date lists of our addresses; and Maxwell, on his mobile, quickly established that the Davies residence was in Norman Street – named after some Norman. Re-entering the car we proceeded thither – northwards down Turner Street – named after some Turner – in which, in those old days, another of my ancient South Wagga primary school friends had abided, and where there was an orchard where we…but that is for the Memoir and I must press on; right and eastwards along Coleman Street – named after George of that name, solicitor, alderman and mayor 1893,1895,1898-9; past Inverary Street – many of our local colonists were Scotch – whither my maternal grandparents retired from their Lockhart farm; and then left, northwards again, into Norman Street.

'Do you see that blue car a couple of blocks behind us?' Maxwell said, indicating our wing-mirror: 'I'm pretty sure it's been following us all afternoon.'

Perhaps; but it didn't follow us into Norman Street; and Maxwell, than whom nobody could be more observant, was sometimes supererogatively so.

The necessary address, if Heather Whittle was as knowledgeable as usual, was a garishly-patterned brick erection, approached across a tract of pink gravel ornamented with urns and gnomes. At the third buzz the lady of the house appeared, and after Maxwell had introduced us as Wagga High Old Boys on a mission of some importance she said she could recognise him, people she knew had pointed him out, and she invited him in. Even after Maxwell had identified me as the well-known Wal and she had allowed me in too she still couldn't recognise me, she said. I recognised her, though. She was all that survived of Sonia somebody, the scrubber, whom I saw having S.E.X. with Gary Doggett on the Beach way back at the start – practically *as* the start – of my adolescence.

She led us in and out, out onto a terrace overlooking another tract of pink gravel &c., and asked us what mission? Maxwell explained that in close association with Detective Charlie Parrot we were visiting a wide selection of Old Boys and Girls who might have been acquainted with the late Andrew Kell, in the hope that we might pick up something, anything, possibly relevant to his last days on earth.

She said she scarcely remembered Andrew from school and wouldn't have known him from Adam since, though wasn't he a pretty good runner? He was, I said, and a good dancer to boot. There was no reaction. Billy should be home any moment, she said, and he might have known him. It's a long time since I've seen Billy, I said, and as a matter of fact I didn't even know you and he were married. Maxwell asked her how long they'd been married and if they had any children? Oh about twenty-five years, she said. Only one, a girl, but that was enough, I'm sure you know how difficult children can be, especially girls, she said. Too true, thank heavens they grow up at last, I said, as I trust your daughter has, and is now a comfort to you.

' Comfort?' she vociferated, flashing or gnashing her teeth: 'That'll be the day! Angela walked out on us a year ago and she's scarcely been in touch since, she's gone to Collingullie, she's waitressing out there. Waitressing! Can you believe it? Such a waste! She was given all the advantages, we sent her away to a good boarding school in Albury, and now she's a waitress. In Collingullie! But here's Billy, don't mention her in front of him, she's a very sore point.'

Billy appeared, looking like the difficult bugger he was supposed to be. He clearly resented our presence, and while Maxwell was explaining why we had come and how soon we'd be going he appeared to be readying himself to uphold the family tradition by attacking us without warning. This surly brute of a father sufficiently explained the daughter's flight from home; the wonder was that she hadn't fled further than Collingullie, only sixteen miles westwards.

'Andrew Kell?' he said: 'A stuck-up bastard in my opinion. Just because he could run a bit quick he fancied himself no end; but he bloodywell couldn't run quick enough when it mattered last weekend, could he! Serves the bastard right in my opinion.'

'I'm sure you're right, Billy,' I said: 'You were always one of the clever ones. But I'm not quite sure why you're right. Why did it serve him right, do you think?'

'He had his balls cut off, didn't he? That's what they say. That shows he must have been fooling around with some bloke's woman, it sticks out a mile. He got what was coming to him.'

'I agree, I've just been saying that,' said Maxwell: 'Do you have any idea which bloke, which woman?'

'No,' he said: 'And I'm not interested. Have you finished? I'm going for a shower.'

He went. We also, after complimenting the lady of the house on her urns and gnomes, went. We'd got what we'd come for. The only place in Collingullie where anything like waitressing could occur was the Gullie Store. This Angela, Andrew's ultimate inamorata, was now in our sights.

As we drove back to Maxwell's farmlet, up and over our Hill, we considered how we could delve into the strangeness or otherwise of Donny Parker's death and the credibility or otherwise of the suspicions about it. We neither of us knew Donny's widow nor, if any, their children; and it was hard to imagine how, if we managed to get into conversation with any member of the family, we might raise the subjects we needed light on. 'I hear he was wearing his Wagga High tie when he passed away? Is it your impression that he was really capable of stringing himself up in that interesting position without any help?' No, no. Maxwell, however, had a plan. The Parker case had been extensively, though ever so discreetly, reported at the time in Wagga's paper, *The Daily Advertiser*. He knew its editor, Gordon Gibbs, whom I now remembered as a small spotty boy in the Opportunity class. Through G.G. we could examine the paper's files and perhaps obtain sight or hint of what had never reached print. A good plan.

I also had a good plan. I planned to plumb Veronica's depths, with particular but delicate reference to her understanding of the background to her mother's final act. I could not be bothered to practise our old weapons. After a light repast – spaghetti on the rocks – I sped downtown to Romano's.

I had booked a room – 33, naturally – in case we needed it. We needed it. I do not propose to gratify the prurience of a certain class of readers by giving them another blow-by-blow account of my exchanges with Veronica. Take them as read. Or read them again, pp.60-64. Our conversation, however, was at various points significantly different, and highly significant.

'I nearly forgot to tell you,' I said at one point: 'You might be interested in this. You remember how I was trying to put a name to poor Andrew Kell's tangoing-and-wrestling partner at your Christmas dinner-dance?'

'And afterwards,' she said: 'The way Brenda described them out at the Wagga Winery they were going a lot further than wrestling.'

We wrestled a bit, and then we went a lot further.

'I wouldn't be surprised. The name of this goer would seem to be Angela Davies.'

'Never heard of her. Is she a Wagga girl? Keep doing that.'

'An out-of-towner, I gather. I also gather that she was sent away to school, which is why, dear God dear God, you and Brenda wouldn't have known her.'

'Did Doug? Yes, yes, yes.'

'Yes, yes, yes. Doug did. Or he knew her parents. She didn't get on with them. She might have been looking for a mature man as a father-substitute.'

' It's just the old story, isn't it? Us young women, I mean, we're always being hunted by older men, including the married ones, especially the married ones. I know all about that.'

'I'm sure you do. Poor you. Have you been dreadfully plagued by Wagga's older men? By Andrew, for instance? If I'd been Andrew, working in the same office, I would have found you utterly irresistible. As I have, as I do.'

'Not by Andrew, though he liked looking at my legs. But there've been plenty of others, some of them really horrible. That Mike McClure, for example, he really turns my stomach. Let's try it on the floor.'

We tried it on the floor.

'Rex likes it down here. Which reminds me of my important news. I meant to tell you before we started. Rex and I have decided to become engaged.'

'Congratulations. He's a very lucky man. How those horrible older men will rage and rave! That particularly horrible one you singled out, Mike McClure: his name rings a faint bell. What was the matter with him?'

'What wasn't! Ugh. I'm surprised you don't know him. I'm sure he was at school with mum, when you were there too.'

'He must have been in one of the lower classes. How was he so horrible to you?'

' As soon as he met me he was trying to grope me. My mum was scarcely out of the room before he made his first grab and then it just went on and on, for months and months, he was always trying to fuck me but my God he was hairy all over, it was disgusting. He's had a few goes since, whenever he sees me he tries to touch me up, but he makes my flesh crawl, I loathed him from the start, he's a really filthy old man.'

In other circumstances I might have drawn her attention to the incredible fact that Mike and I were the same age, but I was too busy wallowing in the realisation that I was here and now achieving a conjunction that mighty Mike had tried for and failed. Andrew had beaten him to Yvonne thingamy and I, even I, than whom nobody was ever regarded as less appealing to our homegrown talent, was beating him to Veronica. Rigid with elation I recognised that I was experiencing one of the high points of my underachieving life.

We continued. After a while we paused, and while we were taking a breather I massaged her back and massaged her back to the filthy old man and her mother.

'That disgusting old groper must have been at you in your tenderest teens. Did your poor dear mother ever find out what he was up to, the swine?'

'I couldn't tell her. I was thinking of trying to but she took her life before I could. But I don't think I could've. How could I? She was crazy about him, she was really happy for the first time for years, she thought he was going to divorce his wife and marry her. How could I tell her that he was trying to fuck her daughter? Let's try it round this way.'

'Let's. You go first.'

While she was going I was thinking. It was tolerably obvious that my next question would have to be something along the lines of 'Of course you couldn't tell her but I wonder whether she might have become aware of it, especially if it went on for months and months; and if she was really crazy about him and hoping to marry him, might that not be the solution to the mystery of her suicide?' The tolerably obvious answer to this question was yes, or very possibly. But the tolerably obvious effect of this question on Veronica – to whom (and to whose mother) I was deeply indebted – would be to induce a fit of the horrors and to load her fresh young life with guilt. If she hadn't suspected this before, or if she had and had suppressed or overcome it, it was cruel, unnecessary and ungentlemanly to shackle her with it now. I did not put that question. Besides, I was already sure I had the answer. Besides, also, it was now my turn to go.

After a while, while we were recruiting our energies for another bout, 'People in general,' I said, 'must have been horrified by your poor dear mother's passing. And puzzled. They must have wondered why, and why she went in that particularly strange way. They must have mentioned it to you.'

'Nobody mentioned it to me. You're the first one, and you're distracting me. I suppose they thought it would upset me. I'm ready now.'

'Not even Andrew? Not even the disgusting McClure? Nobody at all?'

She shook her head, and directed me to... But no. Over the rest of the evening I cast the cloak of propriety. As we were drawing our proceedings to a close Veronica suggested that in view of her engagement perhaps we shouldn't be doing this any more, or at any rate not so often. I agreed, and complimented her on her scruples. I undertook to contact her only after a decent interval. We parted on satiated terms.

When I returned to the Maxwell establishment its inmates were asleep, indignantly asleep.

CHAPTER SIX

I didn't notice breakfast. While eating it I tabled my evening's findings and we began to address their implications.

Robyn's death, fairly obviously, had never been included in the chaps' list of strange Wagga High deaths because it wasn't strange to them – they knew all about it; and because one of them – one of *us* – was implicated in it. So far, so understandable. Perfectly understandable as well was, would be, their probable wish to deter us, and in particular me, from wasting valuable investigating time on an incident that could have nothing to do with Andrew's death. They had been reluctant to mention any of these strange deaths because of their distracting effect on a Wal who was always meditating his Memoir and living or partly living in the past. Perfectly understandably also, I said, they –

'I've been having second thoughts about some of that,' Maxwell said: 'I find it rather peculiar that the very chaps who were urging us to guard against your unfortunate historical tendencies and not to wander off among so-called strange deaths in the past pretty quickly came up with tempting details about one of them.'

'Second thoughts, as you say. They first thought that they didn't have anything to do with Andrew, and then they second thought that they might have. What's peculiar about that? I have second thoughts all the time.'

'That's because you don't live here any more. In Wagga, second thoughts come very slowly. In months rather than weeks. Two days is too quick.'

'Come, come. Even in Wagga, revelations and breakthroughs can occur. Especially when stimulated by the strange death of a mate, and by the presence of admired investigators. But as far as Robyn's death and the chaps are concerned, they –'

'Excuse me for asking,' Maxwell asked, 'but who are this they?'

'If only Miss M.E.Paddock could be here to hear you. They, fairly obviously, are some of the chaps.'

'Exactly. Some of them. You are one of the chaps every four or five years for a week or so. I am one of them every few weeks, year in, year out. Robyn's not-so-strange death occurred all of three years ago. Year in, year out I have never heard the faintest hint or half-rumour about Mike's part in it. Why not? Who are these some of them who knew all about it?'

'Mike, obviously. And Artie and Dunny too. The fact that they don't refer to her shows us that they knew. Roy almost certainly knows – he practically chased us out of the house as soon as we mentioned Robyn. Why not you? That's easy. You are widely known, loved and respected as a man of high and delicate morals. The chaps would have been very careful to conceal this scandalous affair from you.'

'What about Andrew?'

'What about Andrew?'

'Andrew wasn't a man of high and delicate morals. He wasn't only one of the chaps, he was one of the boys. If there'd been a rumour of a scandal going around he would have known about it. They couldn't have concealed it from him. And he would have had no reason to keep me in the dark about any scandalous affair involving Mike McClure. He and Mike were chaps, but they weren't mates, they were always a bit edgy with each other. I simply cannot believe that he could have kept mum on something like this for three whole years.'

'Perhaps, perhaps. He kept mum on the other possible strange deaths; and if he and Mike were not quite mates he might not have been let into the secret of Mike's role in Robyn's suicide. Still, it was a strange sort of suicide, it arrests the attention. I can't understand why it's not marked on his map.'

'Strange, yes, but not suspicious – that's why. All along, though, we've been attaching too much importance to those marks on that map. They could refer to anything. One thing two of them don't refer to is an actual strange and suspicious death, whatever Andrew may have been meaning by them. And you have all along attached far too much importance to the absence of a mark. Whatever the other marks mean the non-mark for Robyn means that nobody has the slightest interest in her strange fate, poor Robyn, except you.'

'Perhaps, perhaps. But by nobody just now we mean Mike and Artie and Dunny and Andrew. Roy was interested enough in it to want to have nothing to do with it. But I take your points, for the time being. For the time being, I think, we shouldn't entirely abandon the marks on the map. They're clues to something, even though we don't seem to have got what right. The hints and rumours pointing to Tommy's involvement haven't been right, either. Charlie and Dunny have invariably picked up and passed on wrong rumours about Tommy and these deaths. If all the deaths are wrong and all the rumours about Tommy are wrong there must be a pattern here that we aren't yet seeing. The last cross on the map is Donny Parker's. Ring G.G. and set up a session at *The Advertiser*. Then we'll hit the road for Collingullie and Angela. I long to make her acquaintance.'

G.G. was not only only too pleased, he declared, to throw open *The Advertiser's* files; he also undertook to introduce us to Barney Reilly, the reporter who had given the Donny Parker story, poor Donny, to the world. That being settled for anytime tomorrow, we set out towards Collingullie, sixteen miles out West on the Sturt highway. The journey was uneventful, except for Maxwell's regular impressions that this, that or the other car was following us.

Collingullie ('boggy ground', aboriginally), in the present era, is home to over three hundred souls. In the era of these events, there might have been two hundred of them. In the days when I knew it well, passing through it every month or so on the way out to the western division of my aunts and uncles, nobody had bothered to count them. Throughout history, however, there had always been five public buildings there – two churches, the Memorial Hall, the pub, and the Gullie Store. The pub – currently the Cross Roads Hotel Motel – was even more famous than the Gullie Stores: because it was situated at, right on, the point where the road to Narrandera goes to the right and the road to Lockhart goes to the left, and at that point the drunk drivers, of whom on Friday and Saturday nights there were not a few, had to take the turn to right or left in time to take it, which not a few could not quite manage in time, going straight ahead into the heavily-barricaded pub's bar instead, sometimes at sixty miles an hour. But the Gullie Store was pretty famous too, particularly for snakeskin belts, obsolete but still useful tools, shotguns and lollies galore, and on account of the two-week siege when Constable Carruthers holed up in it and blazed away at everything that moved until Detective Sergeant Herbert Truscott came through the roof and fell on him. In recent years the Store had added a coffee lounge and diner to its range of attractions. We entered it and ordered cappuccinos and lamingtons. The only waitress in evidence was as dowdy as possible, and seemed a most unlikely Angela; nevertheless we accosted her.

'Angela,' I said, 'these are excellent lamingtons.'

'I'm not Angela,' she said: 'She's not here any longer. I'm Brenda.'

'Where's she gone, Brenda?' said Maxwell: 'When did she go? We were chatting with her parents only yesterday and they expected her to be here.'

'I dunno. Nobody knows. She just didn't come in last Monday, and Mrs. Bartlett told us she packed up all her things and went off without a word. She was very upset, Mrs. Bartlett said.'

'Mrs. Bartlett?' I said: 'We should just have a word with her. Is she a friend of Angela's? Where might we find her?'

'Mrs. Bartlett's was where she stayed. I'll show you where to go.'

We went out and she gave us directions. I regret that I cannot at this moment remember whether Mrs. Bartlett dwelt half a mile out on Thirteen Mile Road or on Twelve Mile Road, but we found her house without difficulty; it was the only one out there.

Mrs. Bartlett was one of those small, cross and useful women around whom the world revolves. She apologised for receiving us in rollers, she was trying to make herself a bit decent, she said, her hair took a long time to come to order, and there was a C.W.A. meeting over in Boree Creek tomorrow morning that she didn't want to look a fright at, but she was just putting the kettle on and she hoped we would join her in a cup. We'd be delighted, we said; and Maxwell explained that we'd happened to be passing through Collingullie and had popped into the Store to say hello to Angela, only to discover that she wasn't there anymore and nobody knew where she'd gone and why. Which was more than she could say, Mrs. Bartlett said, flaring up, which was an unexpected return for nearly a whole year's boarding at a reduced rent and lots of extras. The kettle boiled, the morning tea's makings were accomplished, and a plate of those delicious Monte Carlo biscuits was set before us.

'This is most disturbing,' Maxwell said, while I got among the biscuits: 'Perhaps you can tell us what happened.'

'It was last Monday,' she said: 'She had a phone call in the morning before breakfast. I've never seen such floods of tears, she was beside herself, she wouldn't say why, she locked herself in her room and sobbed and sobbed all day fit to break. I couldn't get a single word out of her but it could only have been a very close death probably from the state she was in. And when they went off that evening they didn't say a thing after nearly a whole year, no forwarding address, nothing except goodbye and scarcely even thankyou. I ask you.'

'They?' said Maxwell: 'Who's this they?'

'Her father came for her. He must have done all her packing up, she wasn't capable, she was still completely prostated. You'd think he would have given me some idea of why it was all so sudden but no, nothing, just a grim goodbye.'

'Her father?' said Maxwell: 'I can't believe it. We were talking about her just yesterday with her mum and him and there was no mention of anything like this. Are you quite sure it was her father?'

'Well, she calls him daddy and he answers to it. He came here to see her every few weeks and of course she introduced him to me. There was never any sign of the mother.'

'He seems not to have been telling her about his trips to Collingullie,' I said, abandoning the Monte Carlos, 'for some reason. Angela's father can be somewhat grim and difficult on occasion.'

'I'll say he can, and on almost every occasion he came here. I'm sorry if he's a friend of yours but I never took to him. I'm afraid I've never really warmed to very tall thin men' – here she glanced at me: tall, thin and full of her Monte Carlos – 'but when there's a beaky face and a snooty manner as well, well, grim and difficult are what I've learnt to expect.'

Maxwell and I gaped at each other. Grim and difficult were certainly two of Billy Davies' adjectives, but tall, thin, beaky and snooty did not match him at any point.

'True. Too true,' said Maxwell: 'And many Wagga people would agree with you. These days he's not only grim, he's really grumpy; because of his car apparently, it doesn't work properly. Was he driving that old red thing he's having so much trouble with?'

It was blue, she said, not that she knew anything about cars. Then I wondered whether he was wearing his glasses when she saw him, it being a well-known fact that not being able to see people clearly tended to make one rude to them. She'd never seen him in glasses, but he was certainly rude enough to need them. Further artful questions enabled us to establish that this tall, thin, beaky, snooty, grim, rude, blue car daddy also looked as if he was a pretty heavy drinker, had a bit of a limp, didn't shave or shower as much as he needed to, and had a tense and fractious relationship with his daughter, especially lately.

'Fathers and daughters, as I know to my cost,' quoth Maxwell, 'are often at odds. Over boyfriends, for example. Did Angela's boyfriend visit her here?'

'You mean Andrew? Every few days, and she used to take the bus into Wagga every Sunday afternoon to visit him. Such a nice friendly man, Andrew, he always brings me chocolates. I must admit I think he's far too old for her but she adores him, that's obvious.'

'These Sunday afternoon trips certainly show that,' said Maxwell: 'What time would she get back?'

'Sevenish, although that Lockhart bus has no sense of time. Oh. Do you think she could have been in such a state because something serious has happened to Andrew?'

'That is precisely what we think, Mrs. Bartlett,' I said: 'There will be no more chocolates, I'm afraid. Something very serious indeed has happened to Andrew.'

We told her all, or as much of it as a respectable woman living in Collingullie needed to know. We assured her that we were leaving no stone unturned in our pursuit of Andrew's murderer. We gave her Maxwell's mobile number, in case she heard anything of or from Angela. We thanked her for her invaluable help, and her tea and Monte Carlos, and expressed the hope that the C.W.A. meeting in Boree Creek would be productive of much good. If she chanced to observe another tall, thin, but emphatically ginger-haired and utterly un-snooty man thereabouts, I said, who was an old friend of mine, she should ring Maxwell without delay. We took our leave and headed back to Wagga, followed by several cars, none of them blue.

So. Apart from apparently having two fathers, a circumstance into which inquiry had to be made, it was a fair bet that Angela had spent that Sunday afternoon as usual with Andrew in Wagga. She then, as usual, bussed back to Collingullie; there to receive, early on the following Monday morning, and soon – strikingly, suspiciously soon – after his body was discovered, the dreadful news of his death.

'It's also a fair bet,' I said, 'that the lovers were canoodling on the Hill, since that's where Andrew has been jogging off to. They seem to have had a regular Sunday service up there.'

'Where?' said Maxwell.

'On the Hill.'

'Where on the Hill? If the Hill is now as heaving with intercoursing couples as Charlie says it is, our lovers would have needed a very private place to canoodle in. Where, all possibilities considered, might that have been?'

'When we find Angela we'll ask her to draw us a map. It might have been anywhere. It – '

'Where would you take Veronica, to take a purely random example, for canoodling purposes?'

'I see where you're going with this, Maxwell. And yes, I would certainly *think* of going there, in that purely hypothetical case, because it is certainly the secretest spot on the Hill; but of course I would go elsewhere, probably somewhere down by the creek. I would not defile our sacred haunt with gross amours.'

'Others wouldn't regard it as defiling. That's peculiar to us. It's not sacred to anybody else. Others would have no compunction. Andrew, for instance.'

'Others wouldn't be able to find it. Unless you know it's there it's impossible to find. How could Andrew have found it? Did you tell him?'

'Of course not. You did.'

' ! '

'In *Secret Landscapes*. You noticed, with some surprise, that Andrew had a copy of it on his shelves. If any reasonably literate person happened to be looking for a hidey-hole on the Hill a reading of 'On the Hill' in that vol. would enable him to work out roughly where such a specially secret spot might be found. A few pokings-about in the likely area would enable him to find it. It's a fair bet that that's exactly what Andrew did. And somebody else found it too – that bit of jersey and the pennant didn't drop from the skies. I never expected to be saying this, Wal, but you have seriously underrated your descriptive powers.'

It was that last remark that convinced me. We sped on towards Wagga, and as we sped – we were just then passing through Sandy Creek, I recall – everything we thought we'd learnt began to change position.

We drove straight to the Museum car-park. We followed the exercise-trail up towards Andrew's fatal tree. Halfway up we were accosted by that idiotic trio of Wagga High security guards, who demanded to know what we were doing there and whether we had any chooks. Apparently chooks were disappearing from the School Farm at the northern foot of the Hill, and these loons were now inclined to regard us as a pair of hardened chook-rustlers. We showed them that we had no chooks. We went on to tell them that we had been natives of the Hill for far longer than the earth had been cumbered with them and that if we should happen to come upon catchable chooks in this our territory we would regard them as fair game and bear them triumphantly home. While we were explaining these matters to them they wandered off. We continued up to the fatal tree and took the (evidently) not-so-hidden pathway through thickets of thorn and scrub to the olives and kurrajongs of our secret sanctuary. We regarded the cache of condoms with a melancholy eye. These, we suspected, were the last relics of Andrew's sexual life. This sanctuary, I observed, observing them, has forever been changed, changed utterly, in what it means in my mind and memory. My Memoir, I declared, will scarcely be able to deal with it. We cast ourselves down under a welcoming olive and engaged in some serious, systematic imagining.

We imagined Andrew and Angela meeting, mid-afternoon, somewhere on the verge of the Hill, perhaps in the Museum car-park, perhaps further in, in the shade of a chosen tree. We saw them proceeding – excitedly, delightedly – up the exercise-trail to the turn, opposite Andrew's fatal tree, where the hidden path stole off into the boscage. (We noticed – surely not for the first time? – that the branch from which Andrew was to hang pointed like a signpost towards the entrance of the hidden path.) We watched them making sure that they were not watched before they slipped away. We watched somebody watching them as they slipped away. We contemplated them enjoying themselves for some time in our sanctuary – this time for the last time. At close of play, as the evening shades drew on, we saw them emerging from their love-nest, strolling back down the exercise-trail, parting perhaps in the car-park or, under cover of the gathering dusk, going together down to the bus-stop in front of the South Wagga Primary, she to return to Collingullie, he to resume or commence his jogging on the Hill before returning home.

'It's a fair bet that he never got back home,' I said: 'I think he was nabbed mid-jog on the Hill.'

'Probably,' said Maxwell: 'He may well have been already dead when the nabbers broke into his house and took his car. We know they got into the house to get hold of that blasted pennant to decorate the site of his final trysting-place; but why did they go to the trouble of taking and planting his car? That doesn't seem to have anything to do with the rest of it.'

'The car must be a huge clue to the rest of it if only we can read it aright. It was full of clues, carefully planned and planted, as we suspected – but clues to what? They don't point to anything we've seen so far. So what haven't we seen so far? What are we missing, apart from Tommy Anderson? He's evidently still missing; the Tourists would have rung if there'd been any sighting of him.'

'One thing we're missing, I'm happy to say, because we've been seeing a great deal too much of it, is the whole nonsensical non-history of the Wagga High murders. Not only does it now seem clear that they never actually happened, it is also therefore clear that they can have had nothing to do with Andrew's murder. They've been a total distraction. Andrew's murder has to do with his doings with Angela, as I have long maintained. *Cherchez la femme.* And it's surely a fair bet that one of her two fathers knows a fair bit about it.'

'It certainly looks like that. But the Wagga High murders have not yet quite run their course. Donny's strange death in the Victory Memorial Gardens is admittedly the weakest link in the chain but we can't leave it untested, if only to finally free Tommy from every last suspicion. The puzzle, though, is that the story of those murders seemed to have so much going for it. You were right – the fact that Andrew apparently thought so too should have been a warning to us; but there were clear signs of it everywhere we looked. Even here, where we could not possibly have been mistaken about anything, we seem to have been mistaken. It was a powerful confirmation of the Wagga High crux of that story that Andrew had plainly been hung up on that tree in such a way as to make sure he looked his last across and over at Wagga High. We utterly overlooked the obvious fact that much more directly and immediately in his line of vision was the grove in which he and Angela had fancied themselves secure. How could we have possibly missed seeing that?'

'Because once we got into that Wagga High story it told us what to see.'

'Told *me*, I'm afraid. I have been carried away, not for the first time. My only consolation is that I have never been carried away by the scatter of indications that my old mate Tommy was involved in any of those deaths. It's tomorrow, isn't it, that we're due at *The Advertiser*? I must admit that I'm keen to put Tommy absolutely in the clear. We'll visit the Tourists this afternoon. It may be necessary for us to go to Boree Creek to hunt for him. It – '

'Here we go again. You keep forgetting that we are supposed to be investigating Andrew's murder. You are fixated on your old mate Tommy. What we ought to be doing now is trying to identify Angela's other father.'

'I was hoping you wouldn't say that. We appear to have two obvious courses of action, both of which give me the trembles. We can interview Mr. and Mrs. Davies again, from whom we may or may not receive useful information, in the obtaining of which we are extremely likely to have to sustain an assault from the resident father – it runs in the family; and we can of course always hope to escape with a few flesh wounds. Or – and this gives me treble trembles – we can pay another call on Miss M.E. Paddock, who will certainly know what we want to know but who might not choose to divulge it to a person who has borrowed but not returned one of her books. There is, too, the risk of the fathomless horror of the Mother.'

'It would help if you could at least remember the title. I think we should go the Paddock route first. Until we know more about these two fathers we should keep what we already know under our hats. Besides, despite appearances, I sense that Miss Paddock is really rather fond of you. She even seems to have read your books. After the first ten minutes I fully expect her to be eating out of your hand.'

'It's those first ten minutes that put the fear of God into me. But all right, so be it. Miss Paddock, here we come. Later this afternoon, pre-tea, is the time to creep up on her. She'll be lunching or napping now. Let us have a spot of luncheon *chez* Maxwell. Then collect your keys and we'll pay a quick visit to *chez* Anderson. Humour me. I've agreed to go head-to-head with Miss Paddock before nightfall. I feel the need to do something for Tommy before I do or die; and that hullabaloo in his house last Monday night nags at me. I want to take a look.'

Maxwell humoured me. Half a dozen chops and twenty winks later we drove to 13 Moani Place; and prepared to employ Maxwell's keys. These keys were fabulous keys: no lock has ever been able to withstand them; except, of course, the famous one on the dunny on the old Bulgary station - but that's another story. (You can find it in my second collection of short stories, *Lockhart & Other Woes*.) We didn't need them. We banged on the front door for a while in case Tommy had come back; but he didn't seem to have, so we went around into a rear jungle where we could just make out a collapsed garage and a ruined dunny – a survival from the days when Wagga's incomparable sewerage system had yet to extend its tubes to these remoter suburbs. We tried the back door. It opened at a touch, some sort of jemmy having apparently been there before us.

Inside was an unholy mess, which anybody who knew Tommy could have expected, but it was utterly amazing that a really very sparsely-furnished house could harbour so many bits and pieces scattered in such confusion in so many noisome heaps. Tommy must have wallowed in here as in a sty. His kitchen was an absolute chamber of horrors. His bathroom has left a permanent scar on my mind. 'Dearie me,' I said to Maxwell: 'What would his mother have said?'

While I was trying to find the words for her Maxwell was noticing and saying things of the first importance. He was noticing that all these bits and pieces were *in* bits and pieces – they had been rent asunder; and not merely scattered, really chucked about. This house had been trashed; these heaps were the spoil-heaps of what, once I had been helped to get the hang of it, looked like a furious ransacking. The jemmied back door pointed in the same direction. Somebody, probably in the plural, had been tearing this place apart. And they must have been pretty sure that Tommy would not be coming back and interrupting them while they did it.

The unholy mess did not, however, extend to all parts of the house equally. Tommy's bedroom was a side sleep-out and in there there were markedly fewer signs of disturbance – a few drawers half-open, a wardrobe ajar, an upturned bedside table's contents strewn across the bed. Had the disturbers given up or been disturbed or found what they had come for? I saw, with some surprise, that Tommy's bedside table had had books on it. Naturally I bent to inspect them, recalling Tommy's reported enthusiasm for my *Eric Connolly's Comeuppance*. There was no sign of it here. He was evidently reading a couple of Zane Greys. And *Fiona Gets Her Fill.* I turned to page 169. There was no page 169. It had found its way into the back pocket of poor Andrew's track-suit pants, and its last words there, in red biro, had been *museum carpark on Hill at midnite.* The other items on the bed, as Maxwell was meanwhile establishing, included a packet of Wrigley's spearmint chewing-gum and the butts of three cigarillos. A rapid rummage through the half-open drawers produced nothing of significance; but the half-open door of the wardrobe seeming to half-invite me to try a further rummage within, the second shirt I extracted from it came incomplete with a single cufflink, round, blue, with a silver spiral. Above the bed, half a dozen *Playboy* centrefolds adorned the wall, drawing all our eyes; and, pinned beneath them, we descried a row of four *Welcome to Wagga Wagga, Garden City of the South* postcards. On their behinds, as usual, nothing – even so, they were eloquent enough.

'I expect we'll find cans of Foster's in the fridge,' said Maxwell: 'There's no sign of them under the bed.'

'There seems to be no sign,' I said, 'of a spare copper bracelet. He must surely have kept a spare, in case he should happen to lose one in a scrap, say, in a car, say.'

'We don't seem to have any matches,' said Maxwell, 'although it's possible that they've been chucked out of the window. Everything else is here. I particularly noted the array of *Garden City of the South* postcards, or do I mean the *Playboy* full-frontals that attract our attention to them?'

'So,' I said: 'It's now suddenly stunningly clear that Tommy is deeply implicated in Andrew's death. Are we agreed?'

'Agreed,' Maxwell agreed: 'Nothing could be clearer. Have we been expecting this, or does it come as a complete surprise?'

'Both,' I said, 'and neither. And until *that* becomes clear we ought not to rush off to Detective Charlie and excite him with our discoveries. Tommy's disappearance has now moved centre stage, as I prophesied. Next stop, the Tourist hotel.'

The next stop was not, on this eventful day, the Tourist hotel. As we turned into The Boulevarde we beheld Mr. Jackson, a-mowing of his nature strip. We could not but stop by him for an exchange of greetings and compliments; and, inescapably, a chin-wag.

'It is a troublous time,' he informed us: 'Speaking generally, wherever one casts one's eyes one constantly sees – *I* certainly see, and any observant person, particularly persons of a certain age, with some experience of Life: particularly too those of us who went through the War and learnt to appreciate the fundamental decency of our fellow-men of that generation: the women, of course, as well, who made an outstanding contribution to our victory and can never be rendered sufficient gratitude for all they did for us, keeping the home-fires burning, in those dark and threatening days, and continue to do, indeed, many of them, even now, in a world going swiftly, heedlessly, I'm afraid I must say, to wrack and ruin, where wherever one casts one's eyes one cannot but see scenes of a degraded and aggravating nature.'

We could not but agree. 'Examples abound,' I said, 'on every side; even here, in this haven, in The Boulevarde itself. We understand that this superb nature strip of yours has been subjected to wild parking by wild parkers unknown. Can this be so?'

'It can, it has indeed been,' he replied; 'only once, I must in fairness say, so far, but every morning now I expect more of them. These vicious and irresponsible acts are highly contagious. It's very distressing to Enid, not knowing what might be out here when she opens the curtains. Enid ... '

'Do you have any idea at all who might have parked that car out here on that occasion?' Maxwell inquired: 'Or about what time?'

'I remember now that young Parker – a coincidence, indeed, that I had missed until this very moment – told me later that the car belonged to poor Andrew Kell. He must have been one of your contemporaries, and you, as I infer, are naturally anxious to find out more about his unfortunate death. I should be delighted to be of assistance. But, alas, on Sunday evenings Enid and myself remain up until practically one o'clock enjoying the transmission from England of *Songs of Praise*, during which no sound of parking in the immediate vicinity is audible; and thereafter we consequently sleep very deeply indeed until nine or so in the morning. We are literally dead to the world, I'm afraid, in the intervening hours. We knew nothing whatsoever of what was occurring outside until the curtains were opened and it stood revealed.'

'Never mind,' I said: 'We must be getting on.'

'But,' he said, 'there are some real ruffians in Tichborne Crescent, to the rear of us, who are capable of anything.'

'We must be getting on,' said Maxwell: 'Be so good as to give our warmest regards to Enid.'

'She will be most gratified. Allow me to express the hope,' he said, ' that the person or persons responsible for poor Andrew's death will soon be brought to book. Speaking personally, I have much confidence in young Parker. Or perhaps Parrot. If anybody can get to the bottom of this dreadful, but in a certain sense typical, crime, it is he. Do call again whenever you're so inclined.'

We undertook to do so in the near future and accelerated away. The next stop was the Tourist hotel, where we confabulated with Rory, Bill and a couple of ancient characters, Harry and Les, who might or might not have been former classmates of ours. Bill reported that there was nothing to report from Boree Creek, several really reliable blokes had been scouring the district, hunting high and low, even Constable Collingwood was baffled, Tommy seemed to have vanished off the face of the earth, it was bloody worrying.

'Constable Collingwood?' I exclaimed: 'Is he still out there? I gave him a starring role in *In the Course of Events*, one of my early novels.'

'He's long retired,' Bill said, 'but he stayed there. After you've spent more than ten years in Boree Creek you're not fit for anywhere else. He still does a bit of local investigating to keep his hand in.'

'We were wondering,' Maxwell said, 'whether Tommy had dropped any hints lately about expecting trouble from somebody?'

Rory said he was always expecting a bit of trouble, there was always somebody who was gunning for him for some reason or other, that was normal. But lately no, not more than normal. In fact when they saw him last last Saturday he was in a very good mood, very jokey, because of being on to that something that was going to make him a mint; but why were we asking?

As far as the general condition of Tommy's house was concerned, the Tourists needed to know only the half of it. The particular state of Tommy's sleep-out was a different kettle of fish entirely, and demanded a different audience.

'We've been out to his house,' I said: 'Somebody or somebodies have ripped it apart from top to bottom, probably searching for something. Have you any idea what they could have been after?'

'The thing he said he was on to, it could have been a thing, I suppose,' Rory said: 'I thought he meant a sort of plan he had, but he might have meant he had a thing, something, and somebody might have wanted to get it off him.'

'That sounds pretty possible,' said Maxwell: 'What might it be? What sort of thing would you expect Tommy to be thinking he could make a mint out of?'

There was a scratching of heads and a general view that anything and everything was grist to Tommy's mill so long as there was money in it. Harry, though, said he had to say that a bit of blackmail, nothing too excessive of course, was one of Tommy's favourite areas, he'd got quite a decent return out of that from time to time.

'That's promising,' Maxwell said: 'Blackmail immediately suggests *things* of some sort – evidence, incriminating or embarrassing – that somebody might well be prepared to go to extreme lengths to get back.'

'Perhaps Tommy was being excessive this time,' I said: 'Perhaps he tried to make too much of a mint out of something. His disappearance grows more sinister with every passing hour.'

'But why Boree Creek?' Bill wanted to know: 'I can't believe he could have been trying to blackmail somebody out there, there isn't anybody with enough money to make it worthwhile.'

'It's a good quiet place for a meeting,' Les said: 'That's one reason for going there. Blessed if I can think of another one. You could have a great big meeting in the middle of the main street and if anybody happened to notice it he wouldn't be able to remember it the next morning.'

'Possibly. Very possibly, Les,' I said: 'Boree Creek would fit that bill. But so would Bulgary and Borambola and North Berry Jerry. There must be a special separate reason for being in Boree Creek. We may have to go there, Maxwell old fellow, perhaps tomorrow, to subject the inhabitants to some of our canny questioning. Somebody must have noticed something, albeit subconsciously.'

'Perhaps,' he replied: 'Tomorrow is another day. Today, meanwhile, there is an inhabitant much closer to home to be subjected to canny questioning, and if we're going to get a constructive reception we should be on her doorstep in the next few minutes.'

'I'd been hoping that had slipped your mind,' I said; 'and as a matter of fact I fear the afternoon is already a tad too far advanced for a successful encounter. We would be pre-tea, granted, but not pre-preparations for tea; which is exactly the wrong time to descend on elderly maiden ladies.'

'And when is exactly the right time?' Maxwell inquired.

'They are at their most susceptible towards noon - high noon, after morning tea has had time to settle,' I replied: ' Tomorrow is another day. Sufficient unto today are the revelations thereof, of which we need to take searching stock. Tomorrow morning we should all meet here to devise a plan for finding out what on earth has happened to Tommy.'

This having been agreed, we drove back to Maxwell's toft and croft, and took stock.

As soon as we had entered Tommy's sleep-out and beheld the objects it contained it was of course perfectly obvious to us – and, equally of course, to our alert readers – that this was a set-up. This pudding had been over-egged. Tommy was being framed. Those objects, or exhibits, had been selected and laid out in such a way as to be unmissable, even by the Wagga constabulary, and to draw the minds of the said constabulary to the contents of poor Andrew's car. So matchless a match between Tommy's bits and pieces and the car's would have appeared to them to be conclusive proof that Tommy had been in at the kill, or so soon before it that he must be an accomplice of the deepest dye. That car and its contents had struck us from the start as *staged* – as a crafty collection of planted clues; but what had puzzled us about them was that, as crafty clues, they were strangely useless, because they seemed to lead nowhere: nowhere, at any rate, within the intellectual and imaginative compass of Charlie and his troops. If *we* couldn't fathom them, *they*, needless to say, hadn't a prayer. So why had such care and trouble been taken to lay out clues that nobody hereabouts could possibly have deciphered? Now, at last, all was clear. There was no need for the police to go on hopelessly and haplessly puzzling over them. The matching set of clues in Tommy's house provided the required decipherment. To the obvious question, how would the police be led to discover the clues in Tommy's bedroom? the obvious answer was that a wide variety of local crimes led the police to Tommy on a regular basis, and sooner or later they would be bound to break into his house in search of him and Lo! there would be the clues.

'All this depends on his not coming back,' Maxwell pointed out: 'He'd disturb the careful clues, so he's got to be kept away until they've done their work. Until it's known that they have he won't be let go. If then.'

'I'm trying to imagine his return,' I said: 'He'll be in a pretty dangerous mood, especially after he sees what they've done to his house. He'll deny everything, of course, and he'll say he's been kept locked up somewhere out around Boree Creek. But he's the local villain, nobody believes him, this sudden disappearance while Andrew was on his way out of the world will look infinitely suspicious, it will look like a typically cack-handed attempt at an alibi, and with all this detailed circumstantial evidence in the sleep-out against him the poor beggar's denials will count for nothing. I know you hold no brief for Tommy, Maxwell, but we have a clear duty to save him.'

'Our clearest duty is to solve Andrew's murder.' said Maxwell: 'We think we now know,' he paused to check that the windows were closed, 'that the scene-stagers in Tommy's sleep-out and his captors in or about Boree Creek and the swine who murdered Andrew are one and the same set of murderous swine. We know it; as far as we know, nobody else knows it, except the swine. But we don't actually have any evidence at all. Charlie may marvel at our hunches; the courts won't. Without a bit of evidence your old mate Tommy is doomed and the swine go free.'

'It would help immensely, it occurs to me, if we knew who these swine are,' I said: 'Tommy will know. He'll know who immobilised him in Boree Creek, and he will therefore know, without knowing it, who murdered Andrew. We, though, will know. The present problem, as I see it, is that Tommy's knowledge won't be available to us until he escapes, or is sprung; or until it's known that Charlie & Co. have eyeballed the clues. That could take some time. The swine are surely expecting that the clues will come to light pretty promptly, much sooner than later. I think we'll have to fall in with their expectations, in order to foil them. Unless we can find Tommy tomorrow, the swiftest way to get him and his information back is to let Charlie know about the contents of the sleep-out. We'll tell him to spread the good news of his breakthrough. Then they'll let Tommy go.'

'If then,' Maxwell said: 'You said he'd be in a dangerous mood. It's my impression that your Tommy in a dangerous mood is very dangerous indeed. Once out of Boree Creek he'd be bent on revenge, and his captors would want to put a stop to that. And we're entirely ignoring what we've been assuming so far. Tommy's disappearance, we reckoned, is connected with his plan to make a mint out of something or somebody; and the trashing of his house seemed to point in that direction. If that is even part of the story here the clues in the sleep-out might not bring him back after all.'

'Sufficient unto the day are the conjectures thereof,' I replied: 'Tomorrow we'll test them in Boree Creek.'

'Mention of tests,' Maxwell said, 'reminds me of Miss Paddock, and of high noon in Sunshine Avenue. Tomorrow is another day.'

Before we turned in we took a turn in the back paddock with our weapons. Maxwell's old mastery of the cosh and the socker was beginning to re-emerge. My command of the throwing-stick still had some way to go.

CHAPTER SEVEN

Soon after sun-up Maxwell was assembling an irresistible breakfast, which included black pudding, champignons and caviar, and I rose to it like a trout. After a meet and proper pause for digestion we drove down to the Tourist hotel and greeted the gathering of Tommy's mates.

Of course there was still no news, we were expecting that. Bill reported that the really reliable blokes who were continuing scouring the district were continuing drawing a blank, they were thinking of giving up, they had other things on their plates. Harry reckoned it was no surprise really that Constable Collingwood hadn't managed to turn up anything, he'd brought off some pretty remarkable feats in the past but he was past it by now, he was too long in the tooth to notice anything much. Rory thought Tommy must have had a serious accident, or done a bunk, or he didn't like to think what else, and he couldn't think of anything else we could do that hadn't already been done.

'One thing that hasn't been done is the one thing that we all owe to our old mate Tommy,' I said: 'We owe it to him to go out there and look for him ourselves. We mightn't succeed, but we've got to have a go. Maxwell here is an extremely cunning interrogator, and I propose that we should now let him loose on the good and bad people of Boree Creek and see what he can wring out of them. Meanwhile, the rest of us will fan out in all directions, following our hunches wheresoever they lead. We are Tommy's best hope, perhaps his last best hope, and we must give him our best shot.'

Inspired by this call to action, and by the reflection that ample supplies of pies and beer were readily available in the Boree Creek Hotel Motel, they were all for getting going straightaway. Maxwell suggested that we should meet up in the bar of the Hotel Motel between one and two, he and I having a pressing interview to conduct in Sunshine Avenue about noon.

'Ah yes,' I said: 'I was forgetting about that. But all right, into the deadly breach we'll go. We'll see you in the Boree Creek bar in a couple of hours.'

We went out into Fitzmaurice Street and proceeded towards Maxwell's vehicle. He was mentioning that we were due to meet *The Advertiser*'s ace reporter in the course of this day when his mobile buzzed. He listened to it for a few moments and 'Yes, of course. I'll put him on. It's Mrs. Bartlett,' he said, giving me the phone: 'She wants to speak to the tall gentleman with the friend in Boree Creek.'

'Mrs. Bartlett,' I said: 'Lovely to hear from you. We much enjoyed our afternoon tea with you yesterday; those biscuits were delicious. I – '

' I'm very sorry to have to tell you this,' she said, 'but that friend of yours you described to me, the one who seemed to be missing in Boree Creek, I think it must be the one, he's been found, the C.W.A. have found him, we found him only a few minutes ago in the supper room in the Memorial Hall when we went in to make the morning tea, he was hung up there, he's dead, he's been horribly mauled poor man, he's a dreadful sight, we've sent for Constable Collingwood, some of the younger ladies have fainted clean away, I'd better go and try and help, I'm terribly sorry to have to give you this dreadful news.'

'Dreadful indeed,' I said: 'I am shaken to the core. We are most grateful to you, Mrs. Bartlett, for letting us know. We... '

But she had rung off. I summarised her fell tidings for Maxwell. We went back into the hotel. The Tourists wondered why, but not for long. I summarised Mrs. Bartlett's dreadful news. We resolved to strike out for Boree Creek *instanter*.

Our three-car cavalcade swept through Collingullie like the wind and took the turning towards Narrandera. Soon thereafter we flashed by the road to Bulgary – famous for the unenterable dunny on the railway platform, and as the setting of one of my strangest tales. Shortly before Kywong – where quite a collection of my antique relatives have lived out their lives – we banked southwards and fairly flew along the few remaining miles into Lachlan Street, Boree Creek; at the far end of which stood the S.S. Memorial Hall (1925) and, attached, the C.W.A. Supper Room, opened by Mrs. Nixon,

State President, 18 March 1970. (These facts and figures were at my fingertips because the hall and supper room were central features of my *In the Course of Events* – indeed, as readers of it will be well aware, if that (complex) novel can be said to have a ruling thread of story, it is the story of how the present supper room came into being.) Shattered remnants of the C.W.A. committee were scattered about, still displaying marks of horror and indignation. Several evident natives were sitting smoking on the kerb, waiting to see what would happen next. And the celebrated Constable Collingwood had positioned himself before the door.

I reintroduced myself to him. He regarded me with what was, for him, a baleful eye: his attitude to the fame I had bestowed on him – he is virtually the hero of the novel – appeared to be no more grateful than Maxwell's. I introduced the others and ourselves in general as Tommy Anderson's oldest, closest and dearest friends who, as soon as the C.W.A. had alerted us to the probability that it was Tommy who was dead in their supper room, drove here at once from Wagga in order to identify the body.

Constable Collingwood said that he'd already identified the body, he knew Tommy from of old, so no additional identifying would be necessary. Maxwell then explained that Detective Sergeant Charlie Parrot had asked us to help him investigate the strange death of Andrew Kell over in Wagga, that there were numerous but so far unexplained links between Tommy and Andrew, and that we urgently needed a quick look at the state and setting of Tommy's body to check whether Andrew's and Tommy's were significantly similar. Constable Collingwood said that in that case he didn't see why not, so long as we took our look from just inside the door because the Wagga Scientific Police were on their way and any disturbance of a crime scene tended to make them very surly. We moved towards the door. However, he said, he needed to warn us that Tommy wasn't a pretty sight, we needed to have strong stomachs to experience him. Harry and Les said that they weren't all that sure about their stomachs, they would wait outside. Constable Collingwood unlocked the door. One final thing, he said, he would let me take that look on the condition that if I was thinking of writing one of my blasted books about this I wouldn't put him into it. A book about this couldn't be further from my mind, I said, he could rest easy. Constable Collingwood opened the door, and we peered in.

The face was black, but it was Tommy's. He was hanging – he had been hanged – in a corner, out of sight of the windows. His feet, I noticed, were only a few inches, a torturing toe-touch, from the floor. He was naked, his genitals were intact, but the rest of him wasn't: his whole body was a livid mass of weals, cuts, bruises and punctures. Poor Tommy, he had had a terrible time. Then the stench reached us and we backed out.

'I'm no expert, but I've seen quite a few hangings in my time,' Constable Collingwood said, 'and I reckon he's been dead a day or two, maybe three. The Scientific Police outfit might even push it up to four, you never can tell with those fellows.'

'Apart from Tommy himself,' I said, 'is there anything else? Anything you think might be a clue to who or how or why? Where are his clothes?'

'His clothes aren't there,' Constable Collingwood said, 'and at a glance I'd say there aren't any clues. He might have finally died in there, but the bashing and battering leading up to it must have gone on somewhere else because there would have been signs of it, on the walls and the floor, and there aren't. They gave him a terrible time before they strung him up. They really tortured him, on and on, and what I would like to know is why.'

'It looks as if it might have been pretty noisy,' Rory said: 'Tommy wouldn't have gone quietly, he wasn't that sort. Even in Boree Creek, somebody should have heard it.'

'Probably not,' Constable Collingwood said: 'Boree Creek goes to bed after ten o'clock, and it sleeps very soundly. They probably brought him in after midnight. After midnight you could make quite a racket in this area without anybody noticing.'

'How did they bring him in?' Maxwell asked: 'Could they have had a key?'

'They didn't have a key. They broke in through one of the back doors,' Constable Collingwood said: 'The lock's buggered.'

'They didn't have a key to get inside, but did they have inside knowledge, I wonder?' I wondered: 'Did they know that the body would be undetected until the next C.W.A. meeting?'

'You wouldn't need inside knowledge for that. The notice on that outside noticeboard there,' Constable Collingwood indicated it, 'tells you that the next C.W.A. meeting isn't until today, and it also tells you that there's been nothing happening in the hall for the last two weeks. If you wanted to hide a body for a period this would be an ideal place. I'm very irritated that I didn't think I should be having a regular look around in here. This bloody retirement really dulls a man's brain.'

'Never mind. Maxwell and I are still many years away from retirement,' I said; Maxwell coughed, impolitely, 'and throughout this present investigation we have demonstrated – I speak, of course, for myself – a dullness of mind of truly prodigious proportions.'

'Never mind. We live and learn,' Constable Collingwood said: 'We must take the rough with the smooth. And mentioning the rough reminds me that it's not only the Wagga Scientific Police that are due here any minute now, it's also the Narrandera Detection Bureau, which means Detective Sergeant Herbert Truscott.'

'Truscott?!' I ejaculated: 'I can't believe he's still on the go, he must surely be in his eighties by now. Don't these characters ever retire?'

'He's retired, but he's a bit like me, he likes to stay in touch,' Constable Collingwood said: 'He's out and about quite a lot, and he reckons he's got some unfinished business out here.'

'I see,' I said: 'I take your point. The sight of me might revive unwelcome memories.' Truscott was definitely not the hero of *In the Course of Events.* 'We'll withdraw to the pub.'

We withdrew to the pub. Stiff drinks were in order. We had no appetite for pies. Or, for a while, for words. Harry and Les shook their heads for longer than I would have thought humanly possible. After a while Bill said it was the worst thing he'd ever seen, although there was something like it over in Pleasant Hills about twenty years ago that he'd heard Eric Connolly was involved in. And speaking of Eric Connolly, he said, he thought he'd seen him standing outside the Gullie Store as we flashed by on our way here. Rory said he didn't doubt that Tommy had deserved quite a lot of comeuppance from time to time but he didn't deserve anything on those lines, nobody did, what could make anybody want to torture him to death?

'In the light of what we already know or suspect,' said Maxwell, 'he was most probably tortured to make him give up something or to reveal its whereabouts.'

'He was a stubborn bastard, Tommy was,' Rory said, 'but it beats me why he didn't give it up and stop being tortured before he was killed.'

'We don't know that he didn't,' said Maxwell: 'He might have revealed that he'd hidden something in his house, and the wrecked state of it is explained by the consequent search for it. He could then have been killed to stop him revealing what he'd revealed, as a complete and final cover-up.'

'The wrecked state of his house suggests that the search for it wasn't plain sailing,' I said: 'Tommy's revelations, if any, weren't all that easy to follow. Besides, Maxwell and I are looking at the possibility that he was actually killed for another reason.'

'What other reason could there be?' Bill demanded: 'What could be big enough to need a murder as a cover-up? Another murder?'

'That's precisely what we're looking at,' I replied: 'We might be able to tell you more tomorrow. We might even need your help. Rory, we need your phone number. I notice that the Narrandera Detection Bureau has just pulled in over the way, and I think, on the whole, that it will be to the advantage of all concerned if Detective Sergeant Herbert Truscott and I are not here in Boree Creek at the same time. Maxwell, I suggest we vamoose.'

As we did so, driving out as quietly as Maxwell's defective muffler permitted, the massive figure of Detective Sergeant Herbert Truscott appeared at the door of the C.W.A. Supper Room and gestured menacingly in our direction. We sped back to Wagga, deep in furious thought, muttering occasionally. We passed the Wagga Scientific Police with their bonnet up, scratching their heads, at the side of the road near the Bulgary turn-off.

'I'm afraid it's not a suitable time to approach Miss Paddock,' I said: 'We'll call on her tomorrow morning before we go to the Terminus and the chaps. We have too much to think about already today.'

Maxwell drove directly to Sunshine Avenue and drew up in front of the Paddock bungalow. 'The time has come,' he said: 'In we go.'

In we went.

'You again?' she said: 'Have you brought my book back?'

'Miss Paddock,' I said, 'I regret to say that I have not brought it back. It is not here, in Wagga Wagga. It is sitting in my library in Venice. If you would be so gracious as to forgive me for forgetting to return it to you, and also to remind me of its title, I promise I will put it into your hands as soon as I am next in our fair city, probably next year.'

'I'll think about it,' she said: 'Probably next year isn't much of a promise, is it? Why are you here now?'

'Ah,' I said: 'Perhaps Maxwell will explain.'

'I think you know rather more about this than I do,' he treacherously said: 'You begin, and I'll contribute what and when I can.'

'Ah,' I said: 'Well. As we told you when we called on you and your mother previously, we have been asked to aid the police in their inquiries into poor Andrew Kell's dreadful death. Detective Sergeant Charlie Parker, who, whom you will of course remember as a lively Wagga High lad, has been particularly urgent in his appeals to us to render assistance, which is certainly sorely needed because thus far, a whole week on, the police have no leads, no suspects, no ideas. We, on the other hand, are on the verge of having all three. Before we reach that point, however ... '

'Come to the point, for heaven's sake,' she said: 'Even as a Wagga High lad you were notorious for your long-windedness. You begin to remind me of Mr. Jackson himself. Precisely what assistance do you suppose I might render?'

'Ah,' I said: 'Well. While pursuing these various leads and ideas we have been puzzling over one minor detail – something quite peripheral to the main thrust of our investigation but nevertheless nagging at us, and needing to be tidied away before we proceed to ... '

'Why are you prevaricating with me?' she said: 'It's obvious that this minor detail isn't a minor detail at all. Or if it is, how dare you expect me to waste my time standing here listening to you chattering on about it? Mother is apt to be fretful if I spend too long at the door. What do you want from me? Be quick about it.'

'Miss Paddock,' said Maxwell, 'you are right. This minor detail might not be minor, but until it's cleared up we can't tell whether it's minor or major. To come to the point: a certain young lady appears to have two fathers. One apparent father is obvious. He lives here with her mother ... '

'Not so obvious, these days, here in Wagga,' she said, 'as those of us who fought the long hard battle to hold certain tendencies in check know all too well.'

'Miss Paddock,' said Maxwell, 'you are right. Those tendencies may well have been unchecked in this particular case. There is another apparent father in the offing. We have it on good authority that the young lady in question refers to this latter father as her father. How she refers to the former father we do not know. One or the other might be her father by marriage, as it were, or ... '

'Or both,' she said: 'Or neither. I have known girls to try to convince me that their third cousins, beardless boys, were their fathers. In this particular case, to come to the point, is or was the young lady in question a Wagga High girl?'

'She wasn't,' I said; 'but her mother was.'

'In what period?' she said.

'In our period,' I said.

'I see,' she said: 'A turbulent period, that was. Some of the tendencies in operation then have still to run their course. This detail, you ask me to believe, could have a bearing on the death of young Andrew Kell?'

'We are. It could,' said Maxwell; 'and also – this is for your ears only, Miss Paddock – on the sudden and dreadful murder of young Tommy Anderson. Anything you may feel able to tell us about it we will of course regard as strictly confidential.'

'Come into the hall. Shrubs have ears,' she said, receding into a lavender-saturated gloom. We edged in after her, but not far, because where was the Mother?

'Tommy Anderson has been murdered? I'm sorry to hear it,' she said: 'His misadventures added much to the gaiety of nations. What is the mother's name?' We were momentarily disconcerted – was she setting us a test? how long would it take us to guess the Mother's name? Myrtle? was on the tip of my tongue when light dawned.

'Sonia Davies, she now is,' I said: 'She was Sonia somebody else, naturally, when she was a Wagga High girl.'

'Sonia Kline,' she said: 'The spelling varies. Her daughter would be eighteen or nineteen. She was born before her mother married William Davies.'

'And before that, to whom was her mother married?' I asked: 'Or if not married ... '

'Not married,' she said: 'Her father was not married to her mother.'

'I see,' said Maxwell: 'It is as you forewarned us. There was an unchecked tendency in the case. Was the father generally known at the time?'

'The general view at the time was that the father could have been anybody at all,' she said: 'Sonia Kline had a reputation. Even as a small plain girl in 3E she had it. One might almost describe it as a fame. She figured in several notorious occasions at the Wagga Beach, I recall; on one of which one of you, I have heard, was present.'

'The father,' I said: 'The actual or likely father. The father who is not William Davies. Who was it?'

'What's going on up there?' The Mother was stirring in the depths. 'There's far too much coming and going in this house.'

'Those young rascals we've been speaking of are back again,' Miss Paddock informed her: 'They are on the point of going, having at last come to the point of coming. Your question,' she said to me, 'asks for a more definite answer than the circumstances of the case permit – the circumstances, I mean, of young Sonia's case. But among those likeliest to know, the majority view of your minor detail is that the probable father was one of your former classmates.'

'Throw them out!' Mother cried: 'We want no more of that sort around here. Get rid of them at once! Especially the one who stole your book.'

'Which one?' I said.

'You,' Miss Paddock said: 'Mother is referring to you.'

'Wal is referring to the probable father,' said Maxwell: 'Which of our former classmates?'

'Michael McClure, of course,' she said.

Of course. A lot of light dawned.

'G.K. Chesterton's *Autobiography*, since you ask,' she said: 'I don't want to see you again without it. Now go.'

We went.

We went – there was no need for discussion – up on the Hill. We cast ourselves down in the shade of one of our sacred kurrajongs, within sight of Andrew's fatal gum tree, and took stock.

'Poor bloody Tommy,' I said: 'What an ending he had coming to him! And so dreadfully, eerily, meaningfully similar to Andrew's.'

'Similar, but not the same,' Maxwell said: 'There's a crucial difference. Andrew wasn't tortured. Apart from the removal of his balls, which looks like a punishment, and a sexual punishment at that, as I have long maintained, the rest of him received only a single stab. Tommy, though, was hacked and battered to within an inch of his life. Whoever was doing that really detested him and wanted to see him suffer. Or, and/or, going on what we know about your former old mate's methods of business, he was being tortured to extract something from him. The ransacked house was already pointing us towards that.'

'Granted. There probably was or possibly still is a special something somewhere in the house. The odds, I would say, would be heavily against its still being there, were it not for the circumstance that all that furious ransacking wasn't allowed to spoil the laying-out of the clues that led from Tommy to Andrew. That sleep-out, like poor Andrew's body, was scarcely touched; it was part of a different operation. If these different operations were pulling in different directions in the sleep-out, which couldn't be seriously ransacked because it had to be kept as a sort of exhibition-area, who knows what a no-holds-barred search in it now might turn up? Rory and his mates will be more than willing to lend a hand.'

'Can we go back to poor Andrew now? We seem to be devoting most of our time to Tommy, poor Tommy. Miss Paddock's news from the front directs us straight back to Andrew.'

'Tommy's fate is the key to Andrew's, as I have long maintained. We'll get to Andrew in a jiffy. Just before we do, let's take a last look at what we saw today in Boree Creek.'

We took a last look at poor Tommy hung up in the corner of the C.W.A. supper room in Boree Creek, one of the last places on earth where a live male would wish to finish up. The question, why torturing him to within an inch of his life wasn't enough? had an obvious answer. If you or I had tortured somebody to that extent we wouldn't have wanted to be around and available for acts and purposes of revenge when he recovered, especially if the somebody was somebody like Tommy. We would have to kill him, that was obvious. The real question was, why wouldn't we simply stick him into the ground in the scrub somewhere, anywhere out there, where he wouldn't have been found forever? Because, it now struck us under the kurrajong tree, we would have wanted him to be found; and found quickly, within these next few days. Why? Here Tommy's corpse and Tommy's sleep-out chimed and swung together. One led to, and back from, the other. In both there were two different operations proceeding, one to do with whatever Tommy was being tortured for, the other with framing him for Andrew's murder. Both the corpse and the sleep-out were meant to be exhibits, and the former was meant to be read in the light of the latter. And vice versa, of course. The sleep-out's clues directed the police to Tommy as Andrew's murderer; and now here in the supper room, most conveniently, was the arch-criminal himself, dead as a doornail, wholly unable to say a word in his defence or produce a pathetic alibi or offer a plea in mitigation or anything at all. Case solved and closed. A pity, of course, that Andrew's murder couldn't be officially added to his lengthy charge-sheet while he was alive, but any rate it was now and henceforth a matter of merely historical criminal record. Justice had been served, also at any rate, because he'd clearly been himself murdered in the course of yet another of his notorious nefarious activities, and so good riddance!

That this, more or less, was the killers' plan seemed, through and behind the scenes and clues they had set out, clear or clearish. But why was it, I could not help wondering, that these set-out scenes and clues, if that is what they were, were actually a good deal too complicated and imaginative for the likes of the Wagga Police to have a realistic chance of comprehending? Why all this trouble to lay a trail to Tommy when a note stating *I did it, Tommy* would have done as well and made everybody happy, especially Detective Sergeant Charlie Parrot?

'I wonder, on the other hand,' said Maxwell, 'whether we haven't been exaggerating the incomprehensibility of these clues and underestimating the plain practical *nous* of our local constabulary all along. Because you – we – tend to regard them as a bunch of arrant nongs and no-hopers you – we – have always assumed that the clues must be too hard for them. But actually they're not. It's really perfectly obvious to the meanest intelligence that as soon as you put the car and the sleep-out together Tommy's guilty as hell. It may not be as obvious that the clues have been planted, but if there was any suspicion of that the well-known fact that Tommy was an extremely careless littering sort of character would probably be enough to explain that away. Such as they are, the clues clearly point in one direction; and the reason why we haven't always seen that anybody else can see that as well as we can is because, I'm afraid, we have always overestimated our own intelligence in comparison with everybody else's.'

'We chiefly meaning me, I'm afraid.'

'I don't say that. I may think it, but I don't say it. It might be some consolation to us to think that nobody could have been quicker than we were to detect the planting-plot in the combination of car, sleep-out and supper room. But here comes another wonder. I wonder whether we have failed to detect that very same plot in another place, in...'

'In Andrew's den? I am with you every step of the way. Fare forward, O Valiant-for-Truth.'

'In Andrew's den. The combination could have four dimensions, not three. That haberdasher reckoned the light was on in the den for about ten minutes. It doesn't take ten minutes to remove a pennant. What were the other nine spent on? Planting, perhaps? Let's consider.'

We considered. The absent number of *The Hill* – *my* number – and in its gap the map that provided us with the link between Andrew, Tommy and the three strange, but not so strange, Wagga High deaths. The South Wagga Primary Class 5 photograph – brought to our attention by Ingres' naked houris – which nourished the notion that whatever was going on here our schooldays were at the bottom of it, and the ringed Tommy was the ringleader in it. The *Welcome to Wagga Wagga, Garden City of the South* postcard – hidden, but not so hidden, in my *In the Course of Events* – which linked the items in the den with the contents of the car and Tommy's sleep-out, and which further nourished the notion that the roots of all these events lay far back in these postcards' era, in the golden age, the era of our youth and glory – the era of, precisely, my forthcoming Memoir.

'Not only do I smell a rat,' I said: 'I think the rat is me. I am the missing link. The clues in Andrew's den have been designed to attract and catch *me*. They play on my proclivities. Putting them together to produce Wagga High murders is exactly what I could be relied on to do. I have been made a proper fool of.'

'There, there. It had to happen sometime. And I insist on taking my share. How, for instance, did I – we – not realise that even such dolts as we then supposed the local police to be could scarcely have failed to notice the pennant and jersey stuck up there in that tree?' He indicated the olive tree in question. 'If we hadn't been such dolts ourselves we would have seen that they must have been put up after the police had searched the area, and put up for *us*.'

. 'Still, I think the central comeuppance is mine. Eric Connolly will laugh himself into fits. I have been grandly proclaiming that, unfortunately for them, poor Andrew's murderers have picked exactly the wrong moment to do him in because lo! here comes no less a maestro than Wal himself to confound their tricks and hunt them down; whereas in actual fact they have planned the murder and the discovery of the clues around my being here and my being me. I see it all now. I have doomed them both. Their place and time of death are due to me. I am the real murderer of both Andrew and Tommy.'

'Stop hogging the discredit. Is there no end to your egotism? You didn't murder Tommy, however you look at it.'

'He was murdered in Boree Creek, wasn't he? They could have murdered him anywhere, but he had to be murdered there to insult and mortify me. That is the point of featuring *In the Course of Events* in their display of clues. They have taken over the scene of one of my cunningest fictions and set the murder of an old mate of mine right in the heart of it, in the very supper room in which my murderer perishes. There can be no mistake about it. This is not only an atrocious murder, it's a premeditated act of literary rape and pillage.'

'You might say - I'm not sure I would – that literary rape and pillage have also been perpetrated here, in our former secret sacred spot. You yourself opened the way to it in *Secret Landscapes*, although I doubt that anything approaching rape took place while Andrew and Angela were occupying it; but his murderers sure made sure of spoiling it for us forever by hanging his relics in it.'

'Not only for us. For all sensitive readers for all time. That essay has had evil consequences. But out of great evil great good may come. It occurs to me that we might be able to turn it to account. We don't actually know that they know it, they might just have been tracking Andrew and Angela, but even if they haven't been studying my work as much as I now think they have, we can direct their attention to it and trap them in its coils. We can find out if they've been using *Secret Landscapes* against us, and use it against them.'

'I sense a plan coming on. Perhaps, then, it's time we got *they* and *them* and *who* and *whom* settled and sorted.'

'I remember your remarking to Mrs. Bartlett in Collingullie that fathers often find it hard to accept that their daughters have boyfriends. I find it hard to accept that Andrew was murdered because he was having an affair with Mike's daughter.'

'Because he was having sex with Mike's daughter is how I'd put it. The absent balls were always the vital clue. Whoever cut them off was making a statement; and also a statement about himself.'

'Meaning?'

'Meaning that the cutter-off has a serious hang-up about sexual doings and undoings, and is of a vicious and punitive nature.'

'That fits Mike all right. Does it make it even more likely that he's our man that he's been trying to have sex with the daughter of the late lamented Robyn, a girl of about the same age as his own daughter?'

'That's conclusive, in my view. Girls of his daughter's age are fair game, and probably at their most desirable, but his own daughter is out of bounds, she's forbidden fruit; and if the plucker happens to be a chap of his own age, and an old school rival to boot, no punishment can be too atrocious. It's a well-known syndrome.'

'It would appear to be a sort of Wagga High murder after all. But how do you come to possess this dark and dreadful knowledge of sexual pathology?'

'I live in Wagga. I do not spend my time swanning about Europe. We are at the cutting-edge here.'

'Speaking of which, Mike is likely enough, *ex hypothesi*, to have done his cutting himself. For capturing Andrew and hanging him up he would have needed assistants, fellow-labourers in the fell field. We don't yet know whether those who bore a part in framing Tommy for Andrew's murder, and murdering him, bore a part in both murders, but they have to be accomplices before, during or after the facts; which brings us, to my absolute amazement, to the chaps. Dunny and little Artie must be involved – they kept feeding and misleading us with strange deaths and hints of Tommy. Who else? Roy?'

'Why are you so amazed?'

'Why? Occasionally, *mon cher*, your mighty powers of penetration seem to be on the blink. I am naturally amazed that the chaps have been murdering one of their own – one of our own. I am even more amazed that they have been conspiring to deceive and befool *me*. And of course you.'

'I too am amazed. You have been romanticising our lives and times for so long, and at such a distance from Wagga, that it never even crosses your mighty mind that most of the chaps absolutely loathe you. Your airs and condescendings infuriate them. The thought of what you might be going to say about them in your bloody memoir is a torment to them. No wonder they want to make a fool of you. And of me too, as your oldest and faithfullest friend. You've heard of the death by a thousand cuts. This is revenge for a thousand slights.'

'There is nothing to fear from the Memoir. I can never write it now. They and you have just this minute destroyed all my Wagga life. I can never write about this bloody place again.'

'Good. Thank heavens there won't be a book coming out of all this. But now about the chaps. I...'

'Those bloody chaps will rue the day they took me on, I can tell you. Some of them, though, wouldn't detest me enough to join in this plot, and some are too dim or too nervous to be possible conspirators. You see how I strive to be fair. We've got to separate the lions from the lambs.'

'We've also got to separate Andrew's murderers from Tommy's. They're different sorts of murders and they must be different sorts of murderers, even if they're the same. If you see what I mean.'

'Perfectly. Their motives must be different. Unless, that is, it's to be imagined that they are so keen to conceal the first murder, and to deceive thee and me, that they are prepared to commit another murder to do so. That's possible; but against it we have reason to believe that the motive for Tommy's murder is mainly or at least partly quite different. If we can just about imagine, which we have to, that Mike and Dunny and little Artie, say, participated in the murder of their old mate Andrew, the idea that they or any of them would have had the nerve and bloody-mindedness to go on to murder this time not just an old mate but a notoriously tough and violent local criminal is simply not imaginable. It's pure fiction. They could have concealed Andrew's murder in some other way. They could have made a huge fool of me in some other way. They would have. If they haven't, that must be because they had no choice. If, for example, their first murder was rumbled, the rumbler could have compelled them to take part in the second as the price of his silence.'

'It can't have been quite like that. The two murders follow each other too closely, for one thing. For another, the framing of Tommy and the planting of the clues meant for us took a lot of time and planning. Both murders must have been planned together, and planned to fit the timetable of your coming and going. Which the chaps knew from me.'

'Quite so. I was only giving you an example. They may indeed have been planned together, but the first one must have been the real one for the chaps. The second one has to be the real one for somebody else, for some other reason; and the chaps have been persuaded into it, or manoeuvred or forced or frightened or somehow drawn into it because it could be made to turn Tommy into the first murderer. The plan that brought these two murders together is the key to both. That plan... '

'We need a plan of our own, and quickly. You implied that you had one – something to do with that cursed essay in *Secret Landscapes*. What is it?'

'At present it is only dawning on me. But it is beginning to look quite masterly, Maxwell, and it will play to our special strengths. It will be dramatically appropriate. It will bring us and our cast of conspirators back here, on the Hill, where Andrew, poor Andrew, breathed and looked his last, and where you and I have always possessed supernatural knowledge and power. Let us now be homeward-bound, where whiskies await us. Then and thenceforward it's cut to the chase. But I'm leaping ahead of myself. Before the whiskies we must repair to the back paddock and Practise! Practise!'

Later, during the whiskies, with Elgar on loud and the windows tight-shut, I laid out my plan. Maxwell fine-tuned it. Maxwell's missus added a few lethal touches. One of the cats gave us a really brilliant idea. We ate chicken and chillies. Towards midnight, having gathered several pieces of equipment and loaded them into the vehicle, we drove up onto the Hill. We did not park in the Museum car-park. We parked in an overgrown corner of the Botanic Gardens. We trekked our stuff through the dense dark – accompanied, we were sure, by scores of friendly snakes - to certain selected spots: child's play this, to us, who had operated here on many a blank black night during all our youthful years. I may have mentioned this before. We were in bed by 3 and slept the sleep of the just and the inexorable.

CHAPTER EIGHT

Detective Sergeant Charlie rang while we were munching our muesli. He had received information, he said, to the effect that my old but former friend, Tommy Anderson, Wagga High schoolfellow and leading local criminal, had been found very dead and murdered in Boree Creek, and that Maxwell and I had viewed the unfortunate scene. It was doubly unfortunate, he went on to say, because although he had yet to also receive a preliminary report from the Wagga Scientific Police it appeared highly obvious to him that Tommy had had a severe falling-out with some of his ruthless criminal associates, resulting in his sorry end, which he wanted to extend his personal sympathy to me for, and which very unfortunately made it now impossible for Tommy to be cross-examined regarding the possible connection between him and poor Andrew's murder that it had begun to seem to him that we might have been tending to. Which, he said, probably meant that we were now even further away from solving it, which the Superintendent would be hopping mad about, to say the least.

I thanked him for his sympathetic expressions. The connection between poor Tommy and poor Andrew had lately become, I said, extremely strong, to say the least. Clues abounded, and they were unaffected by Tommy's departure. Indeed, I said, they might even be said to be strengthened by it. But because he was either an extremely artful or a very muddled character, Tommy had had a lot of experience in evading cross-examiners and confusing issues. From that point of view, I said, his murder was probably a help to us, even a godsend, because it greatly simplified all relevant matters and gave us a clear run – in a metaphor that would give Andrew great pleasure – to the finishing-line. This very day, I said, we would bring our clues and conclusions to a climax. The Superintendent was due to be vastly pleased, and his recommendation for an Inspectorship would be winging its way to HQ within the week.

Muesli munched, we rang Rory and fixed a meeting with the Tourists in the Tourist at 10. We were due to take lunch with the chaps at the Terminus. The names and histories of the streets we drove down are of no further interest to me: they have vanished with the Memoir. Rory and Bill and Harry and Les were deep in dejection. They barely lifted their heads when we came in.

'Jesus. Jesus,' Rory said after a while: 'I can't get that bloody horrible sight out of my mind, I never will. Nobody deserves to go like that.'

'Somebody else went pretty much like that about the same time – Andrew Kell,' said Maxwell: 'We're sure they're connected. We think we're on the brink of discovering who did them both in. We need your help today to bring them to book.'

'Indeed we do,' I said: 'Without your help Tommy's killers, and Andrew's killers too, will go scot-free. Justice, gents, is a fine and noble thing, and we must all do that we can to defend it; but we here today are also Tommy's best mates, and what Tommy would want, and what his mates can give him, is revenge. Tommy won't rest easy until he's got it. We are now his only hope of it, his last throw. Let's get out there, strike while the iron's hot, and send these unmitigated bastards headlong to Hell!'

They were sensibly moved by this appeal. They shook our hands and punched the air. Whatever it was, they said, they were ready to do it or to die in the attempt. We said that it was unlikely to come to that, although there might be a few hairy moments towards the end. Our first move would be to assemble at Tommy's house, 13 Moani Place, at 2 o'clock sharp this afternoon; and to come provided with a variety of tools suitable for breaking into, prising up and yanking apart anything that could possibly conceal anything else. The something that Tommy was on to and died for was probably in there somewhere, I said, 'where the murdering bastards who were looking for it before couldn't find it. And even if we can't, we have a second move that will do almost as well, Rory, if anybody, anybody at all, no matter how much you love and trust them, should happen to ask you, especially today, if Tommy gave you a sealed envelope, contents unknown, to give to me in the event of his going away and not coming back, you must reply *Yes, he did*, and you must stick to that, it's a matter of life and death, everything depends on it.'

'Did he?' said Les: 'That's the first I've heard of it.'

'Yes, he did,' said Rory: 'You remember that, Bill?'

'Too right,' said Bill: 'I was right there at the time. "Take this envelope and give it to Wal," he said: "I am now going outside, and I may be some time".'

'Perfect,' I said: 'We meet at 2.'

We took a stroll up to St. John's, the C of E church where – see Chapter Two – Maxwell and I had starred as altar-boys. We did not go there to pray – although I remember suggesting to God that this would be a good time to come to the aid of the party. We went, even Maxwell went, to pay our last respects to the days that were no more, that would not come again. I had thought to resurrect them in the Memoir, but they had been changed, changed utterly by these recent events and revelations. In one way or another the chaps had always been central to them; and my understanding of them – the days and the chaps and myself – had now and forever been uprooted and abolished. St. John's gave us a last moment in that unpolluted past before we went forth to do battle in the dire and desolating present. Then we drove to the Terminus and the chaps.

We were welcomed like conquering heroes.

'This unsolicited applause is highly gratifying,' I said: 'It's evidently a tribute to something or other. To what?'

'To you both. To your success in cracking this great case of poor Andrew's murder,' Bazza Bruce said: 'We decided to congratulate you before you started boasting about it.'

'Who was it?' Trevor Neely wanted to know. 'Is it anybody we know?'

'Nobody we know could have done anything like that,' Roy O'Hanlon said: 'I've said it before and I say it again, there are large numbers of people in Wagga now who've come from the other ends of the earth who wouldn't think twice about doing something like that to you if you gave them any trouble at all. Wagga isn't what it was. Some of us have never got used to that. The people we know all grew up in a town that's not here any more. Outside the Terminus and a very few other places there's a whole new town here full of strange people who'll stop at nothing.'

'True. Too true,' I said, 'and very feelingly put. On the other hand, there are hidden depths in all of us. In certain moods even I can become quite homicidal. Cutting someone's balls off is probably outside my range, but who knows? And actually there are some people we knew and grew up with who stopped at nothing in their day. Surely you remember Tony Thomas, Roy?'

'I remember,' Roy replied: 'But there was a special reason for that. There were three blokes in bed with his wife, and Tommo just happened to have an axe in his hand. This case is completely different.'

'Every case is completely different,' Maxwell said, 'although the same old motives keep coming around. In this case, now, the motives are absolutely traditional. We wasted a lot of time looking for strange motives, ones that seemed to match the crime, but at long last we've got onto the right track and we'll be ready to take the final step later today.'

'Later today? You mean you haven't finally cracked it yet? I don't believe it.' This was Mike McClure. 'I had a bet with Dunny and Artie here that you'd have this murdering bloody bastard in the cells in less than a week. You've lost me twenty dollars. But I've got a side bet on the bastard, and if it isn't Eric Connolly I've lost another twenty.'

'I apologise for the slight delay, Mike,' I said, ' and I'm afraid I have to tell you that we have ruled out Eric Connolly. I didn't have twenty dollars on him but I longed for him to be our man.'

'He's around, you know,' Bobby Fossey said: 'Rob Macklin noticed him down by the river. He said he was looking pretty dangerous.'

'He *is* dangerous. Ruling him out of anything is a big risk,' Humphrey Hooper declared: 'Wal and Maxwell had better be pretty sure of their ground to rule him out. But why is he here?'

'He can smell trouble a hundred miles off,' Bazza said: 'He's here because Wal and Maxwell are about to give somebody else their comeuppance.'

'Who?' Trevor Neely still wanted to know. 'When are you going to tell us?'

'Dunny and Artie,' I said, both of whom suddenly looked distinctly peaky, 'have been a great help to us, without meaning to be. I mean that in the course of casual conversation, and also a week ago here in the Terminus, they mentioned certain apparently unrelated events and persons by which and by whom we were led to investigate other deaths in the past; and those deaths led us back to poor Andrew's and enabled us to home in on our target. Maxwell and I would like to thank them for their assistance, however unwitting.'

Dunny and Artie now looked distinctly less peaky.

'I always had my suspicions,' Artie said: 'I always knew who it would be.'

'Who?' Trev demanded.

'I think we should wait for Wal and Maxwell to tell us,' Mike said, 'unless they don't finally know yet.'

'Mike is half right, isn't he, Wal?' Maxwell glided smoothly in. 'We know, but we don't finally know. There's one more thing for us to do before we close the case.'

'True,' I replied: 'And it is at this point that we must ask you to take an oath of silence. Even Charlie Parrot doesn't know this yet. We have discovered a very significant connection between poor Andrew's death and Tommy Anderson.'

'What sort of connection?' Mike inquired.

'That's the question,' Maxwell said: 'That's the question we're going to get the answer to later today.'

'It's not a surprise to me,' Dunny said: 'Tommy Anderson has been mixed up in most of the crime around here ever since he left school, if not before. He'd be the first person I'd suspect in any case.'

'But not in a case like this,' Hoop said: 'I can't imagine him being mixed up in murder, murder isn't his type of thing. It's not in his nature.'

'Wal has already dealt with that,' Mike said: 'Hidden depths, he said, and who knows? Maybe Tommy's hidden depths got involved. But what's going to happen later today that will finally crack the case?'

'Ah,' I said: 'That would be telling. I'm not sure it would be proper for us to go into details at this stage, before we spell it all out for Charlie and the Superintendent. What do you think, Maxwell?'

'Well, Wal,' said Maxwell, 'among old mates, all old friends of Andrew, and assuming that the oath of silence holds, I think we can say a bit about it. You can tell them about the book.'

'The book is the strangest thing about it,' I said: 'Who could ever have imagined that Tommy had even heard of it, much less – much, much less – that he could have read it? But so it proves. He had read an essay of mine in a book I edited many years ago – *Secret Landscapes*, it was called. Have any of you heard of it?'

'I have,' Bazza said; 'but I haven't read it.'

Nobody else, apparently, had the faintest notion of its existence.

'There you are,' I continued; 'but Tommy has done both. The essay in question is a meditation on the Hill, Willans' Hill; and it describes, in what I must admit is an overwrought and violently adjectival manner, several spots and spaces and recesses up there, in particular three of them, which had a special significance for Maxwell and myself when we were young and easy under the apple boughs about the lilting house and happy as the grass was green, as it were.'

'What has this got to do with anything?' Mike said: 'Where does one of your old books come into this?'

'It comes into it because Tommy read it and remembered it, and because he left me a note about it.' Here I produced and waved an envelope. 'He left it with Rory McFadden – you remember Rory, he was at South Wagga with us; he's been one of Tommy's drinking-pals down at the Tourist for years. He left it with Rory with instructions to get it to me, he knew I was due, if anything happened to him.'

'Has anything happened to him?' Artie said: 'I haven't seen him in months, but I wouldn't want anything to happen to him.'

'*If* anything happened to him he wanted me to see this note. Because Tommy was a very worried man. He told Rory and his pals down at the Tourist that he was on to something big, something that would mint him a lot of money, something that he evidently suspected was dangerous. Having left me this note, he disappeared. I have now read the note. It tells me that Tommy has left me a clue to the whereabouts of this something that he was on to; and that he has left this clue, which he says he's sure I'll recognise although nobody else could, in one of those three special and particular places on the Hill. Why he's made such a complicated mystery of it is a mystery to me. All will be revealed, I suppose, when Maxwell and I find the clue, and the something, later today.'

'But what has all this to do with Andrew?' Roy said: 'This is a clue to something else. How can this help to crack Andrew's murder?'

'Because Tommy has now been murdered,' said Maxwell.

There were cries of consternation. Schooners were abandoned. There were gestures strongly indicative of horror and amazement. When the hubbub had subsided we briefly described what yesterday in Boree Creek had brought forth; after which Roy resumed his queryings.

'OK. Tommy has been murdered. OK. It's hard to take in so suddenly but we've got it. But what we haven't got is why Tommy's murder can help you to crack Andrew's?'

'Wal has already mentioned that we've found a very significant connection between Tommy and Andrew's murder,' said Maxwell: 'The sort of connection we've found tells us that whoever's been involved in Tommy's murder must also have been involved in Andrew's. And when we find this clue, and this something, later today, we'll find our murderer, or murderers.'

'But what sort of connection is it?' Mike demanded: 'You haven't told us yet.'

'Ah,' I said: 'That would be telling. That's what we need to be telling Charlie and the Superintendent first. I think – and I'm sure Maxwell thinks so too – that it would not be proper for us to let slip even a hint of it before they begin the arresting.'

'So,' said Dunny, pale Dunny, 'you're going to go on Willans' hill this afternoon to look for some clue, are you? Tommy Anderson's clues wouldn't be worth much, I shouldn't think. Where are you going to be looking?'

'In those three special places that Tommy found in my essay,' I replied; 'but before we go up onto the Hill we have a melancholy duty to perform. We've promised Tommy's Tourist pals to meet them at his house to help them collect and store his belongings.'

'It's a terrible mess in there,' Trev Neely said: 'Or so I've heard.'

'Is it? How did you hear that?' I asked him.

'I told him,' Mike replied: 'I heard it from one of his neighbours. He took a look through a window, and he said there was a terrible mess inside.'

'Tommy was famous for his messes,' I said: 'I regard it as a real privilege to play a part in clearing up the last of them.'

Soon thereafter – as soon, that is, as we could decently put away a beer and a gathering of chops, and participate in a little desultory conversation – we departed. Hoop said he was sure he spoke for everybody when he said he hoped we would have cracked everything well before our next meeting next Wednesday. We promised to do our best and we said we looked forward to meeting all the chaps who were free to come next Wednesday.

We drove to Tommy's house and waited outside for the pals. While waiting, we recalled Artie's declaration that he hadn't seen Tommy in months, whereas Tommy had told the pals that Artie had given him the story of Mrs. Rossiter and her canary only the day before the day he went to Boree Creek. We further recalled Mike's quick covering of Trev's blurt about the mess in Tommy's house. Some unravelling was beginning.

The pals arrived, bearing implements. We effected entry, as on our previous occasion, through the jemmied back door.

'Jesus. Jesus,' Rory said, beholding it: 'What a terrible mess.'

We reviewed the situation. We reckoned, we said, that this far-reaching mess represented the efforts of Tommy's murderers to find something they reckoned he had hidden somewhere here. This something, we reckoned, must have something vital to do with whatever Tommy was on to that was going to make him a mint. They might have found it, but the fact that they evidently went on and on torturing him suggested to us that he wasn't giving them what they wanted, so there was at any rate a goodish chance that they hadn't found it; and it was evidently worth a murder. The mess, we then demonstrated, didn't reach as far as Tommy's sleep-out; and that, we also reckoned, was because they needed somewhere uncluttered to lay out certain misleading clues to another murder. It was in this sleep-out, therefore, that they should bring their implements to bear, ourselves assisting as far as in us lay.

They fell to with a will. We broke into everything intact, we prised up everything down, we yanked apart everything else. We went into the roof and we went under the floorboards. We disassembled the bed, we dismembered the drawers and the wardrobe, we tore to pieces everything that we had already torn to pieces. We hunted every conceivable hiding-place to its hiding-place; we exhausted our imaginations; we re-ransacked the spoil-heaps in the other rooms; we even dared to go into Tommy's dreadful bathroom and grapple with his cistern. We found nothing. Not anything. Not anything that anybody could have wanted to kill him for or take any interest in – apart, of course, from the *Playboy* centrefolds. It was deeply dejecting. We sat, exhausted, among the ruins, racking our brains, searching, searching for something, anything, that we might have missed.

Tommy's dreadful bathroom was our salvation. Nothing could have looked less like it, but it was a godsend. Harry and Les were simultaneously caught short. Harry got into the bathroom first and entertained us – our spirits needed lifting - with his cries of disgust and horror at his surroundings. Les was not entertained. When these elderly gents need to go they need to go. Desperate, he bethought himself of the derelict dunny out in the backyard, and he shot out into it.

In that dunny, just before proceeding to business, he naturally lifted the seat to check what was under it. This is what those of us who have had a country-upbringing do. Redback spiders might be under it. Snakes – we all knew of somebody who was bitten on the bum by a tiger snake in a country dunny – might be under it. He lifted the seat and peered into the pit beneath. Halfway down, just within reach, a length of twine ran away into unspeakable depths below. He gave it a yank, a cautious yank, because there might have been a tiger snake at the end of it, but there wasn't. There was a package.

'What's this?' he said, bringing it in. 'It feels like a book.'

It was a book. It was *Eric Connolly's Comeuppance*. Between pp.187 – 193 there were six photographs. These, as Tommy had remarked, were the few pages towards the end that made everything worthwhile. The photographs showed Clive Brady buggering, and being buggered by a huge black man.

'At last!' I cried: 'I've got that bastard by the balls! And what bold and busy balls they are! I prophesy that Clive Brady will not be the next Mayor of Wagga Wagga.'

Maxwell rebuked me: 'This outburst, Wal, is wholly inappropriate. You should be ashamed of yourself. Here we are breathing down the neck of your old mate Tommy's murderer, and of whoever murdered Andrew and cut off his balls, and all you can think of is the opportunity it gives you of settling prehistoric Wagga High scores. It's no wonder that these conspirators have been able to play you like a violin.'

'Not all,' I replied, chastened: 'I admit to partly. Thanks to Les's precautionary measures we now know what Tommy was up to, which tells us who killed him or had a hand in it; and why, in part, he was killed. But Clive couldn't have dealt with Tommy on his own. He must have had help, and I think we know the identity of his helpers.'

'Why do you say in part? This here has to be the whole story,' Bill said: 'We can see here why they killed him.'

'Not quite,' said Maxwell: 'They killed him for another reason as well. They had to make him the prime suspect for the murder of Andrew Kell. They needed to kill him to stop him being able to prove that he didn't do it.'

'Jesus. Jesus,' said Rory: 'Who the hell could have thought this up? It's like something out of a book.'

'It is. It is.' I said: 'And it is to another book that we now turn. *Secret Landscapes*, here we come.'

The pals begged us to take them with us. They were dead keen on getting their hands on Tommy's killers. We, they said, were Tommy's best mates, and what Tommy would want is for all of us to be in at his revenge. Put like that, it was hard to gainsay. It seemed somewhat mean-spirited to deny them at the very least a ringside-seat at the final event. Besides, although we felt that the central issues here were really between us and the chaps, it was beginning to occur to us, as that final event loomed, that we might, after all, need a bit of help. Concealing two murders might, after all, call for two more. We might have brought in Charlie; but we wanted, as promised, to present him and the Superintendent with the whole case wholly cracked, and there was no room in our presentation for police assistance – trampling all over our fine-tuned arrangements – at the climax. On the other hand, we were staking everything on our mastery of the skills we had honed on the Hill – skills that were now, after only a few days' practice, still a little rusty. So we compromised. We would stash the pals, together with their implements, in a corner of the Botanical Gardens, on the other end of a mobile, to be given directions and summoned in as and when. Since it was highly likely that we were all being watched we sent the pals off to drive three or four times around Lake Albert at varying speeds in order to baffle pursuit, and to enter the Botanical Gardens by a circuitous route involving Red Hill Road, Bourke Street, Leavenworth Drive and Mimosa Drive – names and histories I can no longer be bothered with. Ten minutes after they left we left. We drove up and over the Hill and parked in the Museum car-park, as visible as anything. We strolled down to the exercise trail and proceeded gently along it. Then, in a patch of shadow, we stepped aside and vanished into the undergrowth.

As its readers well know, the *Secret Landscapes* essay identifies exactly three special and particular places to which I and (the unnamed) Maxwell attached immense significance. Close readers, scanning the text while actually traversing the Hill, would be able to narrow down their probable locations to within twenty or thirty yards; and after a period of further study and a great deal of casting and clambering and crawling about, to arrive at the spots marked x with considerable, but not quite complete, certainty. The chaps were not close readers. Some of them were not readers. But they could be marshalled and positioned by someone who was – someone who had already done his homework on the Hill in preparation for the plot against us. Clive Brady, obviously. We therefore expected to find the relevant chaps awaiting us in the vicinities of the aforementioned special places, primed and ready to observe our hunt for the conclusive clue. We, however, were now hunting them, and hunting them on our own ground.

The first vicinity we closed in on was down near the north-western corner of the new reservoir. I believe I have already referred here to that accursed reservoir, excavated in the 1960s, which destroyed a creek – *the* creek – that ran South-North through the greenest and loveliest of the Hill's vales. A deep, ferny creek it was, cool and dark and misty even at high noon in mid-summer; and in the rainy season it was Alph, our sacred river, coming through who knew what caverns measureless to man and going who knew where, perhaps as far as North Wagga. It was also – but I digress: for further details see *Secret Landscapes*. Destroyed though it was, there were yet a few remains and reminders of it at the reservoir's north-western end, in particular at what we had immediately recognised as an ancient aboriginal crossing-place, descent and ascent, still virtually and uncannily untouched by the horrid pipes and culverts debouching into it and the chugging pumping-station next to it. This crossing-place could be put under observation, we knew, from three adjacent points and angles, and from a fourth, by binoculars, at a point two-thirds of the way up the facing western slope. We checked the last first, there was nobody there. We scrutinised the other three, all empty; and it wasn't until we actually peered down into the pit of the bit of the creek that we saw poor Bobby Fossey concealed, as he supposed, behind a pepper-tree and plainly uneasy, suspicious of snakes. We crept towards him, hissing stereophonically. He never knew what hit him. (He knows now.) What hit him was Maxwell's socker – a long sock, knitted by his wife, containing a selection of remarkably heavy metal objects (patent pending), delivered, while he looked for a snake to his left, just above the right ear, towards the temple. We produced our ball of triple-strength twine, tied him to his pepper-tree, removed his mobile, stuck a gag into him; and vanished into the undergrowth.

Our next vicinity posed several difficulties. My readers will know that another of our special and particular places was a long-abandoned gravel quarry, a semicircular amphitheatrical cavity in an obscure fold of the Hill's south-western flank. This quarry had been the scene of a series of pitched battles, generally at night, between ourselves and hordes of orc-like creatures, in the course of which, when we were several decades younger, we had perfected the complex art of half-scrambling-half-leaping from the top of the rocky ridge above down into the scrubby orc-packed depths below. On one memorable occasion – but no: see *Secret Landscapes*. To observe any goings-on here one would need to have a look-out on the ridge and a lurker in the depths; and the question was, how could we detect and neutralise each of them without alerting the other? It is easy for you armchair-strategists to say, do them both simultaneously. Far easier said than done when working in two entirely different terrains – but timing, as you have realised, was to be crucial in our forthcoming operation. We were aided now by a gathering gloom. Black clouds were hastening to our side, harbingering rain. The enemy's observers would soon be seeking some shelter, and the noise of raindrops would cloak our noiseless approach. Noiselessly, accordingly, we reconnoitred the vicinity. We discerned Artie Starkey crouching in a clump of Lachlan pines above the ridge, and Trev Neely lying doggo in tall grass in the quarry's depths. From our cache of weapons I chose a cosh and one of our throwing-sticks: these latter, originally an aboriginal device, we had sophisticated into a four-armed flying swastika – in, of course, its Indian, not its Nazi, form – with nasty hooks at the ends of its arms and a nasty knobbly centrepiece. An additional feature was that if, as occasionally occurred in very high winds and torrential downpours, one missed the target, the machine would hurtle into the surrounding bush with the sound of a wild pig breaking cover. I had formerly been a dab hand, a pastmaster, at the aiming and skimming of it and our sessions in the back paddock had restored somewhere between some and a good deal of my command of it. But I took a second stick, just in case. Maxwell stayed with his successful socker, but he took too an awful pronged thing, also just in case. I went up above, he went down below.

    Up above, I flitted from pine to pine, stealthily closing in on the unsuspecting Artie. He was too deeply embowered in his clump of pines for me to get at him with my throwing-stick; I therefore needed to lure him out into the open. The open being wet, this was no straightforward matter; but among our Hill skills was a range of strange cries, eerie ululations, primarily signals to ourselves but terrifying to our foes at dead of night and sufficiently unsettling to little Artie in the gathering gloom. I was out of practice, but I gave a good account of myself. The Hill rang with my hoots and howls and warbles. Artie, thoroughly unsettled, jumped out of his clump and looked wildly around. I hurled the throwing-stick. The wild pig broke cover. I blame the gloom. Artie stood stock-still, reportedly the best tactic when faced with a wild pig in his wrath, and offering me a perfect target. The second stick swept his legs away, and before he could even begin to wonder where and why they had gone I coshed him completely. I now emitted a special warble, the agreed signal of victory; and down below Maxwell, a coiled spring, sprang on Trev. Trev, however, had been as unsettled as Artie by my strange cries. He too was up and looking wildly around. He happened to be half-turned towards Maxwell as he sprang. Trev is full of bones and muscles, Maxwell is not. Maxwell had his prong, but he was too close to Trev to prong him or, indeed, in mid-spring, to socker him properly. A sharp tussle ensued, in which Maxwell's superior science and cunning would certainly finally have prevailed but which might at any moment allow Trev to yell for help. I entered the fray, employing that complex art of rapid descent mentioned earlier. The half-clambering half went extraordinarily well, quite like old times, but the half-leaping half turned into a plunge. Fortunately Maxwell saw me coming and leapt aside. Trev, who did not, received the full brunt of me, and was promptly sockered before he could begin to wonder what had hit him. We lashed our chaps to trees, removed their mobiles, stuck gags into them; and vanished into the undergrowth.

The plunge and the bony bits of Trev had left me somewhat bruised and battered. Maxwell had a distressed shoulder and two tender hamstrings.

'We're getting too old for this,' Maxwell said: 'I don't think I'll bother to come up onto the Hill after we finish here today. The past is another country, to coin a phrase. I don't intend to inhabit it any more. Up here we've been trying to stay young for over fifty years, and the effort is damn near killing us. Today is the end of it for me. For me, up here, the past is dead.'

'It's alive, Maxwell,' I replied: 'It's alive in us, even while it's damn near killing us. It's because we are still able – barely able, I admit, but still able – to live in the past that we can do what we are now doing. It's only because we can still do it that Andrew and Tommy can rise from the dead and accuse their killers. The past is *our* country, old fellow; nowhere more so than up here on the Hill.'

We fell silent as we began our noiseless approach to our sacred sanctuary, our last redoubt, the third and most special of our special and particular places. Readers of *Secret Landscapes* will know enough about it. Readers of this thus far will already have acquired a basic acquaintance with its nature and significance. Neither the former nor the latter, though, will have any notion of our route into it. There were three ways in, and there was only a single point anywhere on the Hill from which its interior could be overlooked – that branch on the hanging-tree from which the expiring Andrew overlooked it during his last dreadful moments. Way A, from the East and the exercise trail, had to be hunted for, but it was findable after some toil and trouble. This, we had concluded, must have been Andrew's route; and it was most probable that his murderers learnt of it by watching him enter and leave by it. Way B, from the South, was extremely difficult to find, a whole huge wall of furze seemingly barring all ingress; and my reference to it in *Secret Landscapes* is anyhow purposely misleading. Way C, from the North, is not even hinted at there. Years of painful research went into the finding of it. The secret of its whereabouts has never been revealed. Only on our deathbeds will we whisper it, if we can still whisper, to a chosen disciple. Way C was our way today; and day passed into evening, a louring evening, as we advanced along it. We were ready, we reckoned, for any likely eventuality. I had added a club to my cosh, and I had two knives – a sort of scimitar attached, in full view, to my belt, and a very small very sharp one in my left sock. Maxwell's socker and prong were now abetted by a throwing-stick up his jumper and a garrotter in his back pocket. We appeared in the heart of our secretest spot, as if by magic, from behind a kurrajong. Mike McClure, who was on the other side of it, barely had time to say Jesus before he was coshed and sockered. We struck him two light glancing blows, calculated to render him docile while we tied him to a convenient pine. We intended to have speech with him. He came to promptly, and after a little wild staring-about he focused, with a start, on us.

'Well, well, well,' I said: 'Fancy finding you in this special and particular place! Fancy you finding it! Have you been reading some of my works lately?'

' Why am I tied up? What the fucking hell do you think you're doing?' he said.

'Good questions, Mike. But you haven't answered ours yet,' said Maxwell: 'Let me widen the inquiry. Bobby and Artie and Trev have also managed to find these special spots, and reading Wal's works won't have been the way they got there. Unfortunately they've been detained, they can't be here with us this evening shedding light on how they managed it. We'll explain their absence when you've explained your presence.'

He spat. He strained against his bonds. He said Fuck often. He evinced no sign of joining the conversation.

'The question that really fascinates us,' I said, 'is not just how but why you are all up here on the Hill. It's not your sort of scene at all, especially not as night draws in and the snakes come out. But, dear me, I'm forgetting that you've been up here before, only a week or so ago, in the company of at least one of the chaps we grew up with.' He spat again, still not evincing. 'Maxwell, old fellow, I think the time has come for us to prod Mike into speech. Be so kind as to give him a poke.'

Maxwell brought forth his prong, and after practising a few thrusts moved towards him.

'What the fucking hell do you think you're doing? Keep that bloody thing away from me. What do you mean I was up here before? Who says I was? If any chap says I was I'll fuckingwell stuff his balls down his gullet, so help me,' he said.

'Is that where Andrew's balls went?' Maxwell said: 'We were wondering where they'd got to. I suppose the Wagga Scientific Police will have found them by now. Can we tell them you put them there?'

'Nothing beats a figure of speech for putting a noose round a chap's neck,' I said: 'Of course, if it isn't just a figure of speech Bobby and Artie and Trev have a good deal to worry about.'

'Have they been talking? What have they said? Jesus. I always said they couldn't be trusted not to,' he said.

'You were right, Mike, absolutely right,' I said: 'Who did you say it to? To whom did you say it? Would Clive Brady be a reasonable guess?'

'It would,' said Clive Brady, strolling into our clearing by way of Way A. Behind him Dunny Dunn, all aquiver, was clutching his throat and peeping about. 'The fact that you mentioned my name gives me the idea that you've already found what I've come for.'

'Christ, thank God you've turned up. Get me out of these bloody twines. The others have been talking, Clive. What are we going to do?' Mike said.

'We've been expecting you, Clive,' I said: 'We've been making arrangements for your reception. Your name has naturally come up in various connections in the course of our chats with some of the chaps, but we haven't needed this evening's hunt for Tommy's clue to track you down. You've been in our sights throughout. Ever since we knew that you knew I was due back in Wagga, you having made a point of declaring that you didn't, we've been on your track. We have tracked you from Tommy to Andrew and back from Andrew to Tommy. We have contemplated the conclusions set forth so carefully for us and we have stood them on their heads. All along, Clive, all along, we have detected the odour of you. And as soon as we knew that you'd been visiting Andrew in his home – in his den, I make no doubt - the whole plot was in our hands. It is supremely appropriate, Clive, that we should have our final showdown *here*, in this place of all places, in the very spot where the plot against Andrew and Tommy and us has its centre. We see here how dangerous, how fatal, literature can be. A single paragraph of text drew one of my readers to select this spot for his private ecstasies, and he ended up up above it, looking down into it as he looked his last on all things lovely, yoked in death with an old classmate with whom he had only that death in common. Another reader, the yoker himself, we have here before us this evening, drawn back to this spot by that same compelling paragraph, and by the counter-plot we have based upon it. You have had your plot, Clive. Now you are in the middle of ours.'

'So now you know,' he said: 'You actually have two readers. All along, Wal, all along through that blizzard of words I've been haunted by the feeling that I've heard this sort of stuff before. And of course I have. It's exactly the same old overblown, self-regarding vapouring you were infamous for in those public-speaking competitions that I used to beat you in. People don't talk like that any more, if they ever did. The more you talked, Wal, then and now, the more certain I became that you're a born loser, all wind and piss. You're in the dead centre of my plot, you two. Dead centre, note.'

'Why am I still tied up here?' Mike said: 'Dunny, Clive, shut the fuck up for a moment and get these things off me.'

'By my count, Clive, you won five and I won seven. But I'm a fair man, ever eager to strike a happy medium – I suggest we agree on six apiece. I'm more than happy to concede that your set-speeches were often remarkably accomplished performances, as feats of memory and elocution. But you could never think on your feet. As a debater you were absolute rubbish. I think I'm right in remembering that while I was captain of the First debating team for three consecutive years you were only ever first reserve for the Thirds.'

'I don't believe this,' Maxwell said: 'Can we get on?'

'Let's,' said Clive: 'Just like old times, this conversation, but all good things must come to an end. Give me what Tommy left for you.'

'Perhaps we don't yet have it. Perhaps we are still searching for it,' I said: 'I have the feeling that it's somewhere over there, behind Dunny.' I started to move in his direction.

'Stay where you are,' Clive said. It was then we noticed that he had a gun. We were armed to the teeth (see above), but a gun was another matter. I am reliably informed that it was a .45. The man was a complete and utter rotter. 'I think you've already got it. If you have, give it to me, and we can talk about your future. If you haven't you have nothing to negotiate with, you have no future to talk about.'

'We've seen what happened to someone who wouldn't negotiate,' said Maxwell: 'What I'm wondering is whether anything very different will happen to someone who does negotiate, after the negotiations are finished. I assume you won't be taking us to Boree Creek and hanging us up out there, but Andrew's gallows are unoccupied and close at hand, and you might be thinking of putting them to use again.'

'No no. It's a lovely idea, but I'll go for something much quicker this time,' Clive said: 'Talking of lovely ideas, I hope you think Boree Creek was. I chose that scene specially for Wal, to give him the thrill of coincidence in the course of these events, as it were. Tommy was always a fool, he brought this on himself. He just never believed he would be killed, he thought he could tough it out. In your cases, however, I promise it will hardly hurt at all.'

'Boree Creek was a coincidence too far, Clive,' I said: 'There you fell into another literary trap. But you haven't answered Maxwell's question. If we don't negotiate, that's that. If we do negotiate, that's still that, surely? You can't afford to leave us alive. We know too much. I doubt that you can afford to leave poor trussed-up Mike alive, he certainly knows too much; he's got too much on you, Clive, and he can't run away. Start on him while Maxwell and I think about negotiating. Or shoot Dunny first, he'll be the first to blab if you don't.'

'What's this about me?' cried Dunny: 'I'm no blabber! Ask anybody!'

'Christ, Clive,' cried Mike: 'Don't listen to him! Just let me get out of these and I'll throttle the bastard myself.'

'Shut up, both of you,' Clive said: 'Now listen to me, Wal. And this goes for you too, Maxwell. You've got a simple choice. Give me what I want, and it will hardly hurt at all. Or don't, and it will hurt more than even you, Wal, could find last words to describe. Decide.'

'And afterwards?' said Maxwell: 'Either way you'll have two bodies, probably a few more, on your hands. Are you going to drag us off into the scrub or just leave us lying about here? You can't have given proper thought to the problem of corpse-disposal, Clive, because it was only a couple of hours ago that we let the chaps know we'd be up here this evening.'

'Quite so,' I said: 'I think the bodies will have to be got out of the way very quickly indeed, before our well-beloved Detective Sergeant Charlie Parker arrives, and since,' I looked at my watch, 'he's due here in the next three, no two, minutes, your time has really run out. You're back in the middle of our plot, Clive.'

'No, Wal. You're still in mine,' Clive said: 'By my watch he's due here now. And here he is.'

'Here I am,' said Charlie Parrot, emerging from Way A, accompanied by two grinning constables of the largest size. 'Here we all are. How are you getting on with them, Clive?'

I must admit I was flabbergasted. I was thunderstruck. This put me right off my stroke. Maxwell reported that my jaw actually dropped. So be it. All I can now recall of the moment after Charlie's entrance is that I cast my eyes up towards heaven. The last time I had done this in this place I had seen a bit of Andrew's jersey and his P.S.A.A.A. pennant in an olive-tree. This time I evidently and unsurprisingly cast them up higher, for there, just visible in the gloom, was the branch on the hanging-tree from which poor Andrew had been suspended, and also there, sitting on it and looking down on us as if from a grandstand, also grinning, was Eric Connolly.

I grinned back, generally the wisest course of action in Eric Connolly's vicinity. Whatever purpose he was pursuing, whatever mad motive or wild whim had lodged him in that tree at this critical juncture, he was always and forever a prodigiously loose loose cannon, as violent and unpredictable as anything on the planet; and in this ticklish situation – into which he might be thinking of irrupting – we needed him to irrupt on our side. No effort to awaken the sentiment of mateship in him could be spared. We had foiled him in Narrandera, which I now wished we hadn't; but my *Comeuppance* had made him a household name, and he might be hankering after a second bite of the cherry of fame. I grinned again, radiating an unaffected pleasure in seeing him here, combined with a sincere and steadfast hope that we could be real cobbers from this moment on.

'Wal doesn't seem to be taking this seriously. I haven't observed a grin like that since the one we wiped off Tommy Anderson's face,' Charlie observed: 'Would you like me to wipe it off Wal's, Clive?'

'So Clive is the Superintendent here?' I said: 'The Detective Sergeant is only taking orders. Well, well, well. We had our occasional suspicions but on the whole, yes, you had us fooled. One of these two fine specimens,' I indicated his attendant giants, 'would have to be the passing local checking constable who happened on Andrew's clothes. But why, Charlie? Fooling us is its own reward, I can appreciate that, but Andrew and Tommy didn't have to die for you to do it. I could have shown you plenty of easier ways. How have you come to fall under Clive's spell?'

'I and Clive,' he said, ' have reached an understanding and formed an equal and mutual alliance. As far as Tommy is concerned it was a case of good riddance, he's been a source of numerous crimes for far too long, it was time to get him off the streets on a permanent basis. He was vermin, Tommy was. Having overstepped the mark by attempting blackmailing the forthcoming Mayor of Wagga it was clearly of great convenience for us both to put an end to him.'

'Blackmailing Clive? Really?' said Maxwell: 'What could he possibly have had on Clive that he was ready to be tortured to death to keep from him?'

'I know all about that,' Charlie replied: 'Tommy was a fool, he was just too stubborn to live. Those special unorthodox financial rearrangements are actually highly common in local government circles, but they're exactly the kind of thing that the Sydney C.I.D. is inclined to take the view that it has a right to jump into and take over, and we don't want that lot down here nosing into everything.'

'But to torture him to death, Charlie?' I said: 'If he'd been Christian Brothers' vermin excuses could be found, but he was one of ours, Charlie, he was Wagga High! As for poor Andrew ... '

Maxwell suddenly hurled himself at the wall of furze and disappeared. With one mighty bound he was free. Way B, you'll recall. Consternation broke out. 'After him!' roared Charlie. The two giant constables hurled themselves at the wall of furze and rebounded, cursing, Way B being hard to locate without careful reconnaissance and the furze being at its extremely prickly height. Clive tore his hair. Mike besought Christ to hasten to his aid. Dunny bleated. The constables regrouped, sustained a stream of orders and threats from Charlie, identified the proper channel after some further hurling and rebounding and plunged in, still cursing.

'Don't think that if he gets away,' Clive said, 'you'll leave this place alive. Whatever happens, I've promised myself that you won't live to crow over me.'

'If he gets away,' Charlie said,' I foresee difficulties. It may be necessary, Clive, for us to consider our arrangements in a different light.'

'Christ, Christ, Christ,' Mike continued. Dunny's bleating passed into panting. Clive tore on. Time stood still. Then there came a shout of, unmistakably, triumph; succeeded by 'Got him!' The principals relaxed, Mike ceased his appeals to Christ and Dunny capered. After a brief interval the constables re-entered via Way A, clutching their prisoner.

'As for Andrew,' I resumed, 'not only was he Wagga High, he was one of the Terminus chaps, that peerless band of brothers of which you, Charlie, were never thought worthy to be a member. Worthy members present here and elsewhere on the Hill include Mike and Dunny and Bobby and Artie and Trev. Andrew's membership didn't save him, and I reckon it won't save them either. No civic purpose could be served by getting Andrew off the Wagga streets, so why, Charlie, why?'

'Shut up, Wal. You've run out of time,' Clive said: 'Are you, or are you not, going to give it to me?'

'Wal has asked a good question, Clive,' said Charlie, 'which he deserves an answer to before he comes to a dead stop. He needs to know that I personally, and my nearby officers, did not raise a finger against Andrew while he was a living person. We only helped with the heavy lifting afterwards. The previous executing was wholly and solely - '

'Shut up! Shut up!' Mike bellowed: 'Don't talk about that! Get the silly fucker to shut up, Clive.'

'Don't talk to me like that!' Charlie bellowed back: 'You're forgetting who I am. Keep a civil tongue in your head or I'll tear it out. It was you who killed him, he was practically dead when we arrived. And furthermore and in addition I am not the sort of man who cuts a man's balls off and I owe it to myself to not let it be thought that I could have. I admit the blood came in useful for deceptive purposes but I still say that was the act of a pure bastard which has been preying on my mind ever since.'

'I'm really relieved to hear that, Charlie,' said Maxwell: 'It's been preying on my mind too. We were certain it was Mike, but it's good to have it confirmed. It was obvious ... '

'You thought it was me? That's balls, that is,' said Mike: 'You didn't have the faintest bloody idea. Tell me how you could have known.'

'We're wasting time,' Clive said: 'None of this matters; they're not going to know anything at all in a couple of minutes. We need to concentrate on what we're here for. I... '

'It was obvious, Mike,' Maxwell went on: 'And you're right, it *is* balls. As soon as we discovered that Andrew was in a relationship with your daughter his lost balls had your name on them.'

'In a relationship?!' Mike howled, writhing in his bonds: 'What kind of prissy fucking language is that? He was fucking her! He'd got her fuckingwell pregnant into the bargain! A man can stand only so much. That prancing bastard wormed his way into my little daughter, who I've never forgotten how he wormed his way into Yvonne Gillard just when I'd tuned her up at the Intermediate Social; and if she won't get rid of it I'll be the poor bastard having to put up with having that bastard's bastard in my fucking family. *He was having my daughter!* You don't know how that feels! He's almost an old man and she's still almost a girl. He got his pennant and I got his balls - a fucking fair exchange, I call it. Why am I still tied up?'

'This bastard won't be a McClure, fortunately,' I said: 'It'll be a Davies, just like your bastard, the one that Billy Davies has to put up with in his family. As for... '

'That's really a pretty poor show, I agree,' Charlie said: 'Even Billy Davies doesn't deserve that. But you can't get away from the fact that she's Mike's daughter and as a father he's got a right to his feelings.'

'But maybe Andrew didn't know that she was Mike's,' said Maxwell: 'We can't be always inquiring into girls' parentage. If he didn't, this father didn't have a right to more than his feelings.'

'He knew,' Charlie said: 'Mike has particularly assured me that he received several anonymous warnings, but he still went on with her, and pregnancy, of course, is naturally the final straw.'

' – As for this little daughter of yours,' I also went on, 'who's too young to be having an affair with old chaps like us, what about other people's little daughters if the old chap happens to be you? What about Robyn Lee's daughter for instance?'

'That stupid bitch, she's as stupid as her mother, and by God Robyn was stupid, she was so stupid that she even had a soft spot for you,' he said: 'The daughter's a real cock-teaser but I never fucked her.'

'Not for want of trying,' I said: 'So it's all right for an old chap to try, but not to succeed, is it? But I have to admit to a measure of agreement with you, Mike, about poor Robyn. She was so wretchedly silly that she even fell in love with you. She was so silly that she even thought you were in love with her. And when she learnt that you were trying to fuck her daughter she was silly enough to be distressed enough to leap out into the air over the Base Hospital. I'm sure you remember that incident, Charlie. Another pretty poor show, wouldn't you say?'

'That's water under the bridge, Charlie,' Clive said: 'We can chat about ancient history later. Wal is just playing for time, and we all know he can blether on forever. Let's finish this now.'

'Just before you do,' said Maxwell, 'I want to say a word – a word about ancient history. What we all know about Wal is that he can talk forever and that he is forever going back into the past, into our past, into those ancient Wagga days when we were all young and semi-innocent and promising – the days when a scene like this, strewn with the corpses of our murdered and mutilated schoolmates, was totally unimaginable. But I digress. I have always regarded Wal's obsession with our ancient history as one of his private and personal manias, a mania that I have frequently tried to haul him back from because, since other normal people do not live in the past like that, like him, it gave him a false picture of the present. I have certainly tried to do that during this last week, and I confess I have been doing it with greater gusto than usual because I was slow to see through your cunning plan to exploit his well-known obsession with the past to lure us into the trail to Tommy ... '

'No, no,' I interrupted. It was plain to me that Maxwell had a plan. This unbearable orating reminded me of me, it wasn't his sort of stuff in the slightest: he was evidently talking for time. I struck in to give him an extra helping of it. 'No, no. Allow me to make a distinction. There are two quite different pasts in action here. My obsession is, as you so eloquently put it, with our ancient history, with those glorious golden days when we were all trusting schoolfellows together. That is the past you have frequently urged me to set less store by because, as you also eloquently put it, other people don't live there any more. I must point out, however, that a part of this noxious tied-up creature here has been living in that past ever since because Andrew's whipping Yvonne Gillard out from under him has never left him. But I digress. The past that this particular cunning plan sought to exploit is only a very recent one, a mere matter of the last half-dozen or so years. That is the past that they sought to fill with clues to a homicidal Tommy Anderson. What they sought to exploit was my fondness for Tommy and ... '

'No, no,' Maxwell interrupted: 'Your fondness for Tommy is part and parcel of your obsession with that ancient past. Those two pasts run into one another. What they sought to exploit was your attachment to Wagga High. All your affections and attachments are parts of your obsession with the past. You should have been a historian. Any exercising tourist on the trail of your psyche would encounter, over and over again, only the past, the past, the everlasting, overbearing past. Your affection for me, Wal, is really only part of your obsession with the past. I sometimes think... '

'Shut up! For Christ's sake, shut up, both of you!' Clive shouted: 'Shut up! I'll put your affection for Maxwell to the test, Wal. Give me what I'm here for or I'll shoot him. On the count of three. One... '

'All right, Clive,' I said: 'You win. My affection for Maxwell has undone me. I think...'

'I think you'd better tell him,' said Maxwell: 'I don't like the look of that gun.'

'I am about to tell him, Maxwell,' I said: 'I cannot endure the thought of you being shot. Not, at any rate, right in front of me. I...'

'Two,' said Clive.

'Perhaps I should tell him,' said Maxwell: 'I can see how reluctant you are, but it's time to admit defeat. The fact of the matter ... '

'Get a move on, Maxwell,' Charlie said: 'I'm due back at the station. We need to tie this up quick.'

'Why am I still tied up?' Mike wanted to know.

'The fact of the matter, Clive,' Maxwell went on, 'is that we found Tommy's clue at the old quarry, where we also found Trev and Artie. Mike will be pleased to hear that they too are tied up. The clue directs us to a certain spot, and at that spot we will apparently find, buried, a package; and in that package we are due to find certain photographs – photographs that will apparently come as a nasty surprise to a certain Detective Sergeant who is expecting to find something relating to financial jiggery-pokery.'

'Where is this spot?' said Clive.

'Up near the look-out,' Maxwell said: 'Near the top of the exercise trail. Just off it to the left, apparently. There's a flattish sort of rock there. It's under that. The package has one of Wal's books in it, *Eric Connolly's Comeuppance*. The photographs are inside it.'

'I don't believe this,' Clive said: 'Why would Tommy pick a place like that?'

'Because I know that rock,' I said: 'I happened to be exercising on the trail with Tommy about a dozen or so years ago – more like fifteen or sixteen, really – and he pointed that rock out to me. It meant a lot to him, that flattish rock. He had Deirdre O'Toole on it. Remember Deirdre, Charlie? Clive isn't likely to, his memory is differently inclined. Deirdre was a tremendously active lay, apparently. Tommy said they actually bounced off that rock in the course of intercourse.'

'Let's go,' Charlie said: 'It'll soon to be too dark to look for rocks. I'm surprised to hear that Deirdre O'Toole was a girl of that character. She always struck me as seriously inhibited. Wonders will never cease. Horry,' he indicated the larger constable, 'you get hold of Wal. Frank,' the lesser constable, 'you hang on to Maxwell. If there is any attempt to effect an escape it's the usual drill. Club them down. Quick march.'

The Horry constable got hold of me, very painfully, and relieved me of club, cosh and scimitar in an offensively insolent manner. The Frank one deprived Maxwell of his prong and socker. The throwing-stick up his jumper, however, remained undetected, Maxwell being, as I think I have previously remarked, naturally plumpish, or plain plump. Undetected on me, the attentive reader will have noticed, was the small sharp knife in my left sock. Maxwell's cunning plan evidently envisaged an escape into the now-darkling scrub while we pretended to search for that flat rock. Gripped by constables and covered by Clive's .45 we would be hard put to it to bring that off, and the last-resort weapons we still retained were scarcely suited to our situation. But *nil desperandum* is one of my mottoes. And where was Eric Connolly when we needed him?

As we were dragged off – via Way A, which was now a complete mess – Mike begged again to be released. Clive told him to shut up, he'd be back to attend to him as soon as he'd attended to us. Dunny said he wanted to stay with Mike, he didn't want to be part of what might be going to happen. Clive told him to shut up and come with him and Charlie. Charlie said he'd make sure Dunny didn't slink away, he'd keep a sharp eye on him.

We emerged onto the exercise trail and turned up the slope towards the look-out. No exercisers were enjoying an evening run. There was no sign of Eric Connolly.

'Your *Eric Connolly* and contents had better be up there,' Clive said: 'If not, you're in for a Comeuppance with a capital C.'

'If he's not, as I understand it, we are due to be dead,' I said: 'If he is, we are also due to be ditto. That's an idle threat, Clive, unworthy of a man of your cunning.'

'There are more ways than one of getting to be dead,' Clive said, 'as Tommy and Andrew found out. This is no idle threat, Wal, as a man of your superior penetration should have realised.'

'Penetration is *un mot juste,* Clive. It will shortly be springing to Charlie's lips when he beholds those photographs,' I riposted: 'But speaking of cunning, I assume that the cunning in the cunning plan to pin Andrew's murder on Tommy belongs to you. Characteristically, it was too clever by half. There were too many clues and correspondences. We saw through it at once.'

'Your assumption, characteristically, is only half correct,' he riposted: 'It was my plan, but I had to leave the execution of it to your old mates at the Terminus, who evidently overdid it. Execution is another *mot juste,* as you will shortly be appreciating.'

'I am frankly amazed, Clive,' I said, 'amazed and impressed, that you have been able to excite and harness so much enthusiasm among the chaps for these dreadful deceptions. It marks you out as a worthy Mayor of Wagga Wagga. How did you do it? How did you and Charlie do it?'

'Easy,' Charlie said: 'I and Clive saw eye-to-eye over Tommy, and Mike McClure had a particular job he needed to do as father of a young daughter on Andrew, and although your old mates in the Terminus could not be trusted to lend a major hand in it they simply could not wait to grab the opportunity of helping us to clean up afterwards by well and truly shafting you. We've been waiting for it for more than forty years. You've been parading your superiority over us ever since we were all at school together. This was our chance to not only do what had to be done but to let you let us get away with it by being made a total fool of. If you see what I mean. And we had to do it all against the clock, because we knew you'd be going off abroad in a short period and we had to make sure you would reckon you had it solved before you went. It was a masterpiece. It's a pity it didn't work, because now you know too much to live. It's also a pity Maxwell's involved, but such is life.'

'All I had to do was to remind them of your memoir,' Clive said.

'That bloody memoir!' said Charlie, with emotion: 'It's been hanging over our heads for years. We were all due to be made fools of in it, including me, including that highly amusing story you made me the town's laughing-stock in about the bastards who tried to drown me down at the Beach. You'd make yourself out to be the cleverest person in the whole bloody Riverina, but who's the prize fool now, Wal?'

'Here's another liver in the past, Maxwell,' I said: 'There are more of us about than even I imagined. Detective Sergeant Charlie is still stuck back at the Beach when they failed to drown him. You'll all be relieved to hear that I won't be writing my Memoir. This whole experience has so deeply disheartened and disillusioned me that I've given it up. The sneaky snaky stratagems of deception practised here,' I said, alerting Maxwell to my own cunning plan in this crisis, 'have convinced me that I know nothing worth knowing about my own past and the companions of my youth. My Memoir would be pointless. It will never be written.'

'That goes without saying,' said Clive: 'Where's this flat rock?'

'It's just here, down behind this Cootamundra wattle,' Maxwell said: 'Off to the left, isn't it, Wal?

'To the left, yes,' I said: 'Five or ten paces down the slope, as I recall.'

'I'm covering you both, and I'm itching to pull the trigger,' said Clive.

We entered the scrub. Far below, the lights of down-town Wagga glimmered through the trees. Pretending to be questing for Tommy's depository we drew our escort into ever-darker terrain.

'I see no flat fucking rock,' Charlie said: 'I see no rocks, full-stop. Find it quick. Or else.'

It was now or never. 'Here it is,' I said, bending down and securing my small sharp knife: 'Just here. O my God! The place is alive with snakes!' I hopped, I skipped, I stabbed Horry in the bum. 'Christ! I've been bit!' Horry shouted, also hopping and skipping. 'It's a trick! Keep hold of them!' Clive shouted. Frank and Maxwell were hopping and skipping together. 'I can't see them! Where are they?' Charlie shouted, hopping and skipping in case. 'They're coming this way!' Dunny shouted, hopping and skipping back towards the trail. Even in the agonies of snakebite Horry, evidently a really dutiful officer, still held me close. Eric Connolly sprang out of nowhere with a thing like a baseball bat, shouted 'This will teach you not to put me in your bloody books!' aimed a mighty blow at me, clubbed Horry down instead, and vanished. I was free! This may be the finest modern example of the *deus ex machina*. 'I saw that! You're under arrest!' Charlie shouted. Frank stopped hopping and skipping because Maxwell had managed to skip just far enough off to extract and throw his throwing-stick and it homed in on his balls. Maxwell was free! We were on the brink of a famous victory. No, we weren't. Clive fired two shots into the air; then levelled the .45 at us.

'Don't move,' he said: 'If you move you're dead, both of you. I'm...'

'Where did that Eric bloody Connolly spring from? Where did he go?' Charlie said: 'He's next for the Tommy Anderson treatment. The district will be well-rid of him.'

' – I'm finished with this charade,' Clive continued: 'Tommy's secret will die with him and with you. Not for one moment did I ... '

There came a heartfelt cry – 'O Christ, O Jesus' – from Frank, who had exchanged his hopping and skipping for crouching and crawling. Horry was at peace.

' – Not for one moment did I believe in this flat rock nonsense,' Clive continued: 'The time has come ... '

There came a sudden bleat from Dunny, out on the trail. One moment later the Tourists poured in upon us, brandishing their implements, and sending Detective Sergeant Charlie and Clive and his .45 flying. This is definitely the finest modern example of the *dei ex machina.* I dived for the .45, but it skidded away into the murk. Charlie ended up upended in a clump of something or other, out of which he arose roaring. 'You're all under arrest!' he was roaring when Maxwell seized an implement from Stan, I think it was a bolt-cutter, and fetched him such a biff with it that he went straight back down into the clump he came from. Rory and Bill made a grab for Clive, but he was as always a slippery customer, he writhed out of their grasp and took to his heels.

We took off after him, after tossing our ball of twine to the Tourists and conjuring them to tie up our vanquished foes. Clive was surprisingly swift. Maxwell had never been swift, and was now slow. I had once upon a time been swiftish, but that time was not now. We avoided, more or less, the spreadeagled Dunny. Down the exercise trail we galloped, fleet Clive twenty yards ahead. He sped past Way A – Mike McClure could be heard raving and cursing within; past poor Andrew's fatal tree – which seemed to sway and rattle its branches at his passing; down the westward slope past another pair of puce and panting pensioners labouring upwards; down and then up after a stumble at the south-western corner – he turned his left ankle, we noted, on a (flat) rock, and he was now limping; and then off, off the trail, into the scrub, heading in the direction of the quarry. Trev and Artie were there: if he could free and deploy them, he might be calculating, he might yet make good his escape. His quickest route to the quarry was straight along the trail for another hundred yards to its southern corner and then sharp left up through the pines. He had to be thinking that we'd catch him on the trail now that his ankle had reduced his pace to half Maxwell's, and that he had a chance of staying ahead of us if he took to the Bush. He had no chance of staying ahead of us for long. He was absolutely at the mercy of our superior Hillcraft; and just now, as we plunged into a patch of scrub that we knew every inch of, we felt absolutely merciless. Clive was only twenty or so yards ahead of us. After a minute or two the gap was hardly ten, and Maxwell had his garrotter in his hand. We hungered and thirsted to get him in our grasps. In another minute we would have him. The noise of our joint approach was inspiring thoughts of rescue in Artie, who began baying hopefully. Clive clambered and scrambled towards the sound of him. He stumbled over a perfectly-placed root as he got out onto the ridge at the top of the quarry. He half-lost his balance and regained it. He lost it again by putting too much weight on his left ankle. He over-corrected, falling to his right. And he fell. He fell right over into the quarry. He fell at the very spot from which I had performed my half-scrambling half-plunging descent earlier that evening. Clive's descent was all-plunging, and he did it backwards, which should never be attempted. Furthermore: not only did he lack the half-scrambling half to slow him down, he also lacked Trev – we'd lashed him to a nearby pine – to land on. He landed on an outcrop of quartz, and he landed with a sound – audible to us on the ridge above – as of snapping kindling.

He was barely conscious when we got to him. Maxwell, who has many doctors in his family tree, opined that he had broken his back and his neck, and was a goner. I forbore – it cost me an effort, but I made it – to tell him that he would not be Mayor of Wagga Wagga after all. I told him instead that his speech at the opening of the Clive Brady Reading Room had been really masterly, far better than anything I could have offered on an equivalent occasion. He gave no sign of it, but I think he appreciated that. Maxwell rang the ambulance and went to the Museum car-park to await it. I treated Artie and Trev to words of biting reproof, loosed them, advised them to make themselves scarce, and warned them that the police – definitely not including Detective Sergeant Charlie Parrot – would be calling on them soon. Maxwell returned with stretcher-bearers and Clive was borne off.

As we trekked back up the trail towards them – a naked clergyman passed us, westward-bound - Maxwell explained the sudden saving arrival of the Tourists. When he'd shot out of the sanctuary via Way B he knew he'd have time, while his pursuers were trying to work out how to get through to him, to get through to Rory & Co. on his mobile. Which he did. (Whatever did we do before we had mobiles? I really must get one.) He'd instructed them to drive like the wind to the look-out, to creep down the exercise trail to the big Cootamundra wattle on their right and to hide behind it, and when we came around it to hit everybody except us with everything they'd got. The others with us, he'd told them, would look quite like police but they weren't, they were Tommy's murderers. When we came around the wattle and they weren't there, he said, he'd felt a distinct twinge of despair, but all's well that ends well, especially at the last possible moment; and now that he'd been able to think about it he'd realised that they'd been hiding behind the wrong wattle, because he'd failed to take account of the fact that most people can't tell the difference between a Cootamundra wattle and the ordinary Golden variety, and there was a big Golden one further up. It wasn't until Clive fired those shots into the air that they could tell where we were.

'Where did Eric Connolly come from?' he wanted to know.

'He came straight out of the pages of *Eric Connolly's Comeuppance*,' I said, 'where, to put it mildly, he did not want to be. He was making that point with a club. He's evidently been tracking me for the last few days to make it. Had he been two inches to the right I might never have written another word.'

On our way up to the scene of the final set-to we looked in on Mike McClure. I was about to ransack my vocabulary for words of maximally bitter reproof but he shouted Shut up Fuck off and we went on up to the right wattle. An agitated Rory met us.

'These characters that we've tied up, they're real police,' he said: 'That's Detective Sergeant Charlie Parrot over there,' who was struggling violently and apparently foaming at the mouth, 'and Stan is sure that that's Frank Stapleton. We think the sleeping one is

Horry Dobbs. There must be a mistake somewhere. We're going to have a lot of explaining to do.'

We explained.

Then we rang – that invaluable mobile! – the police-station and demanded to speak to Superintendent Wilkinson. We were told that Superintendent Wilkinson was at home with his family after a heavy day and was not to be disturbed in any circumstances. We replied that Detective Sergeant Charlie Parrot and Constables Dobbs and Stapleton, together with the murderer and mutilator of the late Andrew Kell, were our prisoners, adjacent to the look-out on Willans' Hill; that former mayoral candidate Clive Brady, one of the murderers of Tommy Anderson, was currently in intensive care or worse; and that Superintendent Wilkinson was to be disturbed at once. Even before we had concluded our summary of the situation we could hear the sirens.

Calming a crowd of thirty policemen is one of the most difficult things to do in my experience, and we were still some way short of succeeding when Superintendent Wilkinson arrived and did it. He asked us if we wouldn't mind telling him what all this was about. We replied that all would become clear if he wouldn't mind stepping down the exercise trail with us as far as yonder Cootamundra wattle. He called for a torch and five constables and came. We showed him our prisoners. (Rory & Co. had vanished.) He asked us to explain.

We explained.

Charlie kept interrupting our explanations with explanations of his own, the tendency of which was to present him in a heroic and self-sacrificial light as the saviour of the municipality from the furious depredations of Tommy Anderson. Superintendent Wilkinson's patience with explanations appeared to be quickly exhausted; or he was just keen, as a family man, to get back to his family. He cut us off – he cut me off, to be exact – in mid-description of the misleading clues in Tommy's sleep-out.

'That's enough for now,' he said: 'I'm frankly not all that inclined to believe a good deal of this. You're locally pretty notorious for your numerous fictions. You're probably being too imaginative by half. On the other hand, I know Maxwell here, who's a reliable chap, and I knew his old doctor father, who operated on my wife's uncle for gall-stones; and on the strength of that I'll put Parrot and these others under lock and key until tomorrow. Tomorrow morning, you both come down to the station and make a full statement.'

We took them to Mike McClure and they took him off with the others. Maxwell borrowed a torch and retrieved Clive's .45. Charlie was still explaining and Mike was still Fucking Off as they went off. We went back down the trail towards the Museum car-park. After the evening's exertions we were aching all over, in particular in mind and spirit.

'I don't know about you, Maxwell,' I said, 'but there were moments back there when I wasn't entirely sure that we would bring this off. Taking it all in all, especially after that .45 appeared, it was a damned close-run thing.'

'True,' he said: 'Even right at the end, only my father and a few gall-stones stood between us and Charlie's release.'

'I think,' I said, 'I'll go no more a-roving hereabouts. Our sanctuary is our sanctuary no longer. Our nest has been fouled. It has been sullied and violated for me forever. As it was, as it really is, it's in the pages of *Secret Landscapes*. There let it remain. There let the whole Hill remain. The Hill we grew up on has gone. I cast it into the past. I shall never visit it again. This is the end of my adolescence, Maxwell. I here forswear it and set forth on the exercise trail to maturity.'

'My adolescence ended a long time ago,' he said: 'But whenever you came back, still full of it, I felt I ought to pretend to join you in it. I'm relieved to hear that I won't have to do that any more.'

I was expressing my gratitude for his years of friendly duplicity when, borne upon a breeze from the North, the sound of moaning reminded us that we had forgotten Bobby Fossey. He was really relieved when we got to him, he said the snakes were gathering from all directions, he'd heard that the really poisonous ones hunted at night. True, we said, we got back to you in the nick of time, how did you get involved in this? It was Mike, he said, and it just sort of got out of hand. There was supposed to be some gang from over in Narrandera, he said, which is a place that's full of gangs, who had it in for Andrew for some financial reasons and they were going to take him out, Mike had warned him but Andrew wouldn't be warned apparently, and when they did it these gangsters planned to pin it on him, on Mike, which they would unless we helped him to pin it on Tommy Anderson, who was a totally useless character anyway but he'd be sure to have a convincing alibi, he always did, so he wouldn't come to any long-term harm. And when Detective Charlie Parker came into it, he said, it all sort of became official.

We released him from his bonds and sent him home. The police, we told him, would be calling on him soon, and he could tell his tale to them.

We drove back over the Hill – for me, for the last time, and with never a backward glance.

Afterwards, after enough pasta to fuel the Renaissance and enough wine to halt it in its tracks, we fell into our beds.

EPILOGUE

In the morning, after a brace of heavy-duty omelettes – Maxwell was a dab-hand at these things – we proceeded to the police station and exercised two stenographers until noon. Our story, impressively cogent in itself, became actually believable as the day advanced, as Mike and Charlie and Horry and Frank began to rat on each other. We lunched, with difficulty, on police sandwiches.

Early in the afternoon Superintendent Wilkinson arrived and indicated that we were free to go. He was now firmly in possession of the chief facts, he said, and he would deal with them appropriately in due course. Certain other individuals mentioned by us would also be dealt with in due course, he said. He was happy to take this opportunity, he said, to warmly thank us for the invaluable assistance we had rendered the police in solving these crimes and bringing their perpetrators to book. The Wagga Wagga Scientific Police would be subjecting the whole case to the latest technologies and successful prosecutions would thus be a certainty, he said. There was therefore no call for us to concern ourselves any further about this extremely regrettable set of affairs, under which there now needed a line to be drawn in case of uncontrollable public outbursts, he said. Clive Brady was dead, he said.

This was most disappointing. I had been looking forward to enthralling a packed courtroom with a step-by-step account of how we had penetrated his deep-laid schemes. Instead, it instantly occurred to me, I would be able to put him in his place in his obituary, which editor G.G. of *The Advertiser* would surely be pleased to have me contribute a few salient paragraphs to. All the police in the police station assembled to wave us off – a nice gesture, I thought – when we left the building, mid-afternoon.

It was now necessary to say some careful words to Andrew's widow, Jayne, and to – through her mother – his last and fatal love, Angela. We drove to the Davies residence. Billy Davies, alas, came to the door, looking not merely difficult but ferocious and somewhat unhinged.

'You two again!' he said: 'What the fuck do you want this time?'

'Good afternoon, Billy,' I said: 'We just happened to be passing, and we suddenly remembered hearing that your daughter Angela had ... '

'Stop right there,' he said: 'The less I hear about her the better, so fuck off or else.'

'Or else what?' I said.

'You're just about to find out, which many people in Wagga would long to do the same,' he said, stepping towards me, looking not merely ferocious now but utterly unhinged.

'You can take a swipe at me,' I said, 'but while you're in the midst of it Maxwell here will have your jaw in tiny pieces and your private parts in even tinier ones. Both of us were fond of dear old Archdeacon West, and since your father isn't available at this moment we'll be glad to settle an old score for him with his son. Are you ready, Maxwell?'

Maxwell moved towards him, flexing his fingers and fixing his eyes on Tommy's flies. Billy stepped back.

'You two just fuck off,' he said: 'I don't want to hear anything about Angela.'

'What about Angela?' The mother, Sonia, appeared. 'She's gone to Melbourne, God knows why. She rang on Monday, she said something terrible has happened but she wouldn't say what. Do you know what?'

'Andrew Kell, you'll recall, was murdered. Angela was acquainted with him,' Maxwell said: 'That would be the terrible thing she was referring to. And there's another terrible thing coming, as to which we make no remark. He was murdered by Mike McClure, who is under arrest. Wal and I will now take our leave.'

We left. I looked back – a mistake: the sight of Sonia's white, white face is with me still.

We drove to the Kell house. Jayne came to the door. Before we could open our mouths she told us that Superintendent Wilkinson had already rung and told her everything. She went on to say that she didn't want to hear anything more about it, she was putting it all into her past, she was walking away from it and from Wagga Wagga too, she was going to Canberra to start a new life. She thanked us for our efforts on Andrew's behalf, she said Superintendent Wilkinson had said we'd been quite helpful to the police towards the end.

'I wonder you didn't see through that Detective Parrot,' she said: 'He was most unconvincing. All he did was look at my legs.'

We looked at her legs, which seemed to be longer and lissomer than ever.

'He was a Wagga High boy,' I said: 'All of them were. I cannot imagine him not looking at your legs, but it took more imagination than I happened to possess to see him taking part in Andrew's murder. It just didn't seem possible.'

'Anything is possible in this town,' she said: 'If you don't know that you don't know anything. I have to believe that Canberra will be different. Goodbye.' She slammed the door.

We drove to the editorial offices of *The Advertiser*. On the way we recollected that yesterday, in the days when we were eliminating poor Tommy Anderson from the strange deaths that were designed to lead us to him as Andrew's killer, we had been due to meet the reporter who had covered Donny Parker's demise in the Victory Memorial Gardens. We proffered our apologies to G.G. and explained that that line of inquiry had been overtaken by events, as poor Tommy had been, as Clive Brady had been; and that our business today was strictly obituarial. G.G. declared himself delighted beyond measure at the prospect of printing my golden words in the forthcoming memorial tributes. I then dictated several telling characterisations of Clive, as one of the two finest public speakers of his generation; as one whose gifts, such as they abundantly were, qualified him to be a supremely suitable Mayor of Wagga Wagga, which due to circumstances beyond his control he was not now to be; as one who had enriched the community with a Reading Room in which the works of distinguished Wagga authors could be read and revelled in; as one who, although this was not widely known, was a deep, vigorous and passionate supporter of our homosexual brethren; as one whose dearest wish, confided to a few of his old Wagga High schoolmates, was that the new abattoir at Bomen should bear his name. Then I dictated a brief tribute to Tommy, describing him as a well-known local identity whose rough and forbidding exterior hid a warm heart and a sociable spirit, who was undismayed by the numerous setbacks he encountered but persevered in his chosen line of activity with unflagging zeal and determination, who would be greatly missed and sincerely mourned by a wide circle of friends, fellow-workers and policemen.

G.G. introduced us to Barney Reilly, the Donny Parker reporter, as we were departing. I told him that we had been exploring the extremely remote possibility that Tommy Anderson had been implicated in the strange death of Donny Parker, but that it had since become perfectly clear to us that he was not, and now that he was dead there was no point in pursuing the matter further. Barney said that that was a real pity, he'd got very interested in that affair, he had a fat file on it which the police had taken a glance at but they hadn't really paid much attention to, they reckoned Tommy had a very good alibi and he couldn't have done it. But Tommy and Donny had a lot of deep disagreements about money, and I reckon, he said, that that alibi was cooked up by Tommy and his mates down at the Tourist hotel, who probably also helped him arrange things to make it look like a suicide, but it wasn't, it was a murder, Tommy murdered Donny Parker. Would we like to see the file?

We would not, we said; and departed.

We drove back to Maxwell's farmlet. Maxwell observed that the nights were getting colder these days. I observed that Wagga's weather had a tendency to get colder when it wasn't getting hotter.

'I'm sick and tired of Wagga's weather,' I went on: 'I have had my fill of it. I have already declared that the Hill has seen the last of me, it is out of my bounds forever. I now declare that Wagga too will see me no more. Henceforth, I shall think of it, when I have to, as Wagga Wagga, and I shall never write another word about it. The Memoir, the novel – they will never now see the light of day. I have no wish to go through the motions of fraternising with the remnants of the chaps. The era of the chaps is over. The Terminus has terminated. Roll on, the William Farrer. The mates at the Tourist have been erased from my mind. You and I, old fellow, will never meet here again. Besides, next time Eric Connolly might not miss. I suggest we meet in time to come in, say, Ballarat – heaven's breath, I hear, smells wooingly there.'

'What novel?' Maxwell said: 'About what? You've already said you wouldn't write anything about all these ghastly goings-on.'

'I said it, but I didn't mean it,' I said: 'I planned to call it *Mrs. Rossiter's Canary*. I solemnly swear to you that I shall never ever write a novel called *Mrs. Rossiter's Canary.*'

The news was all over *The Advertiser* the following day. At breakfast – bacon, eggs, brandy – we read, with cries of surprise, of the tragic accidental death of civic worthy Clive Brady, while botanising on Willans' hill; of the mysterious gangland-style killing of notorious regional criminal Thomas V. Anderson; of the arrest of Michael McClure and several other members of a drinking club in a well-known local hostelry on suspicion of involvement in the murder of popular former sportsman Andrew Kell; and of the sterling police-work of Superintendent – soon to be Chief Superintendent – Wilkinson and his team of expert investigators, especially the Wagga Wagga Scientific Police, who had covered themselves with glory throughout. Of Charlie Parrot &c. there was no mention. Maxwell rang the police station and asked for (Chief) Superintendent Wilkinson. He was unavailable, apparently – in the bosom, no doubt, of his family. He then cunningly asked for Detective Sergeant Charlie Parrot. He was also unavailable – on gardening leave, apparently.

Municipal mourning for Clive was in full swing as I drove down to *Klever Kitchens*. Flags were at half-mast, curtains were half-drawn, Council workmen were having a half-holiday.

'I have come here to share with you,' I said to Manager Doug and his congregated staff, prominent among whom were Veronica's lambent eyes and knees, 'your sense of both shock and relief – shock, naturally, that such a foul murder could have been committed by ordinary, seemingly-normal citizens of our fair city, persons perhaps known to you or to your nearest and dearest, persons you might have passed on the street or rubbed shoulders with in one of our places of public entertainment; and relief, of course, that your esteemed colleague's murderers have at last been tracked to their dens, captured and brought to justice. Their motives will appear in due course; I shall not go into them on this occasion. I say to you,

you may believe that Andrew's ravaged spirit is now at rest. And I also say to you, you may believe, irrespective of what you might read in *The Advertiser*, that those murderers were personally tracked and trapped by Maxwell and myself. Maxwell, your valued client, most certainly deserves a massive discount on his next saucepan. Before I go, I need to say a private word to Miss Veronica there, as I believe that her late lamented mother Robyn was slightly acquainted with one of the accused.'

She followed me out and we strolled together up the arcade. She said I knew she knew Mike McClure was a horrible old man, she'd had a lot of hands-on experience of him, but she never would have guessed that he was likely to be a murderer. Murder, I said, took many different forms, some of them somewhat indirect, and although I doubted that that horrible old man had directly murdered anyone before, before Andrew, I thought it probable that he was directly responsible for other, indirect murders in the past. And I cannot help thinking, I said, that although this terrible recent event has of course no connection at all with her, your dear mother, your and my dear departed Robyn, may well be feeling, wherever she now may be, that McClure has at last arrived at his comeuppance.

'I think so too,' she said: 'I really feel she's pleased, she'll have been waiting for this. But it's an awful thing that it had to come through poor Andrew. Why did he kill him?'

'If only I could tell you,' I said; 'but that must remain an absolute secret until his trial. Were it even to be whispered or rumoured before the jury hears of it his lawyers might get him off. However, for your ears – your lovely ears – only, I will just say that it's not entirely unrelated to something that has a distant connection with a certain Christmas dinner-dance at Romano's.'

'It's to do with that girl, isn't it? I knew it all along.'

'Most of life, generally speaking, is to do with girls. Also death. But tell me, when are you to be married?'

'In November. The 16th. Will you be here? I'll invite you if you are. I'd really love to have you there. You're my special link with mum.'

'Alas, no. I wish I could be, you'll make a ravishing bride; but I must be somewhere in Europe at that time of year. I'll send you a wedding-present.'

'I'd like to give you some wedding-presents – from both me and mum, to show you how grateful we are for everything. But the ones I'd like to I can't, it wouldn't be right, not before November 16th. It wouldn't be fair on Rex. But afterwards, after I'm married, I think I'd quite like to visit that room in Romano's again.'

'Say no more. I can't bear it.' I kissed her and turned to go. 'I leave tomorrow on the XTP, bound for Sydney, London and Venice. It's impossible that we should not meet again. And so, *au revoir*.'

That evening, over a parting port, 'Ballarat,' I informed Maxwell, 'is too far away. I think, on second and third thoughts, that I ought not to abandon Wagga, not entirely. Occasional returns, for old times' sake, should continue. After all, there is still a vast amount of invaluable unmined material here – Mr. Jackson, for a start; and it is here, and nowhere else, that we know where the bodies are buried. I thought I might pay you another visit next year.'

'I trust you're not having second and third thoughts about *Mrs. Rossiter's Canary*,' Maxwell said.

'Never,' I said: 'I have solemnly sworn. Have I ever given you cause to distrust me? *Mrs. Rossiter's Canary* is the one novel that I will never ever write.'

I exited on the next afternoon's XTP. I was contemplating a Venetian canal five days later.

Maxwell reports that Mike McClure received a life sentence – whatever 'life' means these days – and is currently in the Goulburn gaol. Charlie Parrot, after a short but tedious period of gardening leave in North Wagga, was relegated on a permanent basis to Tumbarumba, far beyond human ken. Constables Horry and Frank were sent to Ballarat. Jayne Kell is Jayne Higgs, a resident of Canberra. Angela may still be in Melbourne. The few chaps remaining have ceased their meetings in the refurbished premises of the William Farrer. Clive Brady's tomb in the Wagga Memorial Cemetery is a wonder to behold. Miss M.E. Paddock and her mother are on a world tour, which will include a week in Venice. I know they are coming for G.K. Chesterton's *Autobiography*; and I still haven't found her copy.

Manufactured by Amazon.ca
Acheson, AB